BETRAYED IN SHADOW

A CASSIE QUINN MYSTERY

L.T. RYAN

with

K.M. ROUGHT

LIQUID MIND MEDIA

For information contact:
contact@ltryan.com
https://LTRyan.com
https://www.facebook.com/JackNobleBooks

THE CASSIE QUINN SERIES

Path of Bones

Whisper of Bones

Symphony of Bones

Etched in Shadow

Concealed in Shadow

Betrayed in Shadow

Born from Ashes

Love Cassie? Hatch? Noble? Maddie? Get your very own Cassie Quinn merchandise today! Click the link below to find coffee mugs, t-shirts, and even signed copies of your favorite L.T. Ryan thrillers! https://ltryan.ink/EvG_

1

FRANCISCO AGUILAR HAD LEARNED FROM AN EARLY AGE TO KEEP HIS emotions in check. Anger, fear, even elation. It had served him well as he built his business from nothing, rising from a relative nobody to King of Savannah. His enemies never saw him coming, and his friends never felt too comfortable in his presence.

But it wasn't always easy. As his influence spread outside Savannah, it became more difficult to lock those emotions down. Allies he'd once trusted had betrayed him—and for what? Money and a guaranteed bullet to the brain? The cops knocked on his door at least once a week. And it didn't take long before the FBI had gotten involved, too.

And yet, he had no intention of shutting down his empire. Shipping businesses were a dime a dozen these days, but none compared to the deals he could make. Now that he'd expanded into other fields and bought other ventures, he had a hand in close to twenty percent of the businesses in Savannah. If he didn't own them outright, he was at least an investor. Either way, the money rolled in. The illegitimate businesses helped support the legitimate ones, and the above-board ventures hid the ones he wished to keep in the shadows.

Aguilar wouldn't settle for the title of King. He wanted to be an Emperor. Rome wasn't built in a day, and neither was his network. He'd spent decades handpicking those closest to him, sending them off to lead cells in other parts of the country. And all of them reported to *him*.

He shot the traitors. Paid off cops. All in a day's work.

But his anger was closer to the surface these days. A hairpin trigger away from exploding. In the old days, he could let off a little steam by fighting or fucking, but now he had to be careful. His hands were in too many pots. If he killed the wrong person or slept with the wrong man's daughter, his house of cards would come crashing down.

So, he stayed angry.

On days like today, it was harder to contain. Aguilar sat in his own restaurant—a Brazilian steakhouse that netted him a pretty profit—as one of his closest allies fed him bullshit. Everything in the back room was colored maroon—the walls, the benches, the tablecloth, the carpet—and trimmed in gold. This was one of Aguilar's favorite rooms to conduct business in because it was timeless, classy, and a reminder that no one would spot the blood on the carpet if he decided to nick an artery. But not everyone had gotten the memo.

Nicolas Bianchi was older than Aguilar, and worse, he was from an Old-World family. Italian, to be precise. The kind they made movies about. He and his family had been more than happy to let Aguilar bankroll them long enough for the cops to leave them alone after one scandal or another, but Nicolas was getting restless. Someone was whispering in his ear, making him question Aguilar's decisions. Making him act like he knew better. Could do better.

"Hey, it's a drop in the bucket to you, Frankie." Nicolas had grown up in New Jersey, and despite twenty years in the South, his accent was as strong as ever. He was well put together, dressed in a white suit with thick black hair and a trimmed beard, but something about his voice grated on Aguilar's ears. "What do you say?"

Aguilar quelled his anger, both at the nickname and the question. The Bianchi family wanted a cool million to set up shop back in New Jersey. They would run one of Aguilar's cells for him, and Nicolas would give up half his earnings to do it. But Aguilar knew better. They'd take the money and run, then fortify themselves back in Jersey where Aguilar couldn't touch them. The Bianchis were better connected there, both with the Italian community and the police force. Hell, most of them were one and the same.

Did Nicolas think he was stupid?

"I'm not looking to expand right now." Aguilar forced a wide smile on his face. He knit his brows together like he hated delivering such bad news. "You understand."

A flash of anger darkened Nicolas' eyes for a fraction of a second. No, he didn't understand. Aguilar knew Bianchi was pissed that he wasn't taking the bait, but he couldn't allude to that. Not here in Aguilar's restaurant, surrounded by Aguilar's men and the general public. It was suicide by design.

The back room was private enough that Aguilar could conduct his business uninterrupted, and he often did. But the heavy curtain separating them from the rest of the restaurant was a reminder that they were never truly alone. Aguilar held all the cards. Nicolas knew that.

"Frankie—" Nicolas caught anger emanating off Aguilar from the nickname. He cleared his throat. "Francisco, don't you trust me? You know I would never screw you over. You're my best investor."

Aguilar almost believed him. But greedy men were good liars, and Nicolas Bianchi was one of the best.

"It has nothing to do with you. Or your family."

Nicolas accepted the lie, but the double meaning in Aguilar's words was obvious. "Then what? What's going on? Let me help you."

Aguilar bit back a snarl. At one point in time, he might've trusted Nicolas to help. But the man had shown his hand. Aguilar had only two options now: Snap the leash and remind Bianchi where he stood, or cut his losses. Either would result in the Bianchi family's retaliation.

Before Aguilar could answer, a man parted the curtain and stepped inside the room. He was a tall, thin Black man, with bright gray eyes and a thick beard. One of Aguilar's most trusted lieutenants. His name was Jasper Brown, and Aguilar knew exactly why he was there. The man's subtle nod confirmed it.

Aguilar turned back to Nicolas. "Give me two weeks to look into the numbers again. If anything changes, I'll let you know. If it doesn't pan out, we'll find something else for you. How does that sound?" Another lie to placate Nicolas until Aguilar could decide what to do with him. Nothing would change, but Nicolas didn't need to know that.

Nicolas smiled, but he was grinding his teeth together. "You always take care of me, Frankie. I appreciate it."

"No problem." Aguilar gestured to the door. "I've got some other business to discuss, but I'll talk to you soon. Tell the wife I said hello. And I'm dying for more of her lemon bars."

"She'd love to make you another batch," Nicolas replied, though there was no emotion in his voice. "Stay safe, Frankie. It's a crazy world out there."

It wasn't much of a threat, but nuances weren't lost on Aguilar, not after this much time in the business. But whatever pull the Bianchi family had back in New Jersey, they were startups here in Savannah. Even if they managed to take out Aguilar, those in Aguilar's corner would start an all-out war, which the Bianchis would lose.

As Nicolas left, Jasper took a seat in the now empty chair, pushing a half-eaten plate of steak out of his way. Aguilar waited until he was sure Nicolas had left before turning to his lieutenant, eyebrow raised. "Tell me it's good news."

"You don't pay me to lie to you." It was Jasper's favorite line, but there was something off about it today. His gray eyes usually held some sort of humor, but now his face was somber.

"How bad is it?"

"Zbirak's dead."

Aguilar had to work his jaw back and forth before he could speak. "What?"

"Far as I can tell, the detective took him out."

"Harris?" Aguilar banged his fist down on the table. Cutlery clanged against the lacquered wood. "There's no way she did it on her own. Zbirak was the best."

"There was someone else. A woman named Cassie Quinn."

Aguilar scoffed. "The psychic? She's nobody. Klein liked to parade her around. She got lucky a few times, but she wouldn't have been able to take out Zbirak either." Aguilar had enough connections with the

Savannah PD that he'd heard her name tossed around a few times. He wasn't exactly a believer, but he never did like to take chances.

"Either way." Jasper took a tone with Aguilar that only a select few would dare to. "He's dead. And we're facing hefty consequences."

"I'm aware." Aguilar dragged a hand down his face. "At least I'll save some money on that job."

"There's more."

Aguilar clenched his teeth. "Don't leave me in suspense, then."

"Reed is missing."

Aguilar covered the urge to bang on the table again by running a hand through his hair. "Do we know where?"

"Los Angeles." Jasper had the guts to look Aguilar in the eye as he spoke. It was one of the things Aguilar liked most about the man. "And the two women went after him."

"They've got no chance of finding him, not in a city that big."

"Stranger things have happened," Jasper warned.

Like a bitch detective and a so-called psychic taking out one of the world's foremost assassins? Jasper had a point.

"You have thoughts on the situation. What do you advise?" Aguilar and Jasper had been working together for close to a decade. He knew the way Jasper ran through scenarios.

"You've got people in Los Angeles." Jasper shrugged. "Use them."

"And kill the detective? She's been on my ass for too long. It'll be suspicious."

"She's suspended. Gone rogue, first in Chicago, then in L.A. If she dies out there, it'll be harder for them to trace it back to you. If she finds Reed and comes back to Savannah, it's over. We both know that piece of shit isn't going to jail for you."

Aguilar allowed a growl to escape. Jasper was right. Aguilar pulled out his cell. "It's time to end this once and for all."

2

THE FLIGHT FROM CHICAGO TO LOS ANGELES TOOK LESS THAN FIVE HOURS, but it might as well have taken an entire week. Harris sat somewhere up front in an aisle seat while Cassie sat further back, squished between two middle-aged men. As soon as the plane took off, one of them had promptly fallen asleep on her shoulder. And no amount of polite jostling had woken him up.

By the time they landed, Cassie was stiff, angry, and missing her own bed more than she cared to admit. She hadn't slept a wink, which was likely for the best. The last thing she needed was to wake up screaming from a prophetic nightmare with the entire plane craning their necks in her direction. She felt tortured enough as it was. Cassie could tell Detective Harris had tamped down on her anger, but her feelings about the subject were clear.

The fact of the matter was, Cassie had let Reed get away. She'd had him within shouting distance, yet she hadn't done everything in her power to make sure he never got on that plane. Now, they would have to find him somewhere in the city of Los Angeles. Needle in a haystack didn't even begin to cover it.

Harris waited for her just outside the gate they had exited, looking no worse for the wear. She'd probably gotten a nap and a good snack. By the time the cart had made it back to Cassie, all they had were lightly salted pretzels. She'd decided to starve. At the very least, she should've ordered a glass of wine.

Harris didn't bother with a greeting. "Did you call your sister yet?"

Cassie bit her tongue rather than say the obvious. "Just about to. Give me a second."

Harris took off toward baggage claim, and Cassie rushed to keep up with the woman's longer stride, fighting through crowds of people just to keep her in view. They must've landed in LAX at peak rush hour because there was hardly any room to move as everyone walked in all different directions. The muffled speakers blared overhead, and Cassie had to wonder how Laura would ever hear a word she said.

The phone rang in her ear, and her heartrate kicked up a notch, though she couldn't pin down exactly why. Being in Los Angeles chasing after one of Aguilar's associates? Showing up on her sister's doorstep with no idea how they were going to find someone as slippery as Reed? It could've been either of those reasons or both or a million more.

Being in LAX didn't help either. It was bustling with people, and where Harris could cut a line through the crowd with her presence alone, Cassie had to bob and weave between strangers, tripping over luggage and getting whacked with bags left and right. For once, she wished her ability to keep ghosts at arm's length applied to the living, too.

Cassie caught up to Harris on the escalator, pulling the phone away from her face and hanging up before Laura's voicemail finished its message. "She didn't answer."

Harris didn't look at her. "Keep trying."

Cassie rolled her eyes but dialed again. It was just about dinner time, and Laura was probably on her way home from work, maybe even just walking through the door. Or maybe she was out to dinner with friends, or off to work out, or even out shopping. As close as they had gotten recently, Cassie hated the fact that she still didn't know her sister that well. Did Laura have friends in L.A.? She must've, but what were they like? Laura never talked about them. Or her colleagues, for that matter. She was even quiet about her dating life.

Cassie hung up for the third time as they reached the bottom of the escalators. Harris found their carousel on one of the big screens, and they waited with everyone else until their bags hit the conveyor belt. Then it was straight to the bathroom to change into some more weather-appropriate clothes.

Cassie still had her wardrobe from New Orleans, though she only had one clean outfit at this point—a pair of white linen pants and a green knit shirt that was a little tight on her. She'd brought it as a backup, not thinking she'd actually wear it.

Harris emerged from the bathroom in her jeans and boots, a snug black tank tucked into her pants. The detective had only packed for Chicago, so her options were limited, but they each hoped Laura might help them out. Cassie wondered who would look more ridiculous in her little sister's clothes, and decided it'd probably be her. Something told Cassie that Harris could wear a leopard print leotard and still look intimidating.

As if on cue, Cassie's phone rang. Several heads turned at the disruption, scowling at the shrill sound emanating from the cell. Cassie turned her back on them and answered, unable to get a word out before Laura's panicked voice shrieked in her ear.

"Oh my god, what's wrong?" Laura's words rushed together until they almost made no sense. "I'm so sorry. I was out on a date right after work and I put my phone on silent and I was in my head the whole way home and I didn't even think to check it. I just walked in the door and saw you called three times. Are you okay?"

"I'm fine, I'm fine." Cassie tried to hold back a laugh and failed. "Seriously, everything is okay."

Laura blew out a breath that hurt Cassie's ear. "Thank God. Why'd you call three times then?"

Cassie chewed on her lip before she answered. "We need a little favor."

"A favor?" Laura paused and Cassie could sense her sister's eyes narrow. "We?"

"Me and Adelaide."

"Detective Harris?" Her voice shifted. She sounded surprised and maybe even a little excited. "Of course. How can I help?"

Cassie opened her mouth to explain the situation when the loud-speaker came on. It was distorted by an outdated audio system, but the words *baggage claim* were loud and clear.

"Cassie." Laura drew out her name like she was using the time to fully comprehend what was going on. "Where are you right now?"

"LAX." Cassie winced. "Can you come pick us up?"

Laura sighed into the receiver. "You're such a stereotype. You know that, right?"

"Take your time. We're not in a rush." Cassie looked up at Harris and found her scowling, but there was nothing they could do tonight. "Didn't have time to fill you in before."

"But you're okay?" Laura's voice was softer now, filled with worry again. "Really?"

"Really. I'll tell you everything, I promise. We need a place to crash tonight so we can figure out our next move."

Keys jangled on the other end of the line. A smile filled her voice now. "I'm leaving now. Good thing I just bought two bottles of wine. Maybe this night won't be a total loss after all."

3

TRAFFIC HAD THEM TO LAURA'S HOUSE IN INGLEWOOD AFTER HALF AN hour. Cassie had been out to California a couple times over the years, but her sister had been living in a grimy studio back then. The house was a step up, even if it did look like a relic from the 1960s. Laura seemed happy at least, and that's all Cassie cared about.

They shuffled through the door and dumped their bags in the spare bedroom. Harris insisted on taking the couch, and Cassie had been too tired to argue. Laura had looked between the two of them, watching the way they avoided each other's gaze, and made an executive decision to order pizza and uncork the first bottle of wine. The floodgates opened after they'd each eaten a slice and worked on their second. Between the two of them, they'd told Laura everything that had happened since David's funeral, right up until they'd landed in California.

"Let me get this straight." Laura stood to pour them each a second glass of wine. "I'm supposed to just gloss over the fact that you got shot"—she pointed the bottle in Harris' direction—"and hid a piece of evidence from your boss, then hopped on a plane to Chicago to further investigate a crime while you were suspended?"

Harris wore a dazzling smile. "Yes."

Laura stared at the woman, then shrugged and continued pouring the wine. "As long as we're all on the same page." She delivered Cassie and Harris' glasses, then went back for her own. "So, this flash drive led you to Chicago, where you investigated off-record."

"Again, we're glossing," Cassie said. She was feeling the wine now. "Glossing is kind of a weird word when you think about it too much."

"Then don't think about it too much." Laura laughed. "Harris, you found the dead witness' pregnant wife and got her to safety, but then Cassie got kidnapped by an assassin." Laura turned serious here. "I can't believe you didn't tell me any of this while it was happening."

"I was kidnapped.".

"Technically, it was Cassie's idea." Harris took a dainty sip of her red. "Is intentional kidnapping still kidnapping?"

"You're the cop. You tell me." There was a sharpness to Laura's voice, but there was no telling if it was from fear or anger or a combination of the two. "We'll revisit that topic. Either way, the assassin is dead. A hundred percent?"

"A hundred percent," Harris repeated. "Shot him myself."

"And the body? How will you explain that? What if they trace it back to you?"

"I'll deal with that later."

"That's insane at best."

"That a clinical diagnosis?"

"Maybe."

The word hung in the air for a moment, and Cassie took a loud sip to break the silence. Laura shook herself and continued. "So, the assassin who killed David is dead. That's good, I guess. But you still want Aguilar because he hired the guy. And in order to get him, you have to figure out what Reed knows."

"He's the one who's going to connect the dots for us," Harris said. "The janitor from his office said Reed was playing both sides. He was definitely in bed with Aguilar, so we gotta figure out who else he was working with and why he'd risk pissing Aguilar off."

"I can't imagine that's a decision you make lightly. You have any theories?"

"Not any good ones." Harris thought for a moment, and when she finally spoke, she avoided Cassie's eyes. "But I'm wondering if he was working with David."

Cassie looked up from where she'd been watching her wine swirl around the inside of her glass. "Why would he be working with David? Reed is a sleazebag. David would see through that in two seconds flat."

"We know David was working with Aguilar, though." It looked like it physically pained Harris to say that out loud. "I can't believe—I won't believe—it was of his own volition. My gut is telling me David was trying to take Aguilar down from the inside. Maybe Aguilar found out, and that's why David is dead."

"You think David would try to do that on his own?" Laura's voice was gentle. "Why wouldn't he bring you in on that?"

Harris cleared her throat, but the emotion stayed in her voice. "I don't know. He's been protecting me my whole career. And after what we found on the flash drive, it's hard not to think he got himself into this because of me."

Laura leaned forward and placed a hand on Harris' knee. "It was his decision, Adelaide. His alone. You can't control other people. Don't take the blame for something someone else did."

Harris laughed, but it was watery. "Spoken like a true therapist."

Laura sat back with a smile on her face and shrugged. "What can I say? I'm good at what I do."

Cassie let their playful banter fade out. Not for the first time since David's death, she wondered how well she had known him. From the date and his badge number on the flash drive, they could surmise that David had started working with Aguilar right after Harris had killed Luca White's son in self-defense. David and Aguilar must have made some deal, but how many others would know the details of that? The bookie was dead. David was dead. And it wasn't like Aguilar would confess. That's why they needed to find Reed.

Harris' voice broke through Cassie's thoughts. "You'll have to ask Cassie that."

"What?" Cassie looked between the two. Laura had an eyebrow raised, but Harris was avoiding eye contact. "What about me?"

"How the hell did Reed get away? *He was right there.*"

"I know." Cassie caught that same annoyance from the airport flicker to life on the detective's face. "I panicked. I didn't want to cause a scene and get kicked out of the airport. Or get arrested for falsely accusing someone of planting a bomb or something."

"Harris would've gotten you out of it. And at least he'd be grounded in Chicago. Rather than halfway across the country in a city of, like, *twelve million people*. And that's only if he chooses to stick around."

"Hey, I told her the same thing." Harris kept her voice neutral. Her smile didn't reach her eyes. "Too late now, though. We just—"

Cassie placed her glass down with a *clink* and stood up too fast. She wobbled a little on her feet before finding her balance again. Heat rushed to her face, but she couldn't decide if it was from anger or embarrassment. "Look, I get it. I screwed up. It was stupid. But you can't possibly hate me more than I hate myself right now."

Harris looked up at her with a frown. "Cassie, I don't hate you."

Cassie's face felt like it was on fire. She didn't mean to say that out loud. She hated the way the other two women looked at her now. She fished her phone out of her purse, avoiding eye contact. "I need to call Jason. He'll be worried. And he might know someone who could help us. I'll let you know if he says anything."

Laura called after her, but neither followed her into the back bedroom. She had to get out of there before she said something she'd regret. And she'd be lying to herself if she wasn't desperate to talk to Jason about everything.

Like the rest of the house, the spare bedroom had a midcentury air to it. Laura had replaced the ugly green carpet and had the hardwood floors redone, but she'd elected to keep the eccentric paisley wallpaper because it added *charm*. Cassie had to admit the modern dresser and nightstand pulled everything together, and Laura had kept the bedding plain so as not to compete with the rest of the room.

That annoyed Cassie even more. How dare her sister have her life together?

She slumped back onto the bed and dialed Jason's number. The paisley wallpaper made her feel even more drunk, so she closed her eyes and felt the room tilt around her. She needed to drink some water, but the last thing she wanted to do was walk through the living room and face her sister and Harris again.

Jason picked up on the third ring, with a smile in his voice. "Hey. Tell me you've got good news."

"Define *good*."

Jason groaned like he was settling down into a couch or a chair, and Cassie realized she had no idea where he lived or what his place looked like. "Oh boy. Okay, I'm ready. Lay it on me."

"Not much to lay at the moment." Cassie winced, convinced that was some sort of weird double entendre. "I'm in California now. Los Angeles, specifically."

"That's even farther from Savannah."

Cassie sighed. "Yes, it is. I let Reed get away. I could've stopped him, and I didn't. Now we're here, and I have no idea when I'm coming home."

Cassie told him everything, and when she finished, tears sprung to her eyes, and she had a hard time keeping her voice even. "Everything feels so messed up. I wish you were here."

"I wish I was, too. Look, we all make mistakes. You followed your gut, and if anyone gets a pass for that, it's you. Maybe this is where you're supposed to be." Jason's voice soothed her. Her situation didn't feel so bad with his reassurances in her ear.

"Yeah, I guess."

"Do you have a plan for finding Reed?"

Cassie felt a headache coming on, but she pushed it to the back of her mind. "Not right now. Tomorrow, we're going to track down the body of the woman Reed and Zbirak buried. There may be something to help us flush him out."

"That's a good start." Jason waited for Cassie to say something else, but she didn't feel like being cheerful. "And hey, Rose Sherman is safe and sound. Apollo and Bear are behaving. And work will be here when you get back, okay? You can only do so much. When you find Reed, then you can come home, and we can worry about the rest together, okay?"

She did feel a little better, even if nothing had changed. "Okay. You wouldn't happen to know anyone out here who can help us, do you? Another team of badasses who can track down a sleazy lawyer for us?"

Jason laughed. "Not quite, but I'll see what I can do."

"Thanks, Jason. You always know what to say to make me feel better." The wine was making Cassie drowsy now.

"Any time. I hope you know that." There was a moment of silence before he spoke again. "Get some sleep, okay? I'll see you soon."

"Okay," Cassie said, though it came out quiet and slurred. "Night."

"Sweet dreams," Jason said, a low rumble in his voice.

Cassie didn't bother hanging up the phone. She simply turned to her side and slipped into unconsciousness.

4

A GENTLE KNOCK ON HER DOOR ROUSED CASSIE FROM HER TIPSY SLUMBER. She felt groggier than usual, and the light from the day clawed at her eyes before she even opened them. Wine usually didn't go to her head like this, but she'd hardly had any water or food the night before. She should've known she'd have to pay the price in the morning.

The knock came again before someone opened the door. Laura's voice was gentle. "Hey. How are you feeling?"

Cassie tried to form words, but they came out a jumbled mess. Laura laughed, and Cassie forced herself to sit up. Blink away the blurriness. Turn to her sister. "What time is it?"

"About six. I know it's early, I'm sorry."

"It's okay." Cassie tried to remember what they had to do today. Had she agreed to such an early wake-up call? "What's going on?"

"Adelaide made breakfast. I told her she could have my car today, so she's going to take me to work and then come back for you." Laura paused. "She wants to know if you could be ready in about an hour to, um, track down that woman's body."

Right. That's what they had to do today. Another dead body.

"Yeah, of course." Cassie flipped back the covers and swung her legs over the bed. Her phone toppled to the floor, and when she retrieved it and sat back up, the room swam again. She tried not to let it show on her face. "I'll hop in the shower and grab a bite. I'll be ready."

"Okay." Another pause. "Hey, about last night—"

"It's all good." Cassie looked up at Laura and gave her a tired smile. She wasn't sure if her sister was about to apologize or ask her to do the same, but either way, she didn't want to talk about it. "You're gonna be late. We can talk about it later."

Laura's mouth pinched into a straight line, but after a moment's hesitation, she nodded. "I've got a bunch of t-shirts and shorts in my dresser. Take your pick. Sunscreen is in the hall closet. Advil is in the medicine cabinet. Take a water bottle with you. Adelaide knows where they are."

"Right. Got it. Thanks."

Cassie waited until she heard the front door close before she climbed out of bed. Her phone was dead from not having it on the charger all night, so she plugged it in before padding into the kitchen. Harris had made an entire spread—bacon, eggs, pancakes, and fruit lined a large wooden tray. There was even a pitcher of fresh-squeezed orange juice to the side. Cassie wondered if Harris had made it all herself or if she'd gone to the store. Either way, Cassie couldn't imagine waking up that early, putting together a buffet, and then driving through California traffic.

Luckily, she didn't have to.

After inhaling as much food as could fit in her stomach and drinking two full glasses of water and a glass of orange juice, Cassie started to feel human again. A couple Advil and one shower later, she was operating at eighty percent. Good enough.

No sooner had Cassie picked out an outfit—a white t-shirt and a pair of snug jean shorts—than Harris walked through the door. She wore a light brown tank top and a pair of army green shorts. The only things that had remained the same were her high ponytail and hiking boots.

Harris crossed her arms over her chest. "You're staring."

The detective looked like a different person in the California sun, like she was made to roam the beaches and roller skate down the street. It was such a far cry from the Adelaide Harris Cassie had met and gotten to know in Savannah.

For the first time since they met, Harris looked...happy. Like she belonged. Like she was relaxed. But it felt rude to say that.

Instead, Cassie just pointed to the other woman's boots. "Not exactly beachwear."

Harris cracked a smile. "My feet are too big for your sister's shoes. Don't have another choice. Besides, these are all-weather. Especially if we have to chase someone down."

"You sound a little hopeful."

Harris shrugged. "Maybe."

Any tension that had been lingering in the air from last night disappeared with their easy banter, and Cassie breathed a sigh of relief. As strange as this new Harris was, she was better than having to deal with the one from last night. "I'd be concerned if you had any other answer."

"The beach, huh?" Harris asked, grabbing a pair of water bottles from the cupboard and filling them up. "That's where the body is?"

"Not quite. But there is water involved. She was dumped in the Ballona Wetlands."

Harris looked up with sharp eyes. "That's specific."

"I could be vague if you want me to." Cassie put a couple of fingers to her temple. "She's in a body of water somewhere along the western coast of the United States."

Harris tossed Cassie a bottle. "You're hilarious. I just meant we usually have to do a little more digging to find what we need." She threw a backpack over her shoulder. "Pun not intended."

"Normally, I have to talk to the spirits that I see. Interpret what they're trying to tell me." Cassie followed Harris out to Laura's car, a little silver Nissan Altima. It looked brand new. "But this woman's spirit went right through me. Left her memories behind. She was very specific about where she was buried. It took a minute to piece it all together, but I don't have any doubts. That's where she is."

Harris slipped behind the wheel of the car. "Did she also leave behind a name we could call her? You know, rather than *the dead woman* or *the woman dumped in the middle of the wetlands somewhere*."

"She'd lost too much of her sense of self by then." Cassie slid into the passenger seat and buckled up. "She only hung onto certain moments. Like her death."

"Lucky for us," Harris said.

Cassie grimaced. "Yeah, lucky for us."

Their destination was only a twenty-minute drive north of Inglewood. Cassie had read about the area on the way over. It was the second-largest open space within the city limits behind Griffith Park, and the California Department of Fish and Wildlife worked hard to preserve it both for the sake of the flora and fauna within the estuary but also so residents and tourists alike could appreciate this little oasis in the middle of Los Angeles.

The path leading through the wetlands was nothing more than a dirt trail, and every so often there'd be a neon orange cone sitting off to one side, warning people of danger. They hardly met anyone during their trek. Probably for the best.

The pair didn't talk much. Harris had been around Cassie long enough to know how this worked, and for her part, Cassie tried matching the flashing images in her head with the very real areas around her. It wasn't easy when everything more or less looked the same, but about halfway down the trail and around a slight curve, she came to such a sudden stop that it took Harris a few seconds before she realized Cassie was no longer walking beside her.

"What is it?" the detective asked, looking around like the body might float to the surface at any second. "Is this it?"

"I think so."

Harris crossed her arms over her chest. "You think so?"

Cassie scowled. "Give me a minute, will you?"

Cassie couldn't shake the disparity between the world around them and the horrors that lay just under the surface. She wondered how many people passed through here daily, and how many had no idea who was buried just feet from the trail. As she took a step closer to the edge of the water, that invisible line that sometimes tugged her in the right direction grew taut. They were close.

Closing her eyes, she took a deep breath in and exhaled slowly through her mouth. She blocked out the sounds of the rushing traffic and chirping birds. A peal of laughter rang out somewhere farther along the trail, but she barely registered the sound. She could feel an emptiness below her, just to the right of where she was standing. Any spirit that had lingered was gone now, but even without seeing the body, Cassie knew it was right. She knew who was buried there.

Most of the dead bodies she had encountered weren't as lifeless as people believed. Murder victims wanted one thing—justice. Cassie was used to seeing their spirits lingering, waiting for her to notice them. To help them.

But this body was vacant. The soul that had once resided in it was gone. The woman had used all her remaining energy to get a message halfway across the country to Cassie. And instead of returning to her body until her murder was solved, she had simply dissipated. Just like that.

Whoever this woman was, she had not only been a victim of both Zbirak and Reed, but also of Aguilar. And, with any luck, her one final act of defiance would lead Cassie and Harris to where they needed to go. And maybe, Cassie would be able to get justice both for her and David.

Opening her eyes, Cassie took two small steps to her right. She called Harris over, then bent down and pointed to a random patch of grass growing out of the water. "Right here."

Harris looked from the vegetation to Cassie and back again. "You're sure?"

"Positive." Cassie stood but never took her eyes from the spot. "She's waited long enough."

5

As much as Cassie had wanted to jump into the water and release Reed's victim from her prison, she didn't think it was a good idea. The water varied in depth, and there was no telling how deep it was, even just off the trail. Had Zbirak and Reed jumped into the water and buried her in the silt below? Or had they simply dumped her body over the edge, weighing it down with rocks and other debris?

With too many factors to consider, Harris called the authorities. Reports of bodies in the marsh must not have been uncommon because once Fish and Wildlife arrived, the police weren't far behind. After they cordoned off the area, a small crowd gathered to watch the proceedings. Cassie couldn't blame them for their morbid curiosity—it was human nature, after all—but part of her wanted to chase them off for invading this woman's privacy, dead or not.

Thanks to Cassie's specific instructions, it didn't take long to find her. Two Fish and Wildlife officers were joined by someone from the LAPD, and together, they lifted the body from the water like pallbearers at a funeral. Wrapped in a black trash bag, now torn and covered in mud, it was much smaller than Cassie would've thought. Whether because the woman had been small in stature or because Zbirak had burned the body before disposing of it, she didn't know.

Despair crept through Cassie's body. She didn't know this woman—not even her name—but pieces of her memories existed within her. That love for the ocean. The way the sun set on the California coast. Once, she had been happy. Carefree, even. And now she was gone. Why? Someone had used her as a pawn in their own sick game, and tossed her away when she'd stopped being useful.

Cassie swiped away a tear and thought about what came next. Now that they had a body, the cops would want to question her and Harris. Before they had arrived, the two of them had decided to tell an approximation of the truth. Cassie had a good track record with the Savannah PD and the FBI. If the local cops wanted to look her up, they could. They might think she was crazy, but they'd have to at least give her the benefit of the doubt. Harris would be there to back her up. The fact that she was currently suspended wasn't ideal, but that'd be an issue for a later time. For now, her badge would lend Cassie more credence.

Harris and Cassie stood inside the police tape, watched by one of the officers, and left to wait until the authorities were sure of what they were dealing with. They'd already taken an initial report from them, and soon a forensics team arrived to take pictures and collect what little evidence there was from the marsh. And when the detective finally arrived to question them, he was nothing like Cassie had expected.

She'd been around the Savannah PD enough to know that cops came in all shapes and sizes, but in her experience, most of them had been like David—perpetually tired and worn down by their years on the job. Even Harris, who was more than a decade younger than David, carried herself with a weariness that told Cassie she'd seen more than she'd ever care to talk about.

But this guy looked like he belonged in the movies. Well over six feet tall, with dark, windblown hair, ocean-blue eyes, and a smile so white it actually sparkled in the sunlight. His skin was that perfect shade of tan that let you know he got it by working out in the sun, not from a tanning bed.

"Hello, ladies. My name is Detective Noah Green." He extended his hand for Harris to shake, and Cassie noticed the way his rolled-up sleeve revealed the strength of his forearm. "Wish we were meeting under better circumstances."

"Yes, us too," Harris said, sounding all business. "Detective Adelaide Harris."

"Pleasure to meet you," Green said, not letting Harris' professionalism wear on his charm. There was that smile again, and he turned it on Cassie, extending his hand to her as well. "And that must make you Ms. Quinn, the psychic." When Cassie's eyebrows pinched in confusion, he chuckled. "The other officers were talking about you. All good things, I promise."

"Somehow, I doubt that." She forced herself to look him in the eye. "You can call me Cassie."

"We get a lot of psychics around here, as you can imagine," he explained. "Most of them are just out for a paycheck. Or notoriety."

"Or both," Harris quipped.

He nodded his agreement. "I've seen my fair share of the real deal. Or, who knows, maybe they were just really good con artists. I guess I don't mind as long as they help me solve a case or two."

"Cassie's the real deal," Harris said. "I've seen enough to believe it."

"I don't know whether to be excited or nervous." Green grinned at her again, and the skin around his eyes crinkled. But there was something in the way he looked at her, like he wasn't just going to take Harris' word for it. "What can you tell me about what's going on here?"

"Well, the short version—" Harris started.

"I'd like to hear it from her, actually." Gesturing to Cassie, he winced theatrically. "If you don't mind, that is."

"No, of course not." Harris' voice remained even, but there was a flash of annoyance in her eyes. All she wanted to do was get this part over with. They still had to find Reed, after all. If he was anywhere to be found.

Instead of expressing those frustrations out loud, however, she turned to Cassie. "Go ahead."

Cassie took a deep breath of the humid air. "We were just in Chicago, working on a different case. I had been seeing this shadow all throughout the city, but I didn't know who or what it was. Then, we sort of crossed paths with an assassin." Saying it out loud didn't make it feel any more real. "And I knew it was all connected. The shadow sort of passed through me, sharing its memories with me."

Green wrote everything down like she was describing something as mundane as a burglary at the corner store. "I assume this shadow was the ghost or spirit of the woman here?"

"Yes." Cassie pushed through her discomfort, not used to being so open about all of this. But at least he wasn't laughing in her face. "I could see how she died and where she'd been buried. We came here to make sure it was all real. And it was."

"That's a remarkable talent you have there, Cassie." His face was somber as he looked at the body laid out on the trail. "You said you know who killed her? And how she died?"

"She was hit over the head with something heavy. She didn't see it, so I didn't exactly see it either."

More notes. "Makes sense."

"Then someone set her on fire. I think—" Cassie cleared her throat. It wasn't a guess. She knew. "I know she was alive when it happened. She died in agony. Then they wrapped her up in the black bag and brought her here. Buried her where no one would find her."

Green looked up from his note pad. "You said you knew who killed her?"

Cassie swallowed. This was the part she and Harris hadn't been sure about. Should they mention Reed and risk having him locked up where they couldn't get to him? They wouldn't have a chance to interrogate him. Harris had wanted to play it by ear, see how cooperative the LAPD would be.

"The man who set her on fire was named Joseph Zbirak, the assassin we came across in Chicago."

"Do you know where he is?" Green asked. "Still in Chicago, maybe?"

"Still in Chicago," Harris answered. "Dead."

"I see. And we'll be able to confirm this?"

"I imagine it won't be too difficult," Harris said.

Cassie cleared her throat to get Detective Green's attention. "I'd like to see some missing women's reports from the last few years. I think I can identify her." Cassie licked her dry lips. She'd finished her water ages ago. "I'd like to know her name."

"So would I," Green said. "You'll need to come into the precinct for that."

Cassie glanced at Harris. "Is that necessary?"

"We're looking at thousands upon thousands of potential victims, and that's just in Los Angeles alone. You mentioned to the officer who took your initial report that she was a California native, but do you know for sure she wasn't from San Diego or Sacramento? We can let you go through our missing persons folders to see if anyone matches who you saw, but there are far too many binders to drag out here." Green paused to peer at Cassie, that assessing look back on his face. "Is that a problem? Something you're worried about?"

Other than the fact that she hated police stations—had been inside them too many times—and didn't know anyone on the LAPD? It was one thing to go down to the Savannah precinct with David or Harris, who knew her, trusted her, and had her back. But what if the LAPD thought she had something to do with this woman's disappearance? What if they thought she'd been involved in Zbirak's machinations?

Before Cassie could come up with an excuse, Harris spoke for her. "No, it's not a problem. Right, Cassie?"

Cassie frowned as both detectives stared at her. Expectant. "No," she finally said. "No problem."

6

As soon as they arrived at the police station, Green had Harris wait in his office while he led Cassie to a private room. "A colleague of mine will swing by with some of our missing persons cases. She might also ask you a few questions." He dazzled Cassie with that smile again. "Just standard procedure. We want to get as many details as possible."

Then he left.

Cassie sat facing the two-way mirror, as would be expected of her. The metal table, the stark white walls, the blinking camera in the corner of the room all sent a wave of panic through her that she had to suppress. It didn't make sense for them to think she was a suspect—why would she uncover and report the body of a missing woman years after the fact? Sure, some people wanted notoriety, but Green hadn't batted an eye at her claims. There was nothing to worry about.

Then why couldn't she control the nervous jiggle of her leg?

The door opened, and Cassie turned to see a tall, lean woman enter the room. Unlike Green, she had pale, delicate skin, though she shared his dark hair, pulled back into a bun. Her eyes were dark brown, almost black, and looked sharp and intelligent. A beauty mark sat just under her left eye, though no one needed further confirmation that this woman could've been a model, but for some reason chose to be a cop.

"My name is Officer Yu." She placed a glass of water on the table in front of Cassie and held out her hand. "You must be Cassie. I hope you haven't been waiting long."

Cassie shook her hand. "Just a minute or two."

"Great. Give me a second to roll these in here." Officer Yu pulled the first cart, then a second, through the door. Both had three tiers, each piled with binders.

"Are those the case files?" Cassie asked.

"Not exactly. They're headshots of missing persons. Can you believe we haven't gone digital yet?" She laughed, and Cassie liked the rough sound of it. "The Chief is a bit of an old-school guy. He's paranoid about hackers. Thinks if we let people sit down at a computer and go through the pictures, they'll find their way into his personal email."

Cassie surprised herself by laughing. There was something comforting about Officer Yu, something real and tangible, unlike Green's otherworldly attractiveness. "Yes, I've known some people like that."

After the officer finished rolling the carts into the corner of the room, she slipped a manila folder off the top and sat down across from Cassie. "Detective Green filled me in on a few of the details, but I'd just like to confirm them with you."

Cassie was transported back into a reality where she was sitting across from a cop being asked about a dead body. Even the glass of water couldn't keep her mouth from drying out. She hated how tiny her voice sounded in the room. "Okay."

"Great." Officer Yu flipped open the folder and scanned the first page. "Now, it says here you came in from Chicago, right?"

"Right," Cassie said. Was she meant to expand on that? "With Detective Harris."

"And how long have you known Detective Harris?"

"A few months." Cassie winced. "But we have—um, had—a mutual friend that we'd both known for years. He was also a detective for the Savannah PD."

"Had?" Officer Yu asked.

"Yes." Cassie had trouble swallowing. "He died. Recently. On the job."

Officer Yu's eyes softened. "I'm sorry to hear that." She looked back down at her notes. "Detective Green said that while you were in Chicago, you came across a man named Joseph Zbirak. Can you tell me how that happened?"

"Oh, well, he kidnapped me." Cassie tried to sound nonchalant, but she still remembered the fury in his eyes when he'd realized she wasn't Rose Sherman. "But I managed to escape."

"And now he's dead?"

"Yes."

Officer Yu didn't break eye contact. "How did that happen?"

Cassie glanced at the binders full of missing women. "What does this have to do with identifying the body we found?"

"We need to know about the circumstances that led to you arriving in California." Officer Yu's voice was patient but unmoving. "You also said Joseph Zbirak killed the woman who was dumped in the wetlands. If he's dead, we can close the case. But we need proof. And an explanation."

Cassie swallowed and nodded. She knew this. And no matter how difficult it was, the truth was better than a lie, even if the truth could get Harris into hot water down the line. It was better than the alternative.

"Like I said, he kidnapped me. Harris came to my rescue. She saved my life."

Officer Yu jotted something down, then looked back up at Cassie. "Is that it?"

"More or less," Cassie said. "He had a gun to my head. She put a bullet in his before he put one in mine. I'm still here because of her."

"And we're glad you are." Officer Yu looked down at her folder, but this time she hesitated before speaking again. When she looked up, there was a wary look in her eye. "Before he died, Zbirak told you the location of the woman's body?"

"Uh, not exactly." Cassie adjusted herself in the seat. The rigid metal was digging into her thighs. "I had an experience. With a shadow."

Officer Yu lifted one eyebrow. "An experience," she repeated. "With a shadow."

"It passed through me. It was a spirit. A ghost. And I gained her memories. She showed me where she was buried."

"And I suppose you have no proof of this?"

28

"No." Cassie was used to people not believing her, but it never got easier. She never stopped feeling crazy. She couldn't explain it to herself half the time, let alone anyone else. "Other than the fact that I knew exactly where she was buried."

"There could be a lot of reasons you knew that."

Cassie took a deep breath to control the sudden spike of anger that spread throughout her body. This was exactly why she didn't want to come here, why she was so nervous about leaving Harris' side. "I'm not here to prove whether or not I'm psychic, Officer Yu." Cassie smiled to take the edge out of her words. "I'm here to identify the woman I helped find today."

Officer Yu studied her for a moment, her thoughts indiscernible. Would she keep pressing the topic? Would she go back to Zbirak's death? Would she make Cassie describe, in painful detail, what it was like to feel yourself burning to death? None of these were ideal, and Cassie had no interest in spending more time in this room than necessary.

But Officer Yu surprised her by saying, "You're right." Then she got up and started piling binders onto the desk. "Unfortunately, these binders are separated by year, which means we don't have a way to distinguish blondes from brunettes from redheads, et cetera. It's an inefficient system, but like I said—"

Cassie put a hand out as Officer Yu placed the third pile on the table. She pointed to the middle binder. "That one."

The woman furrowed her brow. "What?"

"This one." Cassie pulled the binder free. "She's in here."

"How could you possibly know that?"

Cassie looked up at the officer. She couldn't help the smile that tugged at the corners of her lips. "Psychic."

"But how?"

Cassie ignored the woman. It wasn't something she could always qualify, like a strange heat or a tugging sensation. Sometimes it was like the answer had always existed in her mind, and she just needed the right set of circumstances to occur to reveal it. How could she explain that to someone who didn't believe she had these abilities in the first place? It was impossible.

Closing her eyes made it easier to forget Officer Yu was in the room with her. It allowed her to concentrate on the pages before her. Pressing a hand against the first set of pictures, she could tell the woman from her memories was buried deeper, at least halfway through the book. She flipped to the middle and pressed her hand against that page, too. Closer. The tips of her fingers tingled. Her heart rate sped up. A heat that hadn't existed a moment before began to run up her fingers, into her wrist, and through her arm. Not painful like a fire, but encouraging like burning embers. It was life—maybe not for the woman, but for her story.

Cassie turned the page. And again. One more time. Then she stopped. Opened her eyes. Pointed to the woman who had shared a part of her soul with her. "Here." Cassie's voice cracked with emotion. "This is her."

Officer Yu gaped at Cassie, caught between disbelief and distrust. Cassie swung the binder around to face the officer. "Emily Washburn, thirty-six, five-three, brown hair, green eyes, reported missing three years ago." She looked up at Cassie. "How did you—" She broke off. Shook her head. "Never mind. I already know your answer."

"I wish I had a better explanation," Cassie said, and it was the truth. It would be a hell of a lot easier if she did. "But this is her. I know it is."

"We'll see," Officer Yu said, though not unkindly. "We'll work on identifying her right away. Dental records might be our only hope."

Cassie nodded. That could've taken weeks if Cassie hadn't been able to pick her out of the book. Maybe now Emily's family could find solace much faster. "Is that all you need?" Cassie asked. "I'd really like to get back to Detective Harris."

Officer Yu looked like she was trying to come up with an excuse to keep Cassie longer, but curiosity had gotten the best of her. Cassie could see it in her eyes. She wanted to track down this lead, to see if Cassie was blowing smoke or if she was the real deal.

"Yeah, come on. She's still in with Detective Green."

Officer Yu gathered the binder under her arm, her finger saving the spot where Emily Washburn had been relegated to existing as a picture and a few key details. A sense of relief washed over Cassie as soon as she was released from the room. The hard part was far from over, but at least they were on the right path.

Cassie waited for Officer Yu to knock on the door and for Green to call out before she entered. She barely registered Officer Yu telling him they had a lead on the woman's identity and closing the door behind her. It wasn't until both detectives were looking at her that she realized they must've said something.

"What?" Cassie asked. She was staring at Harris, who had a cup of coffee in her hands and looked happier and more relaxed than she had since David's murder. And Green looked totally at ease, with his feet kicked up on the desk and his hands hooked behind his head. "I'm sorry, did you say something?"

"I said congratulations," Green repeated, his smile firmly in place. "You helped identify her. Emily, was it? You blew this case wide open." He dropped his feet to the ground and leaned forward onto his desk. "If you can believe it, I actually remember this one. It was from a few years ago, but something just struck me about it. She had a sister. It was tough watching her realize she might never see her sister again."

"Some cases you just don't forget," Harris said. She looked up at Cassie and frowned. "Are you okay?"

Cassie blushed. "Yeah, I'm fine." She wasn't, but she didn't want to discuss it in front of the other detective. "What have you been up to in here?"

"Noah agreed to help us look for Reed."

Cassie froze. "What?" They'd decided not to tell anyone about Reed. What if the LAPD didn't let them question him? "Why?"

"A little tit for tat," Green answered. "You two helped us solve a cold case. I couldn't let you walk away without some kind of reward. Harris here told me all about David, and how Reed might know something about—what was his name?"

"Aguilar," Harris supplied.

"Right, Aguilar." Green's blue eyes brightened. "Who knows, if Reed was involved in Emily's case, he might be involved in others. Or could give us more insight into Zbirak's criminal past. This could be huge for both of us."

"With my suspension, we need this, Cassie." Harris shrugged when Cassie's eyes widened. "He would've found out sooner or later. It's better to be honest up front."

"Always," Green said. He tapped a knuckle on the desk. "I don't know about you, but I'm starving. Let's grab some lunch before I knock on a few doors. My treat?"

"We've got plans," Harris said, which was news to Cassie. "But we'll talk soon."

"You can count on it."

Cassie didn't miss the way the two of them looked like they were sharing an inside joke, and she definitely didn't miss the way it made her feel like she was the odd one out. She had just spent the last forty-five minutes defending her knowledge about this case, protecting Harris, and trying to get justice for Emily. And what had Harris done as thanks? Shared a coffee with a complete stranger and laid all their cards on the table.

Whatever their mystery plans were, Cassie hope it involved a stiff drink.

7

Lunch did not, in fact, come with a stiff drink, but the blow was softened by the fact that Laura had met them at a little bistro within walking distance of her work. They ordered their sandwiches to go and walked down the street to a miniscule park with a couple of picnic tables set up in one corner. It was strange to Cassie that just a couple days ago she was freezing her ass off in Chicago, and now she was enjoying lunch outside in the sunshine.

Harris caught Laura up on everything that had occurred at the marsh and what had happened in Green's office. Laura took it all in with wide eyes as she munched on her turkey sandwich.

When she was finished speaking, Harris turned to Cassie. "Did I forget anything?"

She hadn't. Mostly. "Just the part where I was interrogated for forty-five minutes while you shared a coffee with Detective Green."

"Did something happen?" Laura asked, sitting up straight. "Are you okay?"

"I'm fine. Officer Yu was very professional." Cassie meant it. Even though she hated the way police stations made her feel, she couldn't complain. If she was truly being treated like a suspect, she would know it.

But constantly having to defend herself, her abilities, was exhausting. "I was just worried about how much we were going to tell them."

"You're mad at me for telling Noah about Reed," Harris said. It wasn't a question.

"We hardly know him." Cassie spoke around a bite of her ham sandwich. "He could use that information against us."

Harris set her own sandwich down and took a swig of water. "Well, I trust him not to."

"And what about me?" Cassie tried to keep the bitterness out of her voice, but the look on Laura's face told her she'd failed. "Does my opinion matter?"

Harris' eyebrows knit together in confusion. "Of course it does."

"But?"

"But," Harris said slowly, "I read the room. You weren't there. Green was grateful we helped him solve this case. It was a big one a few years ago. Got a decent amount of media attention, especially in a city where women go missing all the time. This could mean a promotion for him."

"And why does that matter to us?" Cassie asked.

"It's good," Harris said, starting to lose her patience, "because he'll return the favor. He's taking all the credit. I'm not supposed to be here, so he can't thank me publicly. And I doubt you want your name in the news." Harris waited for Cassie to answer, but they both already knew how she felt about that. "So, we landed on a little exchange of information. He'll do some digging on Reed for us."

"This is a good thing," Laura said, trying to placate Cassie. "He's a cop."

Cassie couldn't help but snort. "We have an entire flash drive full of cops who can't be trusted."

"Those cops are back in Savannah," Harris said, picking up her sandwich again. "Where Aguilar's influence is strongest. I doubt he's got some missing person's detective in Los Angeles on his payroll." She took a bite and looked at Cassie thoughtfully. "Look, if you've got some sort of bad feeling about Noah, let me know. I'll rein it in."

Cassie twisted her mouth to the side. She wished she had some insight, some reason to give to Harris, but she didn't. "No, I don't have any feelings about him. I just want to be careful. We're so close. I don't want to make any more mistakes."

"We won't." Harris said it with such confidence, Cassie actually believed her. "Trust me. We'll find Reed. One way or another."

"Speaking of." Laura shoved the rest of her sandwich in her mouth, brushing the crumbs off her hands. "I did a little digging of my own this morning."

"You what?" Cassie looked from Harris to Laura and back again. "Now we're involving my sister in this? When did we make that decision?"

"You involved me in this the minute you landed in L.A. and asked to crash at my place." Laura didn't give Cassie time to fumble through a response. "Adelaide and I talked about it this morning. I know a few people in the area—cops, parole officers, lawyers, social workers who might be able to find something. Don't worry, I was discrete. Gave them an excuse about having a client in trouble who said he only trusts one person—Reed."

Cassie couldn't argue with that, as much as she wanted to. "Did you find anything?"

"Most people hadn't heard of him. It was a longshot, anyway." There was a glint in her eye. "But we got lucky. A parole officer. Nice, but super intimidating. Tends to get the tougher clients. The shadier ones. The ones who definitely did it, you know?"

"What'd he say about Reed?" Harris asked.

"Said he had to deal with him—his words—some years ago, before he moved to Chicago."

"So, he used to practice here?" Harris waited for Laura to nod in confirmation. "That's good. We might find a record of him and his associates. Maybe he's laying low with one of them."

"I had the same thought." Laura brought out her phone and scrolled through a page. "It's not like the guy was big on social media. No website, no reviews. The parole officer, Dan Jenkins, said he always had the same type of clients. Probably worked on referrals. Didn't always take payment in money. Sometimes it was favors."

"That'll be even harder to track," Harris said.

Laura nodded and looked back at her phone. "Exactly."

The table was silent while Harris finished her sandwich. Cassie forced the rest of hers down, too. They didn't stick to a schedule when they were on a case, and she had to make sure she had enough energy for whatever the day would throw at her.

Harris leaned over her own phone, and it was only when she held it up that Cassie realized someone was calling her. "It's Green."

The detective put the phone to her ear. "Harris." She furrowed her brow, then nodded a few times, listening intently. "Yeah. Sure, yeah. No, it's not a problem. Now?" She cut a glance at Cassie, frowning. "Are you positive? Oh, okay. That's fine. Got it. See you soon."

Cassie cocked her head to one side. "What was that about?"

"He wants to pick my brain about something, and said he'd appreciate having a female detective," Harris said.

Cassie could tell there was more. "And he doesn't want me to come along?"

"Apparently not. He said no hard feelings, But he just didn't want to freak out the witness he needs to talk to."

"And there are no other women in the department who could do it?" Cassie thought of Officer Yu. She was stern, but compassionate. She'd be able to handle it just fine. "Why you?"

"Said he's gonna pass me off as a social worker. Seems his other contacts are busy." Harris crumpled up her garbage and tossed it in a nearby trash can. "Look, I don't exactly want to get roped into another case, but having someone in the LAPD on our side is important. It could be the difference between finding Reed and letting him escape again. If I feel like he's wasting my time, I'll let him know no more favors, okay? But while we're out, maybe I can get him to knock on a few doors for us."

Cassie couldn't argue. Worse, she didn't want to. They hadn't even been in L.A. for a whole day, and it already felt like everything was falling apart. "Are you taking the car?"

Harris tapped something on her phone before she answered. "No, you keep it. I'll Uber there. It's not far away. I'll try to be home by dinner, okay?" She looked down at Laura as she stood. "Still want me to make that casserole?"

"Yes." Laura's eyes sparkled. "I'll have Cassie stop at the store on the way home from work." As though only just remembering that Cassie existed, she said, "Is that okay? Come pick me up at six?"

"Sure, yeah." It's not like Cassie had anything else to do, anyway. She turned to Harris. "What about you? Do you need a ride?"

"Nah, I'll make Green bring me home. Least he can do." Harris stood up and pointed to a car idling on the other side of the park. "That's me. I'll keep you updated, okay?"

Cassie nodded but didn't answer. As soon as Harris got into the car, Laura turned to Cassie and raised an eyebrow.

Cassie scowled. "What?"

"What's going on with you?"

"I don't know what you're talking about."

"You can lie to Adelaide, but you can't lie to me," Laura said. The wind ruffled her curls, and she pushed them out of her face. "Spill."

"I feel..." Cassie searched for the right word. "Unsettled."

"About what?"

"About this." She gestured around her, like she was talking about all of Los Angeles. "I'm not sure why."

Laura leaned closer and stared her sister in the eyes, like she could pull the answers from Cassie's mind. "You're annoyed at Adelaide."

There was no point in denying it. "Yes."

"Do you feel replaced by this other detective?"

"No." Cassie's answer was too fast. She forced herself to think about it. But she'd told the truth. "No, I don't think so. He's a stranger, so I'm cautious. Harris seems uncharacteristically trusting. And optimistic. I don't like it."

Laura nodded like she'd noticed, too. Then she stood and tossed their garbage away. "Walk me back to work?" She waited until they were on the sidewalk to start talking again. "It seems like she's on the brink of cracking this wide open. Reed is close. You just need to find him, get him to talk, and he could explain the whole situation with David. He could even turn on Aguilar. He'd be a star witness."

"*If* he talks," Cassie pointed out. "There's no guarantee of that."

"Adelaide thinks there is. She's confident."

"Confident or cocky?" Cassie asked.

"A fair point." Laura chewed her lip. "Maybe a little of each, but we both know not to underestimate her. I'm sure she's got a plan." They stopped at a crosswalk and waited for the light to change. "I think she feels unsettled, too. This whole thing with David ripped the rug right out from under her feet."

"And it didn't for me?"

"I never said that." Laura smiled patiently, and Cassie had to resist the urge to roll her eyes. Her sister could be so superior when she wanted to be. "Her reaction is going to be different from yours, and expecting it to be the same is the quickest way to find yourselves at odds. She's coping in a way that makes her feel most comfortable. And so are you."

The traffic light turned red, and the pair of them crossed the street.

"So, her coping mechanism is to be reckless?"

"Yes." Laura laughed at the dubious expression on Cassie's face. "She wants answers, and she wants them now. She'll do anything to get them. It's why she's such a good detective. She doesn't give up until she solves the mystery."

"And me?" Cassie asked, though she wasn't sure she wanted to know the answer.

Laura stopped outside her office building and turned to Cassie. "You're the opposite. You shut down when things get tough." Laura held up a hand to stop Cassie's protests. "It's not necessarily a bad thing. Look at everything that's happened to you. You've learned to be cautious, to conserve energy. You want to make sure whatever move you make is the right one."

"And that's why Reed got away."

Laura shrugged. "Yeah, but that kind of thinking has also saved your life." Laura checked the time on her phone and sighed. "I need to go, but do me a favor? Don't be too hard on her. She's going through the same thing you are. You should be a team. Both of you need to learn balance. In fact"—she waited until Cassie met her eyes—"you balance each other out. That's why you work so well together. You just need to get back on the same page."

"Hard to do when she's leaving me behind."

Laura nodded. "True, but this is all in service of the bigger picture. She's off working the Noah angle. What are you going to work on?"

Cassie had no idea, but she didn't want to say that out loud.

Laura checked her phone again. "Okay, I really gotta go. See you tonight."

"See you." Cassie watched as her sister pushed through the doors and headed up the stairs to her office. Then she turned back to the street and took it all in—the traffic, the trees, the sun, the breeze. She had all of L.A. at her disposal.

The only question now was, what would she do with it?

8

ON THE RIDE OVER TO MEET DETECTIVE GREEN, HARRIS TRIED TO WIPE Cassie's hurt look from her mind. She kicked herself for not thinking about how Cassie would feel at the station. Sometimes it was easy to forget everything the other woman had been through, from her attack to the countless times she'd had to convince a group of strangers that she wasn't crazy, that she knew exactly where to find the victim or the dead body or even the killer.

It was true that Harris should have waited to loop Green in until after discussing it with Cassie first, but there had been no time for a sidebar. Harris had made a gut decision, and there was no current evidence suggesting it was the wrong one. Sure, Green was cocky, and something about his Hollywood-handsome face rubbed her the wrong way, but that didn't mean he was untrustworthy.

A flicker of doubt passed through her. Harris hadn't liked the way he'd requested Cassie stay behind, but she couldn't blame him. Cassie was a capable woman full of compassion and empathy, but her abilities weren't always received well. And if this witness was as squirrely as Green had made her out to be, they couldn't risk it.

Harris sighed loud enough that her Uber driver looked over his shoulder to make sure she was okay. She was used to following her gut, but ever since they'd found out the truth about David working with Aguilar, her world had been flipped upside down. She knew she was pushing Cassie's buttons and taking risks she normally wouldn't, but the truth was right there, just out of her grasp. All she had to do was stretch another few inches and she could grab onto it, once and for all.

The Uber pulled up along a curb, and Harris got out with a hasty thanks. Detective Green was waiting for her outside a café, holding a clipboard and a small stack of folders. The smile he gave when he spotted Harris almost blinded her.

"Twice in one day," he called. "Lucky me."

Harris tried not to grimace. If he wanted to flirt his way through this investigation, he'd be disappointed. "Lucky you," she repeated wryly, then pointed to the paperwork in his arms. "What's that?"

"Your props." He handed them over. "Our witness' name is Ginny Dupont. She knows who I am, but she didn't respond well to my questioning. I've told her you wanted to follow up with her, offer her some free services. She probably won't take them, but I've included one of your *colleague's* business cards in case she changes her mind."

"Got it." Harris flipped through the folders, but they were mostly full of blank paper. "And what kind of information are you looking for here?"

Green turned serious. "Ginny is friends with a missing woman, one of my open investigations. Norma Mitchell." He paused and studied Harris, maybe weighing how much detail he should give up. "When I last talked to Ginny, she didn't really want anything to do with me. Told me she saw Norma get into a car with a man, but she didn't know his name."

"But you think she was lying?" Harris asked.

"Yeah." He shook his head. "Look, I can't blame her. She's probably been through the ringer. Maybe she didn't want to tell a cop who this guy was. Maybe she's afraid of him. But if she thinks you're a social worker—"

"That's kind of a loophole." Harris looked beyond Green, to the front of the café behind him. It was a hole in the wall, some place local that sold damn good coffee, judging from the bustling inside. "Is this where she works?"

Green nodded and checked his watch. "She should be going on break any minute now."

"You just need the guy's name, right?" Harris asked. "And then you'll see what you can find out about Reed?"

"His name, yeah, but anything else you think would be relevant would be a huge help." He pointed to a table farthest from the door, just as a woman with short black hair stepped out into the sunshine.

"That's her. I'm going to sit there and make some phone calls. Hopefully, we can help each other out today."

Harris fixed a shy smile on her face and approached Ginny. She stuck out her hand and tried to radiate warmth. "Ms. Dupont? My name is Addie. Detective Green said you'd be willing to talk to me for a few minutes."

"You're the social worker." She shook Harris' hand, dropping it almost as fast as she'd taken it inside her own. Ginny couldn't have been older than mid-twenties, but the weary look in her eye and dark makeup on her face suggested she'd seen more than her fair share of life. She looked over at where Green was pointedly not looking at them. "He said you had some questions?"

"Come on, let's sit over here." Harris led the younger woman to a table farthest from Green. When they were settled, Harris leaned forward, resting her elbows on the folders, and gave Ginny all of her attention. "How are you? Everything going okay?" She looked up at the sign for the café. "You like working here?"

Ginny seemed surprised for a moment, like she wasn't used to people inquiring about her wellbeing. After a second's hesitation, she shrugged and leaned back in her chair. "I'm okay. And it's a job. Wish it paid more, but I've had worse."

"I hear that. I worked in some pretty shitty places before I got this gig." When Ginny didn't continue the conversation, Harris sat back, giving the other woman a little more room. "Thanks for taking the time to talk to me, by the way. I know you're on your break right now. I just have a few questions, and then I'll let you get on your way."

Ginny was looking anywhere but at her. "Okay."

"We're pretty concerned about Norma, and we want to find her as quickly as we can."

"Do you even know her?" Ginny asked, looking Harris up and down. "Why do you care? You're just a social worker."

"Detective Green is a friend of mine," Harris said. "He asked me to help. I have some experience with cases like this, and he wants to make sure we dedicate all possible resources to Norma's investigation." It must've been a satisfying answer because Ginny didn't argue. "When's the last time you saw her?"

"A few days ago."

"And she got into a car with a man, right? Someone you know?"

Ginny nodded but didn't say anything else.

"Do you know his name?"

"I don't."

"I know you're scared. And I know you don't want to get caught talking to the police. But I'm not the police, okay?" Harris hated that, right now, that was mostly the truth. "I don't want to get anyone in trouble. If we can find this person, we might be able to find Norma. And no one needs to know that you were the one who told us."

Ginny pressed her lips together, and it looked like she was holding back tears. "I just want her to be okay."

"So do I." Harris tried another tactic. "Are you worried this man might hurt her?"

Ginny nodded.

"What does he do?"

"He helps people." Ginny laughed wryly. "At least that's what he says. The people he helps end up getting hurt. Or worse."

By the look in her eye, Harris knew Ginny didn't just mean getting killed. There was a fine line between getting this information as fast as possible and scaring Ginny off completely. "We can only help her if we know who she got into the car with. And if we can find her, maybe we can find others, too. This is about more than just Norma. You can really help a lot of people here."

Ginny blew out a shaky breath, and Harris knew she'd said the right thing.

"His name is Dom Lindholm." Ginny stood. "But you didn't hear it from me."

Harris stood, too, forcing herself not to grab the other woman's wrist to keep her in place. "Anything else? Anything at all that you can tell me? Where he lives, or—"

"No." Ginny's voice indicated that she'd already shut down. "That's all I know. My break is almost over. I need to get back inside."

Harris knew pushing wasn't going to get her anywhere. And at least they had a name. That was a start.

"Here." She pulled out the business card Green had left for her. "This is a friend of mine. She can help you with whatever you need, if you change your mind. All you have to do is call that number."

Ginny took the card without looking at it and slipped it into her pocket. Then she turned around and walked back inside.

As soon as she was gone, Green joined Harris at her table. "Well? Any luck?"

"Does the name Dom Lindholm mean anything to you?"

Green blinked at her a few times before answering. "It does. He's a piece of shit."

"That's who Norma got into a car with. But she didn't tell me anything else."

Green stood up. "That's great. Thank you. This might be exactly what we need to blow the case wide open." He brought his phone to his ear and walked away.

"Wait," Harris called out. "What about Reed? Did you find anything?"

"None of my contacts knew anything," Green called over his shoulder. "But I'll keep asking around."

Harris couldn't stop the disappointed slump of her shoulders as she watched the detective disappear around the corner.

9

After some debate, Cassie decided to go back to the one part of L.A. she'd already visited earlier that day—the Ballona Wetlands. It had only been a couple hours, but most people had dispersed, onlookers and police alike. A few members of the forensics team were still sifting through the vegetation, hoping to find clues, but mostly coming up with garbage. The tough part was knowing the difference, so they'd bagged everything they'd found and hauled it back to their lab. At the very worst, they were providing a cleanup service for the marsh.

On the other side of the caution tape stood a handful of onlookers. As Cassie approached, she saw one or two break away and a few others take their spot. Most of the onlookers passed by without stopping, not wanting to admit to their morbid fascination about what had been discovered that morning. A few bystanders seemed to have been there for a while, if their sun-kissed noses and shoulders were any indication.

Cassie approached to the caution tape near one of the officers. He was a short, stocky man with a balding head smeared with sunscreen. Either he hadn't realized it wasn't rubbed all the way in, or he didn't care. His job was to stand there and make sure no one crossed the line without permission. Nobody dared, but a few people pestered him with questions.

"Come on, Jerry. Just a nudge in the right direction? Something off the record?"

"Nothing is off the record with you, Piper." Officer Jerry still had his back to them, but Cassie caught the hard edges of his words. "I learned that the hard way."

"It was an honest mistake," Piper said, but the grin on her face said otherwise. She was a short woman with long brown hair and black glasses. Her nose and cheeks were pink, but if she was worried about getting a sunburn, she didn't show it. "I swear it won't happen again."

"It won't happen again." He turned around. The jovial smile on his face didn't reach his eyes. "Because I will watch everything I say to you from now on."

He caught sight of Cassie. "Hey, I know you."

Everyone turned to look at her, and Cassie had to force her voice to remain steady. "You do?"

"You an actor or something?"

Cassie was flattered until she realized that was a very real possibility around here. If you thought you knew someone but couldn't figure out why, your first thought was whether you'd seen them on TV.

She shook her head. "No."

Officer Jerry narrowed his eyes at her, then they widened and he snapped his fingers. "You're the psychic lady. You were here earlier."

"Yeah." The people around her started whispering amongst themselves, and Cassie had to force herself not to listen. "I was wondering if I could come back in? Check out the scene again? I might've missed something."

The officer looked over his shoulder at the edge of the trail, then back to her. "You really a psychic?"

She tried for breezy, but it came out strangled. "That's what they tell me."

"Let me ask." He stared her down and pointed at her feet. "Wait here."

Cassie nodded and planted her feet. What did he think she'd do, bum-rush the crime scene? That wouldn't get her what she wanted. But stranger things had happened, and she wasn't about to ruin her chances at crossing the tape and picking up something she hadn't noticed before.

Piper approached Cassie. She pushed her glasses up the bridge of her nose before holding out a hand. "Hi, my name is Piper McLaren. I run a true crime podcast." She pulled her hand away just as Cassie was about to shake it. "Are you going to, like, see when I die if you touch me?"

"Unlikely," Cassie said, "but not impossible."

The woman stuck her hand back out. "I'll take my chances. What's your name?"

"I'd rather not say."

If anything, that made Piper more curious. "You're one of those mysterious types, aren't you? Do you do this a lot? Help cops solve crimes?"

"I wouldn't say a lot—"

"I'd love to have you on my podcast." Piper produced a card and shoved it into Cassie's hand. "What do you say?"

Cassie put the card into her shorts without even looking at it. "Oh, um—"

"Ma'am?" Officer Jerry was back. "We can give you ten minutes. Supervised."

"Perfect," Cassie said, grateful for a reason not to answer Piper. "Thank you."

As Cassie ducked under the tape and walked away, Piper called out from behind her. "Hey!" Cassie turned, just in time to see the woman lift her phone and snap a picture. "Give me a call if you change your mind."

Cassie half-smiled with no intention of following up. She'd probably throw the card away as soon as she got back to Laura's. The last thing she wanted to do was broadcast her ability across the entire the internet.

Officer Jerry led her to the edge of the trail. He pointed to the few people still in the water, sifting through garbage. "Let them work. Don't go in the water. And don't touch anything. If you find something"—he gave her a pointed look—"you tell us."

Cassie flashed him a winning smile. "Got it."

She must've been convincing because he sighed and turned back toward the crowd. "Ten minutes," he called over his shoulder, then took up his post, keeping a wary eye on her.

She felt like the whole world had its eyes trained on her, but she ignored the feeling as best as she could. Emily wouldn't be making an appearance, but this was still the spot she'd been buried in for several years. There had to be some residual energy. Something to point Cassie in the right direction.

Cassie tried to relax. She breathed in the salty, humid air, and the breeze felt nice under the direct sunlight. It was a good thing she'd slathered on plenty of sunscreen.

Seagulls cried out above them, and she could just barely make out Piper's voice from the other side of the tape. The forensics team along the water fiddled with plastic bags and empty beer cans. Someone's radio went off, and they mumbled their response.

Cassie tried to erase each noise and each person from the crime scene until she was only left with the dirt beneath her feet and the water in front of her. What would it have been like when Emily was here? Nighttime, that was for sure. Cassie ignored the sun on her shoulders, and tried to imagine stars above her instead. The ice-cold water on her feet. The chill in the air.

Goosebumps rose on Cassie's skin as she pictured Reed and Zbirak making their way down the trail. She had bits and pieces of the scene stored in her memory from her last interaction with Emily, but she had to connect the dots. There had to be something here that could help them.

Emily had been tiny, even more so after Zbirak had burned her body. It hadn't been long enough to turn everything to ash, but she wouldn't have been recognizable in the state they'd found her in. Zbirak would've carried her in the black garbage bag over his shoulder. Reed would've carried whatever tools they thought they'd need. Between the two of them, they would've filled her bag with rocks and dumped her in. Under the cover of night, no one disturbed them, although Zbirak probably had a plan in case they'd been interrupted.

Cassie watched in her mind's eye as they dropped Emily into the water, her spirit looking on, helpless. Zbirak was a man of few words anyway, but he seemed quieter than usual. Reed, who loved to hear himself talk, didn't say a word either. They both felt the heaviness of this moment.

But why? Who was Emily to them, if not just another victim?

The two men waited until the bubbles were gone from Emily's final resting place. Then they grabbed their belongings and headed back to the car. Neither looked back. Even if they had, they wouldn't have seen Emily standing over her own grave, screaming silently in pain and anger. Spirits might not have felt the same way humans did, but they experienced their agony for eternity. At least until someone like Cassie helped them move on to a better place.

Cassie tried to sift through Emily's memories. So many of them were mere snapshots of her life. Hugging a woman with long blonde hair. Shopping at a toy store. Seeing a dog running around a park.

Others were more relevant, like meeting Reed in a parking lot and arguing with him. Feeling the flames lick up her skin and not being able to move a muscle in protest. Watching as Zbirak murmured a prayer of forgiveness. Fighting against the pull to move beyond this world, unable to let go of the tragedy she had endured.

Emily was gone now, having expended all her energy to pass her final message onto Cassie. There was a clue, an answer, somewhere inside Cassie's mind. If only she could tap into it. What had happened here still lingered in the air. There was still an energy here, a buzz Cassie could reach out and touch.

She opened her mind.

Emily and Reed had been arguing. About what? Where? A large building loomed behind them. Its silhouette looked familiar, but Cassie couldn't put her finger on it. Some sort of famous landmark? Writing was scrawled along the top in bold, white letters, but they were too blurry to make out. The memory kept refocusing on Reed's face, the anger in his eyes. But Cassie pushed harder. If only she could make out what it said. Even a single word—*Hotel.*

They were arguing outside of a hotel. Which one? Cassie willed her eyes to focus. The answer was within reach. Or, at least, a clue to an answer. She had no clue why this was important, but for the first time since she'd landed in Los Angeles, Cassie felt like she was on the right track.

"Ma'am?"

Cassie blinked her eyes open as the world came crashing back into existence. The sun made her skin prickle, and the wind had spun her hair into knots. The traffic just beyond the wetlands roared in her ears, and a nearby seagull's squawk made her jump.

"Ma'am?" the voice asked again, this time a little louder. "Are you okay?"

Cassie blinked against the bright sun and shielded her eyes as she looked over at Officer Jerry. "Yeah, yeah." She bit back her frustration at being interrupted. "I'm okay."

"It's been ten minutes, ma'am. Did you, uh, see anything?"

Had she? Knowing that Emily and Reed had been near a hotel—not even *in* one—wasn't the breakthrough she had hoped for. It was no breakthrough at all, really, but it felt important. Still, it wasn't something tangible she could hand over to the cops.

"No." She didn't have to fake her frown. "No, I didn't see anything."

"In that case." Officer Jerry let the phrase hang in the air as he swept his hand back toward the caution tape.

Cassie peered beyond him and saw the small crowd still gathered on the other side. Piper was watching them, speaking into her phone like a microphone.

"Actually," Cassie said, "do you mind if I walk around to the other side? I'd like to avoid"—she waved a hand in that general direction—"all that."

Officer Jerry looked over his shoulder, presumably zeroing in on Piper. When he turned back to Cassie, he had a knowing look in his eyes.

"Sure thing," he said. "Follow me."

10

By the time Cassie and Laura got back from the grocery store, Harris was already chopping vegetables and sauteing meat in a pan. The air was heavy with spices, and Cassie's stomach growled in response.

"Hey, honey, we're home." Laura set the groceries on the counter. "How was your day?"

Harris tipped her head back and laughed. "Don't expect me to be this domestic all the time. It's Cassie's turn tomorrow night."

Cassie looked between their smiling faces and forced one of her own. She couldn't figure out why she didn't feel as carefree as they did. Maybe the crime scene still weighed heavily on her. Or maybe it was the fact the other women seemed so easy with each other. It was her own sister's house, yet she felt like a third wheel.

Cassie changed the subject. "How was it with Detective Green? Find out anything useful?"

Harris sliced tomatoes while she talked. "About Reed? No, not yet. Noah's good at reading people. He was right that the witness would open up to me a lot more easily than him. She was friends with a woman who disappeared last week. Saw her getting in a car with a man she recognized. But she's scared of the guy. Scared of most guys, actually. But I got her to give us a name. Hopefully, it helps."

Laura set a box of pasta and some cheese next to Harris before tossing the plastic bags under the sink. "It's a good thing you were there."

Harris shrugged, but she looked happy with the compliment. "Just glad I could help. Feels good to make some forward movement. Even if it's not on our case."

Laura pulled down three fresh wine glasses. "Speaking of forward movement, you should hear what Cassie saw."

Harris's head snapped up. "You saw something? Like actually saw it, or—"

"I don't know what I saw," Cassie said. Saying it out loud to Laura in the car had felt good, but now her face flushed with embarrassment. Harris wouldn't think much of it. "Nothing concrete, anyway."

Laura picked up the spoon and stirred the meat in the pan, taking a big whiff of it and sighing happily.

"The trick is to use ground turkey. Less grease," Harris said, then poured the tomatoes in, then the beef broth, then the pasta, covering it and bringing it to a boil. Then she started grating the cheese. "Well, go on," she said. "What did you find out?"

Cassie sighed, thinking the story would be easier to tell now that she'd already recited it once. "I went back to the crime scene." When Harris looked up sharply, Cassie faltered. "What?"

"Without me? Don't you think that would look suspicious?"

"Maybe. But I'm not a suspect." Unless Green had mentioned something to Harris, detective to detective. "Am I?"

"No, of course not."

"One of the cops recognized me. He remembered I was the psychic, so he let me through. Gave me ten minutes to look at the crime scene again." Cassie hadn't told Laura about the reporters or Piper the podcaster, and she wasn't about to tell Harris either. "I just stood there and tried to see if anything came to me."

"I wish you would've told me," Harris said. "We could've gone together."

"And I wish you would've told me you were going to ditch me for *Noah*, but that didn't happen either."

"I didn't ditch you." Harris grated the cheese with more force. "You were there when he called. I had no idea he would ask for my help. The witness was squirrelly enough. Too many people, and she would've shut down completely. Why are you being weird about this?"

"I'm not being weird. I'm just saying, you left, and I had to figure out what to do. I ended up back at Ballona. And I found something. It was worth it."

"You said you didn't find anything concrete," Harris said, lifting the lid on the pan and stirring the pasta. "So, which is it?"

Laura handed Cassie her glass of wine. "Guys, can we just take a second—"

"I saw Reed and Emily arguing outside a hotel."

Harris replaced the lid on the pot and took a sip of her wine. When she looked back at Cassie, her eyes were cool. "Emily died several years ago. I doubt there's any evidence left."

Cassie bristled. "Yes, I'm aware. But it could be a hotel Reed frequents. He could be there right now. At least I did something relevant to the case."

Harris ground her teeth together. "I'm trying to stay on Noah's good side. I know you don't think it's the right call, but he could be a huge resource for us. Why are you fighting this so hard?"

Because it doesn't feel right wasn't a perfect excuse. "All I'm wondering is, why are we wasting time on someone who may or may not help us, rather than just looking for clues ourselves?"

"I told you. Noah is a good resource. It may not feel like it now, but this is a much more efficient way of tracking down a lead on Reed. The LAPD will be able to find him a lot faster than we will."

"So, you're not even going to consider the hotel angle?"

"I never said that. If you've got a solid lead, we'll follow it. Which hotel was it?" Harris walked around to the other side of the counter and stood in the living room, across from Cassie.

Cassie looked away, not wanting to see Harris' reaction. "I don't know."

"Really, Cassie? After all that? *You don't know.*"

Laura clutched her glass of wine like it was her only tether to reality. "She said it looked familiar. Maybe it's a famous hotel?"

"Do we even know if it was in Los Angeles?" Harris asked.

Cassie's face flushed. "It was a big building with white letters on the side. It won't be that hard to find."

"Even if you do figure it out," Harris said, "what are you expecting to find? It's a one-in-a-million chance Reed is there. And if he's not, any records of him or Emily will be years old. Evidence will be gone."

"I saw it for a reason," Cassie snapped, finally looking back at Harris. "It means we're meant to figure this out. I'd rather do it together, but if you're too busy—"

"Too busy?" Harris spat. "What has gotten into you?"

"I'm tired of being left out of the loop. Of feeling like I don't have a say in this partnership. I spent forty-five minutes getting grilled today. I didn't even want to go to the precinct. Do you know what it's like there for me? What kind of memories it brings back?" Harris' jaw went slack, but Cassie pressed forward. "I spent the entire time trying to protect you, worrying about saying the wrong thing and getting one of us in trouble. Only to find out you already told Noah about Reed. I know you trust him, but what if you're wrong?" Cassie had to blink back tears of frustration. "What if the LAPD get their hands on Reed and don't let us talk to him? What if we never find out what he knows? What if we never figure out what happened to David or why he was working with Aguilar?"

Silence fell around the room. Harris looked at Cassie like she was seeing her for the first time. "Don't you think I want answers too? Don't you think I'm doing what I think is best for us? For David?"

Cassie thought of what Laura said earlier that day. Harris was too reckless, and Cassie was too cautious. They had worked well up until this point, but what if that had just been luck? Maybe they were too different.

"I do," Cassie said. "But sometimes I think you forget I'm in as much pain as you are. Sometimes I think you don't know when to stop being a cop and start being a person."

Harris' mouth fell open, but whatever she was going to say was cut short by the doorbell.

Laura set her glass down and hurried over to the door, grateful for the distraction. Cassie didn't bother turning around. She stared at Harris, half wondering if she'd gone too far, half not caring. Chicago had been tough for them, had changed their relationship. Not everyone was meant to stay in your life forever. Maybe after this was all over, when they finally made it back home, she and Adelaide would part ways.

"Cassie." Laura's voice was deadly serious behind her. "It's for you."

Cassie turned around, not knowing what to expect. It took her the span of several heartbeats to realize who was on the other side of the door. Blinking once, twice, three times to make sure it wasn't an illusion. Was he really here?

"Hey," Jason said. "I heard you might need some help."

11

IT HAD BEEN SO LONG SINCE AGUILAR LET LOOSE THAT HE'D THOUGHT HE'D forgotten how. Years had gone by without getting blood on his hands—that's what he had his men for, after all—but it was like riding a bicycle. Once he got started, instinct took over, and he found himself remembering all his favorite ways to make a man scream in pain.

He had a sudden urge to tell Zbirak about it—the only person who would appreciate how he felt in this moment. But then he remembered, the man was dead. He still didn't know how some second-rate detective had gotten the drop on one of the world's best hitmen, but it hardly mattered now. It was fuel for the fire building inside him.

A low moan brought Aguilar back to reality, and he surveyed his handiwork.

He was standing inside a modest four-bedroom home in the suburbs outside Savannah. The area housed some of the wealthier families from the city. Each home sat on a decent amount of land, and no neighbors were close enough to hear the screams.

The dining room had rich hardwood floors, elegant green walls, and a bay window that looked out on the sprawling backyard. A cabinet to his right housed the family's fine China—the type of dinnerware you passed down from generation to generation.

Upon the mahogany dining room table—which sat twelve—was a stark white tablecloth now stained red. Not from wine, as might normally be the case, but blood. Pietro Bianchi's blood, to be exact.

Pietro Bianchi was a twenty-something upstart with a temper, a flare for dramatics, and no business sense. When he'd heard Aguilar had turned down his Uncle Nicolas' generous offer, he'd gotten a bright idea in his head. Why not torch one of Aguilar's beloved restaurants? And what better one to start with than his infamous Brazilian steakhouse? No one would ever know, and it'd help Pietro and his friends let off a little steam.

Only someone did know. Jasper Brown, Aguilar's steadfast righthand man, had been passing by the restaurant just as the flames hit their peak. In fact, he was the one who had reported the crime. He'd also been the one to see Pietro fleeing the scene after pissing on one of the walls and almost getting third-degree burns on his dick.

Jasper's first call had been to the cops, and the second had been to Aguilar. Less than an hour later, Aguilar had waltzed into Pietro's home —the one his father had given to him for nothing at all—shot three of his friends, and knocked Pietro unconscious, pinning him to the dining room table with his own knives.

It was brash, even for Aguilar's usual taste. Normally, he'd let one of the Bianchis—most likely Nicolas himself—come to apologize. Aguilar would've accepted even a half-hearted apology. They'd laugh about how impulsive kids could be, Aguilar would demand Pietro pay a significant price for his crimes, Nicolas would talk him down to something they could both agree upon, and the debt would be settled.

But Aguilar's temper had gotten the best of him. The situation in Chicago had added fuel to the fire, and he wanted to see the Bianchis burn. Were four lives really worth one restaurant? No. But Aguilar needed to send a message. The Bianchis had forgotten who they were dealing with. They would remember now. And if it led to an all-out war? Aguilar had more resources, more friends, more of a will to live. They wouldn't win.

Another moan, louder this time, told Aguilar that Pietro was waking up. He had driven a knife into each of Pietro's hands, stretched high above his head, and hammered them through the wood until they could go no farther. If Pietro attempted to free himself, it would be agonizing.

Aguilar had then slit Pietro's Achilles tendons. As blood seeped from the wounds, soaked into the tablecloth, and dripped to the floor, Pietro grew weaker. His screams got quieter. Every time he lost consciousness, Aguilar drove another knife into a different body part—his liver, his thigh, his chest. Eventually, the screams turned to moans. Pietro had very little life left to give.

Jasper stepped back into the room, his hands clasped in front of him. "Sir?"

"Yes?" Aguilar was sweating, but he didn't dare remove his jacket. "What is it?"

"An update from Los Angeles."

Aguilar turned toward him, interested. Pietro wasn't going anywhere, and he was hoping for good news. He tried not to let it show on his face. "What is it?"

"Shepherd has eyes on the detective."

A smile bloomed across Aguilar's face. That was excellent news. Shepherd wasn't the man's real name. It had something to do with dogs, but Aguilar couldn't care less. Shepherd was Jasper's contact, not his. The more distance between them, the better. He'd met the man once and hadn't been impressed, but Jasper had vouched for him. And, right now, he was the only one in L.A. who was in a position to help them.

"Where are they?" Aguilar asked, ignoring more moans from their host. "What are they doing?"

"In Inglewood. The psychic has a sister there. And her friend, Jason Broussard, hopped on a plane before our guy could make his move. He's now in L.A. too." Jasper shifted from one foot to the other. It was a subtle move, but Aguilar knew he wouldn't like what came next. "They found Emily's body, sir. The investigation's been reopened."

Aguilar forced himself not to react. "Good job getting eyes on them so quickly," he said, more to give himself time to decide how he felt about the other bit of news. "Having all of them in the same place, Broussard included, could be good for us. Much easier to kill them all at once."

Jasper nodded. "And Emily, sir?"

"An unfortunate development." Aguilar turned back to Pietro so Jasper couldn't see his face. "But it doesn't change anything. We still need to find Reed before they do. Any luck?"

"Not yet, sir." Jasper's voice was even, to the point. "Shepherd is also looking for her sister. Just in case."

"She was always smarter than Emily. If she knows what's good for her, she'll stay gone." Aguilar didn't think the woman would grow a spine overnight, but he couldn't take any chances. Now that Emily's body had been uncovered, it could be just the incentive she needed. "Anything else?"

"No, sir." Jasper paused for a beat. "We should get going. Just in case."

It didn't matter. Aguilar was bored with Pietro now. He'd lost too much blood, endured too much pain. On any other day, Aguilar would let him live his final moments in agony, but he wanted this last moment of control. And he wanted to send a final message.

Taking the last knife from the block, Aguilar drove it into Pietro's right eye, killing him. The boy shook once and deflated, the last of his breath exiting his lungs. No more crying. No more moaning. No more begging.

An eye for an eye.

Aguilar picked up the dead man's phone and used Pietro's thumb to unlock it. He scrolled through his text messages until he came across Nicolas' name. Then he tossed the phone to Jasper. "Wipe everything down. Send a message to Nicolas to meet here. Make it convincing." Aguilar stopped before he passed Jasper on his way out. "Lock the door. Make sure no one sees you leave. Prepare the men. Keep it quiet."

Jasper's eyes were resolute. "Yes, sir."

It was all the confirmation Aguilar needed. Jasper would make sure it got done. There would be no evidence Francisco Aguilar had ever stepped inside this house, but Nicolas Bianchi would know who was responsible. They would all know.

Aguilar planned on it.

12

The room fell silent as Cassie, Harris, and Laura stared at Jason standing in the doorway.

He stared back. "Surprise?"

Harris was the first one to break the spell. "What are you doing here?" She looked at Cassie. "Did you invite him?"

It took a second more for Cassie to find her voice. "Not exactly."

Laura laughed and shooed Jason inside. "Come on, don't let the bugs in. Dinner's in the oven, and I've got plenty of wine. Or something stronger. You know what, something stronger sounds great."

Jason set his bag down on the floor while Laura hurried into the kitchen. But he only had eyes for Cassie. Eyes filled with worry. "I'm sorry to drop in on you like this. If I'm interrupting something—"

"No!" Laura called from the kitchen. "You're not interrupting. Please stay."

Jason's brows furrowed, and the worry in his eyes turned to confusion. "Cassie?"

"Not interrupting." Cassie walked over to him and wrapped her arms around his waist, feeling him relax against her. "I'm glad you're here," she whispered, just for him. Then she took a step back. "But when you said you'd help us find a way to track down Reed, I didn't think it meant flying halfway across the country."

"Yeah, that wasn't the initial plan." He wrapped a hand around the back of his neck and looked up at the ceiling. "But then I got to thinking. And worrying. And, well, here I am." He dropped his arm and looked back down at her. "I'll admit it was an impulsive decision."

"Well, we're glad you're here," Laura said, pushing a glass of something into his hand. "Do you like vodka?"

"Uh, yes?"

"Great! Me too." She had a manic smile plastered across her face. "I'm Laura, Cassie's sister. We met once, very briefly. At the pizza place? Cassie was very rude and pushed me away."

Jason laughed. "I remember. It's nice to see you again."

Harris called out from where she'd retreated into the kitchen. "How did you know where Laura lived?"

"Oh, right." He took a sip of his drink before he spoke. "Well, Cassie had mentioned once that she lived in Inglewood. And last night, when we were on the phone, she'd mentioned how she liked that all the streets were named after fruits, and especially that the house was on Cherry Street." Jason took a big breath of air, like he was trying to get through this as quickly as possible. "So, I drove up and down the street until I saw Laura's car, which I recognized from her Facebook profile, which I can see because I'm friends with Cassie."

"Huh," Laura said. "I don't know if I should be impressed or concerned."

Jason held up his hand. "I would prefer impressed."

"Impressed it is." Laura threw back half her drink. She also retreated into the kitchen. "How much longer till dinner's done?"

Cassie didn't hear Harris' answer. She was too busy staring at Jason. "You flew all the way to California for me?"

"It sounds crazier the more we say it out loud. But yeah. After Chicago, I just couldn't stay home and do nothing."

"What about work? What about Bear and Apollo?"

Jason chuckled. "They're both okay. I have Magdalena looking after them. They were a little confused, and I think they miss you a lot. But they'll be okay for another couple of days. I promised them I'd bring their mom home safe and sound."

Cassie's smile was brief. "But what about work? They're already so mad at me—"

"Mad isn't the right word," Jason said. "Concerned, maybe. Magdalena is holding them off for now. She has complete faith in you. Everyone else is following her lead."

"For now." Cassie shook her head in disbelief. "She's a superhero. I need to bring her something. Or take her out to dinner. Or buy her a car."

"That woman can barely accept a free cup of coffee, let alone a brand-new car."

"It doesn't have to be new," Cassie pouted. "But what about you? Aren't they mad you're taking off now, too?"

"I got the other guys to cover my shift. I only plan on being here a couple days. I just wanted you to know you have someone in your corner." He glanced at Harris and lowered his voice. "Are things getting any better between you two?"

"I don't know," Cassie whispered. "I may have just ruined everything. I think she hates me now."

"I doubt it." Jason leaned forward and kissed the top of Cassie's head. "You'll figure it out."

Cassie's entire body lit up at the touch. It was such a casual thing to do. With everything going on, they hadn't talked about their kiss outside her hotel room in New Orleans. Were they both interested? Yes. But Cassie's life wasn't exactly stable. She didn't want to ruin what they already had.

"Dinner's ready," Laura called out.

It saved Cassie from having to say anything more.

She took the stack of dishes from the counter and set the table. Harris placed the casserole in the middle of the table, and Laura passed out bowls of salad she'd thrown together. It felt normal. Pleasant. But there was still some tension in the air.

"So, Jason," Harris said, scooping up a heaping pile of the casserole and placing it on Laura's plate first. "Cassie tells me you might know someone in the city who can help us track Reed."

"An old MP buddy of mine." Jason held his plate up for his serving. "Thanks. Looks amazing."

"What's he do now?" Harris asked, serving Cassie and then herself. She sat down, and they all dug in. "And how do you seem to always know someone everywhere you go?"

Cassie shot Harris a look. It was a fair question, but something in her voice bothered Cassie, like she was interrogating her little sister's boyfriend after meeting him for the first time.

But if Jason heard it, he didn't react. "Perks of having led an interesting life before settling down into the security business." He shoved a forkful of food into his mouth. "Terry's a bounty hunter now. Very good at his job. And very, shall we say, twitchy."

"That's probably what makes him good at his job." Harris' tone was lighter now. "I'm guessing he wouldn't have talked to us without you?"

"He's a good guy. Just doesn't trust people. But I think he would've taken one look at Cassie's big blue eyes and done anything she asked of him." Jason winked, and then laughed when Cassie blushed. "But it'll go quicker if I'm there."

"We'll take all the help we can get." Harris' voice was genuine, but Cassie noticed the other woman still wouldn't meet her eyes. "We'll need to come up with a gameplan for tomorrow."

"Later," Laura said, her eyes bright. She was drunk now. "Can we not talk about murder for, like, a solid hour?" She looked around the table. "Please?"

The four of them managed to have a conversation full of stories, jokes, and plenty of laughter. Jason's presence eased some more of the tension out of the room, and for the first time in weeks—maybe months—Cassie felt normal. And happy.

Jason and Cassie washed the dishes while Laura and Harris put the food away and poured another round of drinks. Everyone was yawning by the time it hit ten o'clock.

Jason stood first. "I should get going. I need to find a hotel. Laura, do you have any recommendations? Something that won't cost me my first-born child?"

Laura blinked up at him. The alcohol made her brain slow. "Hotel? Why? You're staying here, obviously."

He blinked back at her. "I mean, if you have room, that would be great. But I don't want to intrude. I can just meet up with you tomorrow."

"There's room." Laura tapped her chin. "Adelaide is sleeping on the couch, and Cassie's in the spare room. You could bunk with Cassie"—she paused here to wink, and Cassie's already flushed face burned brighter —"or she could sleep in my bed and you can have the spare room. Or Addie can sleep with me"—it was her turn to blush now—"and you can have the couch."

"I don't want to put anyone out." Jason turned to Cassie. "Seriously, no pressure. I can just meet you in the morning."

"We're all adults," Cassie said, trying to keep her voice even. "And it's a big bed. You can stay if you want to." She cleared her throat. "I would like it if you stayed."

Harris groaned, but there was a smile on her face. "Thank God. You two need to bang it out."

"Hey." Laura stood. "There'll be no banging in my house."

Jason held up his hands. "I promise only late-night chats and distant pining."

Laura clapped her hands and headed toward the back as Jason and Cassie followed, grabbing his suitcase along the way. "This is just like the 'they only have one bed' trope!"

Jason cut a glance at Cassie. "Huh?"

"She reads a lot of romance." Cassie waved her hand. "Ignore her."

13

CASSIE NEVER KNEW WHETHER SHE WOULD GET A GOOD NIGHT'S SLEEP. IT wasn't always up to how much caffeine she'd had before bed or how early she turned in. Even if she didn't have to answer to the alarm, the universe might be feeling cruel enough to send a nightmare her way. And her nightmares were worse than most—closer to prophetic than she cared to admit. Sometimes dreams were the easiest way for a spirit to get their message through the veil. It was thinner there, while she was sleeping. Easier to cross.

But last night, Cassie got some of the best sleep of her life. Crawling into bed with Jason, far enough away that they weren't touching, but close enough that she could feel his warm breath on her cheek, she was at war with herself. On the one hand, she wanted to cuddle close, and on the other, she needed to keep her distance until all this was over. Needed a clear head. But that was impossible with him just inches away.

It wasn't like it was the first time she'd had a man in her bed. There had been plenty of them before her near-death experience ten years ago, and a few since then, too. Mitch Tanner came to mind, and she found herself missing the Philadelphia homicide detective's friendship, wondering what he was doing at that very moment. Their relationship had been brief, but she didn't regret it. And she didn't think he did either.

But it was different with Jason. He was different. This was the first time she felt like she could be herself. Most men, other than Mitch, didn't know about her abilities, and she preferred it that way. Few people would understand, and even fewer wanted to. She could even see it in Mitch's eyes—a wariness that had nothing to do with her and everything to do with what she could see. It unsettled him.

Jason had been the opposite. When he had found out, he seemed to relax, like he had finally solved the mystery of Cassie Quinn. She felt like an open book around him. That ability to be herself was freeing, knowing that he accepted her for who she was and what she could do. It was a strange sort of vulnerability that wasn't always comfortable, but for the first time in her life, she was more excited than scared about what came next.

"I'm glad you wanted me to stay," Jason had said as soon as they'd slipped between the sheets.

"I missed you," she admitted. "And I didn't want you to leave so soon."

He had smiled and pulled her close, kissing her gently. Cassie had melted into him, turning off her frantic brain for a few seconds, allowing herself to enjoy the sensation of being so near to him. Gasping for breath by the time they separated, Cassie could see the same regret on Jason's face that she had felt in her bones.

She'd groaned. "Why do we have to be in my sister's house. Investigating a murder, no less."

"Several murders," he'd added.

"You're not helping!"

She could feel the low rumble in his chest as he chuckled, and the sound made her smile. "Savannah will be waiting for us."

Cassie had curled up against him then, laying her head on his chest. There'd been no need to talk, to discuss what they were to each other. He had flown out here to help her, had known exactly when she needed him most. For the first time since she'd left for New Orleans, Cassie was excited to go home and see what the future brought.

The next morning, she woke early, a smile already on her face before she opened her eyes. She felt refreshed, despite the fact that the sun had barely crested the horizon. Jason was dead asleep, snoring next to her, and even when she rolled out from under his arm and stood next to the bed, he didn't move or wake up.

Not bothering to fight the happiness bursting in her chest, Cassie backed out of the room and into the hallway, shutting the door as quietly as possible. When she turned around, she didn't expect to be face to face with Harris, and she yelped in response.

"You're up early," Harris said, trying not to laugh.

"You scared the shit out of me," Cassie hissed, clutching her chest. "Why are you sneaking around?" Expecting Harris to have a quip for that, the detective looked at the floor to avoid Cassie's eyes. That was when Cassie realized where she'd come from. "Did you spend the night in my sister's room?"

"I need coffee before I have this conversation." Harris padded toward the kitchen with her bare feet.

Cassie trailed behind her and waited for them both to have a cup of coffee in front of them before she repeated her question with a quirked eyebrow. "So?" she asked. "Did you spend the night with my sister?"

Harris took a slow sip of her beverage. "I did."

Cassie looked from Harris to Laura's door and back again. "Is she going to regret that in the morning?"

"Nothing happened," Harris said. "We didn't have sex." She sighed, like she knew she had to start from the beginning. "Last night, after you went to bed, we stayed up talking for another hour or two. Laura was pretty drunk, and I decided it'd be best if we both went to bed. I made her chug a glass of water, and then I made sure she didn't trip and die on her way to her room."

"That's sweet," Cassie said.

"You don't have to sound so surprised," Harris replied. "I can be sweet."

Some of the tension from last night seemed to be forgotten. "Seems I'm learning new things about you every day."

Harris rolled her eyes. "She wanted me to stay, and the couch isn't exactly a five-star accommodation. When I crawled into bed, she kissed me. I didn't let it go further than that. Not when she'd been drinking."

There was a beat of silence, and when Harris looked up, she seemed worried. "Did you know? Have you two ever talked about it?"

"Not really." Cassie took a sip of coffee and let the hot liquid slide down her throat while she thought. "I mean, it tracks. Laura's only ever dated men, and could never figure out why it didn't click. Even the good ones never worked out. She's never really cared what a person looked like or who they were on the outside, you know? Never really had a type." Cassie looked over at the detective. "I'm guessing you didn't talk about it then?"

Harris shook her head. "Laura passed out pretty quickly, and I wasn't far behind. She was still asleep when I left the room." Harris set her cup down. "Cassie, I hope this doesn't change anything between us or you and your sister."

Cassie was already shaking her head before Harris had finished the sentence. "I just want her to be happy." There was a nagging question on her mind, though. "But what happens when we go back to Savannah?"

"I haven't figured that part out yet."

"Do you like her?" Cassie asked.

Harris held a glimmer of vulnerability that Cassie had never seen before. "Yeah, I do. Thought she was pretty cute when she came to visit you in Savannah, and we went out to dinner that one night without you. Had a really good time. Didn't think I'd ever see her again, considering she lives out here."

"No one could've guessed we'd end up here."

"Exactly." Harris took another sip of coffee. "And then when we got here, and I saw her again, all those same feelings came back. But it's not just about the distance, Cassie." Harris was serious now. "She was drunk, and she kissed me. That's a lot different than doing it while you're sober. I have no problem helping her explore her sexuality"—Harris quirked a smile here, like she enjoyed that idea, and Cassie rolled her eyes—"but I've been with straight women before who just want to use me to satiate their curiosity and then scamper off back to their ex-boyfriends." She held up a hand before Cassie could argue. "I'm not saying Laura's going to be like that. I don't think she is." Harris sighed. "Maybe I'm overthinking this. It's early, and you caught me off-guard."

"What I'm hearing is that I can interrogate you before your first cup of coffee and actually get some answers?"

"Don't push it, Quinn," Harris said, but she was smiling.

"You've known for a while, then?"

"That I was a lesbian? Yeah." Harris laughed. "Remember how I went off to college and discovered myself? I wasn't just talking about being Puerto Rican and figuring out what that meant for me. Not everyone back home took it well, but I had my parents, and that was the most important part."

"And I'm guessing the rest of the officers back in Savannah—"

"—have no idea," Harris finished. "Not worth the heartache. Like I said before, it's bad enough being a woman in a man's world. They find out I'm Latina *and* queer?" She shook her head. "That would be game over for me. It might be the twenty-first century, but not everyone in the South has realized that yet."

"Is that hard for you?"

Harris shrugged. "Not really. I don't have a lot of time to date." She cut a glance at Cassie. "But I find ways to let off steam."

Cassie shook her head. "Just make sure if you're letting off steam with my sister, I'm not in the same house."

"Fair enough." Harris' eyes were twinkling now, and she looked more herself than she had in a long time. "And what about you and Jason, huh?"

Cassie shrugged and tried to hide her smile in her cup. "I think we're finally on the same page."

"You mean you opened your eyes and realized you would lose something great if you didn't get off your ass and do something about it?"

"Ouch," Cassie said. But it wasn't like Harris was wrong. "Speaking of being on the same page," Cassie started, unable to meet Harris' eyes, "about last night—"

At that moment, one of the bedroom doors opened, and Jason emerged, looking bleary-eyed and disoriented.

"Yeah, we should probably talk about that," Harris said, plastering on a fake smile. "Later."

14

THE ONLY THING WORSE THAN HEARING "LET'S TALK" FROM SOMEONE WAS hearing them say "let's talk later." Cassie tried not to let Harris' words worm their way into her brain, but it was tough. Although regretting the way she'd acted last night, she'd be lying to herself if she said she felt any different this morning.

The house was quiet as everyone got ready for the day, as though no one wanted to break the silence and risk another fight. Harris wasn't looking at Cassie, and Laura wasn't looking at either of them as they passed each other every few minutes. Jason was stuck in the middle, just grateful he hadn't had to spend a night alone in a hotel.

Laura was hungover, but refused to call out of work. Harris and Jason spent a solid five minutes debating the best remedy for Laura's pounding headache before plying her with food, water, coffee, and a lot of prayer. Cassie felt a peace fall over her that she'd never felt before, like she'd already gotten used to the four of them spending time together. It was enough that she could pretend they didn't have any pressing plans today. At least for a few minutes.

Before long, however, Cassie and Jason had to pack up to meet his old MP buddy, Terry Ingram. Since Jason had rented a car, that left Harris with Laura's. After she took Cassie's sister to work, Harris could track down some of Reed's old associates, the ones Laura had discovered during her research yesterday. They agreed to meet in the park for lunch again, partly to compare notes and partly to make sure Laura was feeling better.

It was only when they'd all parted ways that it felt like the oppressive silence had lifted from Cassie's shoulders. Buckled up in Jason's car, she was happy to let someone else do the driving.

"So, that was kind of tense back there," Jason said with a laugh.

"I'm sorry about that. Harris and I didn't exactly get to talk about yesterday."

"Looked like you were having a nice chat over your coffee," he pressed.

Cassie shrugged. She wasn't about to out Harris or her sister. "We didn't broach that subject. Probably for the best. At least this way we can spend a little time apart. Maybe things will go back to normal."

Jason glanced at her. "You don't sound convinced."

Cassie looked out the window, not wanting him to see the hurt in her eyes. "Sometimes I have a hard time reading Adelaide. She's doesn't like to let people in. When we first started working together, I thought she had all the answers. Always made the right call. But since David died..." Cassie let her voice trail off.

"She hasn't been the same?"

"She's been reckless." Cassie rolled her eyes. "But it's not like I haven't been reckless too. What happened in Chicago was my idea, and it was stupid. But I feel like she and I are drifting apart. As much as I want to figure out what the hell David got himself into, I just want things to go back to normal."

"One step at a time," Jason said, placing a hand on Cassie's knee, sending a thrill through her. "First, let's figure out where Reed is."

"So, tell me about Terry," she said, to distract from her pounding heart. "How did you two meet?"

"We worked together a few times when I was an MP. He was a demolitions expert, but more than that, he had this uncanny ability to find people. I don't know how he did it, and he didn't share any of his secrets with us. But he got us out of a lot of hot water. I'm grateful for that."

"And what's this about him being paranoid?" Cassie asked, wanting to know what she was getting herself into. "Should I be worried?"

"Probably." Jason said it matter-of-factly. "I haven't seen him in a few years. Didn't have his number. Only a few people do. Had a friend of a friend pass a message to him just before I flew out of Savannah. He should know we're coming."

"Should?" Cassie asked. "That doesn't sound promising."

"It was the best I could do on such short notice. I wouldn't be taking the risk if I didn't think it would pan out. Terry is very good at what he does."

"So, are we talking the-government-taps-my-phones paranoid or the-aliens-are-coming paranoid?"

"Mostly the first," Jason said, sliding his eyes to the right to glance at her. "A little bit the second."

"Great." Cassie didn't know if she wanted to groan or laugh. "Any particular reason?"

Jason shrugged, hitting the turn signal and taking them farther away from the metropolitan area of Los Angeles. She had no idea where they were going. "He's always been like that. I think his dad raised him that way," Jason said. "Got worse over the years, especially after everything he saw while working for the government."

"Doesn't he work for them anymore?"

"He got out a few years after me, as far as I know. Became a bounty hunter. Collected a lot of cash. He still does it from time to time, I think, but mostly he stays home and invents things."

"The demolitions expert is inventing things?" Cassie asked. "That sounds safe."

"That's why you're staying in the car while I make sure he's not going to blow us up."

Cassie whipped her head toward him. "Not a chance. If you think I'm going to let you go in there by yourself—"

"I just want to keep you safe—"

"And putting your life at risk for me and my investigation is unacceptable. We do it together or not at all." Cassie's voice left no room for argument. "Got it?"

"Got it." He sounded like he was suppressing a laugh, but Cassie's glare wiped the smile off his face. "Just don't make any sudden movements."

"Fine." Cassie let her heart rate return to normal before she spoke again. "You don't talk about that time in your life a whole lot."

"I don't have a lot of good memories from back then." Jason's voice faded a little, like he'd drifted off into the past. "I loved being an investigator. Loved helping people. But you see a lot of messed up shit. It gets to you after a while." He turned to her with a sad smile. "Not that I need to tell you that. You've probably seen worse."

Cassie shrugged. "Worse is relative. None of it's great. But the helping people part is. That never gets old." She thought for a moment. "Do you miss it?"

"Sometimes." He chuckled. "Helping you, reaching out to old contacts, doing the legwork and the research reminded me what it used to feel like."

"But it brings up bad memories too?"

He nodded. The car was silent for a minute. Jason pulled to a stop at a redlight and didn't speak again until it turned green. "This whole thing with David reminds me of what happened with my CO. He and his family were murdered. He had two kids. Twins. Not even five."

Cassie caught the emotion in his voice and placed a hand on his arm. "You don't have to talk about it if—"

"You've shared so much with me, Cassie." As he smiled at her, even though it was sad, she could feel his gratitude. "I want to talk about it, but there just isn't that much to say, really. Surprising, considering it turned my whole world upside down." He took a deep breath. "We found him on Monday morning, killed in his own home, in his own bed. They'd killed the kids first, then the wife, then woke him up to make sure he knew. He fought. Took four bullets to put him down. He died in the hospital. Never had a chance, but we had to try. Even if he had survived, what kind of life would he have led?"

"Did you ever find out who did it?"

Jason nodded. "Turns out it was a hit. Some other officer had ordered it. They'd been rivals for close to twenty years. The other guy had finally had enough, I guess. We caught him and six others who'd been in on it. And you know what happened? They arrested the soldiers and sent the other commander off to some god-forsaken post in the middle of nowhere. Then the military covered it all up. No one knew the truth but us. And we were told, in no uncertain terms, never to speak a word of it. I knew I couldn't stay after that. Took me two years, but I got out. Left that whole world behind. That's how I ended up in Savannah. At the museum."

"I'm glad you did," Cassie said. "I can't believe they just covered it up like that."

"Had to save their own asses." Jason turned the car down another road. They were well and truly in the desert now. She remembered seeing a sign for Palmdale a while back. "Corruption is everywhere. In the military, in the Savannah PD. That's why I never want to work for an establishment like that again. I'd rather make my own choices, even if they turn out to be the wrong ones. I hate feeling like I don't have a say in my own life."

"Have you ever thought of working for yourself?"

Jason cocked his head to the side. "What do you mean? Like, own my own security company?"

"Maybe," she said. "Or become a private investigator."

Jason opened his mouth to say something, then closed it and furrowed his brows. By the look on his face, Cassie could tell he'd never considered it. As she was just about to go to bat for the idea, he pulled into the driveway of a large double-wide. It looked innocuous, but there was something threatening in the barren front yard and the way the windows had been boarded over.

"Is this Terry's place?" she asked. It looked like a doomsday prepper's dreamhouse. "I thought he had a ton of money?"

"He spends it on more practical material possessions."

"Explosives?" Cassie asked.

Jason nodded. "Explosives." He hooked a finger through the doorhandle, but turned to her before he opened it. "Are you sure there's no way I can convince you to stay in the car? At least until I go say hello first?"

Cassie didn't dignify that with an answer. Shouldering open her own door, she stepped out under the desert sun. If she'd been smart, she would've packed sunscreen, but she'd been too worried about getting out of the house and away from all the awkward tension.

"Didn't think so," Jason mumbled, standing up and shutting the door behind him. "Just keep your hands where he can see them, okay? And remember—"

"—no sudden movements," Cassie finished. "Got it."

They made it to the front door without incident, and Cassie breathed a sigh of relief. She wondered if the sandy front yard was boobytrapped with mines. There was a very distinct walkway to the wood-and-cinder block front steps, and after everything she'd heard about him, she wouldn't have put it past Terry to punish all who strayed from the path.

Jason raised a hand to knock on the front door, but before he could, it whipped open and the very distinct sound of a shotgun being cocked echoed in the air around them. The barrel emerged from the dark interior, held mere inches away from Jason's forehead.

Someone who'd smoked two packs of cigarettes a day for the past twenty years spoke. And his words were just as alarming as the gun.

"You've got ten seconds to tell me who the hell you are and what you're doing on my property."

15

HARRIS WONDERED HOW HER DAY HAD STARTED OFF SO GREAT AND HAD tanked so fast.

Waking up to Laura's arm wrapped around her waist, her face pressed into her neck, still caused Harris' stomach to tighten in excitement. There was no doubt Laura was beautiful, but it was more than that. Something Harris hadn't felt in a long time. She liked Laura's sharp wit and the way she could keep up with her banter. Plus, her eyes were bright and full of compassion, and with just one look, she could soothe the fire that always seemed to burn in Harris' chest. The fire that got hotter each day Aguilar walked free.

The last thing Harris had wanted to do was move from Laura's embrace, but she'd also gotten the impression that, while Laura's drunken words matched her sober thoughts, this was all very new to her. Harris had no idea if she was ready to talk to Cassie about it, especially with Jason there to witness the conversation.

She had figured it best to slip out of the room before Laura woke up— only to run into Cassie, who'd had a goofy grin on her face as she closed her own bedroom door behind her. The conversation that followed hadn't been uncomfortable, but Harris liked keeping parts of her life tucked away where only she could see them. It helped her compartmentalize. Helped her keep Cassie at arm's length.

Not that she was doing a very good job of that. After losing David, Harris wanted her relationship with Cassie to remain as professional as possible. Blurring those lines between colleague and friend was the quickest way to get hurt, especially when they were chasing after someone like Aguilar.

But it was no use. Harris didn't have any other friends, and Cassie was her closest confidant. And now, it seemed, she had a crush on Cassie's little sister. There was no way this was going to end well, but Harris decided she'd jump that hurdle when she got to it. Until then, she had other problems to deal with.

Like where the hell Reed was hiding out.

The parole officer Laura knew had given them a list of Reed's former associates. Harris had worked her way through the names with no luck. All dead ends in one way or another, and now she was left with one person. Mason Hardy.

Thankfully, it hadn't been difficult to find him. He ran a little pawn shop tucked down a sketchy side road, far off the main strip. Harris had walked into the store with the intent of watching him for a few minutes to see the kind of person she was dealing with. But he just sat behind the counter, reading a magazine and pretending she didn't exist. Harris' patience was already thin, so she decided to make the first move. Part of her hoped he'd put up a little resistance. She needed to blow off some steam.

Approaching the counter—which housed an impressive array of jewelry—Harris decided not to play coy. "Mason Hardy?"

The man folded down a corner of his magazine to look at her. Thin and balding, what hair he did have touched his shoulders. His eyes were a pale blue, and the whites were red and irritated. It could've been allergies, but she knew it was something else. He reeked of it.

He flipped the corner of the magazine back up. "Who's asking?"

"I am." Harris didn't bother being polite. "I'm looking for Don Reed. I heard you know him."

Hardy hesitated for only a second. Sounding nonchalant when he answered, Harris knew better. "You heard wrong."

"Cut the bullshit," Harris replied. "I'm not in the mood today."

Hardy closed his magazine and stood. His height took Harris by surprise, but she didn't let it show on her face. The man was only a few inches shy of seven feet, but while he had a height advantage on her, she had the muscle.

Throwing the magazine on the counter, he stepped closer. "Lady, I don't care what kind of mood you're in. I told you, I've never heard of him. Now get out." He leaned closer, and Harris had to hold her breath against his smell. "Before I make you get out."

Harris tipped her head back and laughed. The adrenaline started to pump through her body. "I would love to see you try."

In one fluid motion, Hardy reached under the counter and brought out a small pistol, cocking back the hammer without any warning. But Harris had been ready for that. She whipped out a hand and grabbed his wrist, pushing it out of her face at the same time she pulled him closer, forcing the top half of his body to lean over the counter. Then she reached a hand behind his neck and slammed his face down onto the glass. It didn't break, but the sound of the impact was satisfying, none-theless.

Hardy yelped in response, and while he was busy checking to see if his nose was broken, Harris wrestled the gun out of his hand. Opening the chamber and spinning it around, she realized it was empty. After pushing the hammer back into place, she set it on the counter and slid it well out of reach.

"And what were you expecting to do with that?" she asked.

The man didn't bother answering. Spinning on his heel, he ran for the back room. Harris didn't fight the grin forming on her face as she hopped the counter and grabbed a fistful of his shirt just as he opened the door. But instead of hauling him back out into the shop, she pushed him forward, propelling him into his desk and causing him to knock half its contents onto the floor.

Without waiting for him to stand and face her, Harris grabbed his arm and wrenched it behind his back, pushing it up as far as it went.

Hardy screamed in pain, and it took her a second to realize he was forming words.

"Okay, okay!" he yelled. "I'll tell you want you want to know!"

"Are you friends with Don Reed?" she asked.

"No." When Harris pushed his arm up higher, he screamed out again. "We're not friends! We used to be. Long time ago." Harris loosened her grip enough to ease the pain in Hardy's shoulder. "I haven't seen him in years. Was surprised as hell when he showed up here asking for help. We didn't exactly part on good terms."

Her mind was spinning. Reed had come to this shop. He'd been *here*. "What did he want?" she asked.

"He was looking for someone. I don't know her name." Harris pulled his arm higher, and he squealed in response. "Natasha! Natasha Michaelson. But I don't know who she is, I swear."

"Then why'd he come to you?"

"Looking for a place to stay. Somewhere to crash and lay low for a few days."

Harris' heart pounded from excitement. "Where is he? Is he staying with you?"

"I sleep in the shop. I didn't have room for him."

Harris looked around Hardy's office and took in its contents for the first time. In addition to the desk in the corner, there was a bed pressed up against the opposite wall. Bedding spilled onto the floor, and the sheets looked like they hadn't been washed in years.

"What did he say when you told him you couldn't help?" Harris asked. "Where did he go?"

"I don't know." Before Harris could make another move, Hardy rushed on. "There's only one other person in Los Angeles who might still talk to him. They used to be a thing, long time ago. I'll give you her name and address if you let me go."

Harris contemplated her options for a moment. Hardy could be lying, but what would be the point? He owned the shop, and she'd be able to find him again if his information didn't pan out. Besides, it sounded like he had no reason to cover for Reed.

Letting his arm slip free from her grasp, Harris stood back and waited for him to turn around to face her. Then she stuck out her hand, a shit-eating grin on her face. "You've got yourself a deal."

16

CASSIE HAD THE URGE TO BOLT FROM THE DOORSTEP AND DRAG JASON AFTER her. But her legs wouldn't move. Probably for the best, she thought. It wouldn't end well for them either way. Even if there were no mines in the yard, something told her that if Terry pulled that trigger, he wouldn't miss.

Before Cassie could get a good look at him—or use her big blue eyes to their advantage—Jason shifted to the right, so more of his body blocked her from the gun. Not that it would make much difference.

"I said don't move!" Terry barked.

"Actually, you didn't." Jason's voice was shockingly calm. "You just said *tell me who the hell you are and what you're doing on my property.*"

Terry's hands were rocksteady. "I would think the gun implied the *don't move* part."

"Terry, it's Jason Broussard."

"Who?"

"It's Duke, goddammit. Will you lower the shotgun, please?"

There was a pause. "Who's the girl?"

"This is Cassie Quinn. She's a friend. We need your help. Hannah should've told you we were coming."

"She did," he said, not lowering the gun. "I didn't believe her."

"Do you believe her now?" There was another moment of silence. Then Jason relaxed, which meant Terry must've lowered the shotgun. "Thank you. Was that so hard?"

"Harder than you think," Terry answered. "What do you want?"

"We need your help finding someone. It's important."

Terry grunted and stepped inside, allowing the two of them to pass through the front door of his trailer. Cassie wasn't sure what she had expected, but the living room was tidy, almost barren. There was a couch and a recliner, but no television. A stack of books sat on an end table, along with a reading light. There were no pictures on the wall or any other decorations. The furniture was either new or hardly used. It looked more like a showroom than an actual place of residence, though the books indicated Terry did use this area once in a while.

"Water?" he asked.

He was tall and wiry in the way older men got by working hard their entire lives. His skin was tanned and leathery from the California sun. Cassie figured he probably had about a decade on Jason, maybe a little more, but life had aged him quick. His sandy gray hair didn't help, nor did the untamed beard on his face. "I can make sandwiches."

"Water would be great," Jason said. "We ate a big breakfast."

Terry grunted again and pulled down two glasses. The kitchen was much like the living room, with minimal furniture and no decorations. There was a table and only one chair. Cassie caught sight of a stocked fridge as Terry pulled out a homemade water filter, but there were no dishes in the sink. Was Terry a neat freak, or did he never cook?

Cassie accepted her glass of water with thanks and took a polite sip. It was cold and refreshing, far better than most bottled water you get in the store. Terry's eyes lit up when he saw the surprise on her face.

"My own filtering system. Finally got it right. Nothing gets through it but pure, all-natural H2O, just the way God intended." He studied her for a moment, then stuck out his hand, which looked clean despite the dirt under his nails. "Name's Terrence Ingram. You can call me Terry. Pleasure to meet you. And I apologize for being rude at the door."

"Cassandra Quinn," she said, taking his hand. "You can call me

Cassie." If that was being rude, she wondered what downright uncivilized looked like.

"What the hell was that about, Ter?" Jason asked, shaking the man's hand.

"Memory's not what it used to be," Terry said, though he didn't look all that sorry about it. "Can't be too careful. Just took me a few minutes to catch up."

"You taking anything for that?" Jason asked. "Eating healthy?"

"Bah." Terry waved away his comments. "Don't put nothing in my body that God didn't put on this earth."

"Technically, God put everything on this earth," Cassie said, before she could stop herself. "Everything comes from something."

"That's what they want you to think," Terry said, closing one eye and touching a finger to his nose. Cassie was struck suddenly by the image of him as a pirate. "That's how they get you." He clapped his hands together so suddenly, it made her jump. "What is it I can do for you, Duke?"

"Duke?" Cassie asked, wondering for the second time where that had come from.

Jason rolled his eyes. "An old nickname, don't worry—"

Terry slapped Jason on the back so hard, he stumbled forward a step. "The Duke could get away with anything back in the day. Got me out of trouble more than once, too." Terry leaned forward. "I like to blow stuff up."

"I've heard." A giggle escaped Cassie's mouth. She wasn't sure when she'd gone from terrified to relaxed, but she was beginning to like Terry. "So, Duke because—"

"Everyone treated him like royalty." Terry slapped his back again, but this time Jason was prepared for it. "And he walked around like he owned the place."

"I wasn't that bad," Jason said, sounding somewhat embarrassed.

"That bad and worse," Terry said with a wink. He seemed to be more lucid now than when he'd answered the door. "So, you need to find someone?"

"It's kind of a long story." Cassie geared herself to tell him about David and everything else that had happened in the last couple weeks.

But Terry held out a hand. "The less I know, the better. Plausible deniability." He held out his hand. "You got a picture?" Cassie produced her phone and pulled up the picture of Reed she'd taken in his Chicago office. Terry took a pair of reading glasses out of his shirt pocket and perched them on his nose, then took the phone from Cassie. "Name? Occupation?"

"Don A. Reed," Cassie supplied. "He's a lawyer. We met him in Chicago, then chased him to Los Angeles two days ago."

"He's slippery," Jason added. "Has his hands in a lot of shell corporations. Tied back to Francisco Aguilar in Savannah, Georgia. We want to know where he is. Hopefully, he hasn't left the city yet."

Cassie worried at her bottom lip. "Can you help us?"

"Can I help you?" Terry snorted. "Follow me."

Jason and Cassie exchanged a look, then followed Terry through the back door, down another set of cinderblock stairs, and out into the backyard. It was just as barren as the front except for a tiny wooden shed that couldn't have fit more than a lawn mower and some basic tools.

Only, Cassie realized, there was no lawn to mow.

Terry pressed his thumb to the lock against the shed, and the door popped open. He turned around with his arms spread wide, those silly little glasses still perched on his nose.

A grin spread across his face. "Step into my office, young lady."

It turned out Terry's office was a spacious bunker beneath the shed, complete with sleeping quarters, a fully stocked kitchen, bathroom facilities, and even a small lounge area. The rest of the room was dedicated to Terry's hobby, which apparently had something to do with electronics.

"Ter?" Jason said, looking around the bunker with a slack jaw.

"Hmm?" Terry was half paying attention, bent over his keyboard so they couldn't see his password as he typed it in. It must've been at least twenty characters long.

"I thought you hated technology."

"Oh, I do," Terry said brightly, spinning in his chair to face them. "But you have to change with the times, right?"

"What is this place?" Cassie wondered.

Terry grinned. "It's where I go to get away."

"Most people go to the Caribbean," Jason said, an eyebrow raised. "Or even Florida."

"Do I look like someone who would enjoy Florida?" Terry asked, shaking his head. "No, I'd rather stay here. I've got everything I need. Food for two months, all my favorite books, and a network of computers that lets me do my job underground and away from people."

"You're a bounty hunter," Jason said. "You have to talk to people sometimes."

"Unfortunately." Terry scowled and scratched at his beard. "But thanks to my system here," he said, patting the side of a monitor, "I can gather at least fifty percent of my intel before ever going back up to the surface."

"You're a mole person," Jason said, suppressing a laugh. "You live in a doomsday shelter."

"When the apocalypse comes, I'll remember this." Terry looked at Cassie. "You, however, are more than welcome to wait out the end of the world with me."

"I'll keep that in mind." What Cassie really needed was to keep them on track. "What about Reed?"

"Right." Terry swiveled back toward his screen. Then he cracked his knuckles in one quick motion and started typing with a fervor that shocked Jason, if his slack jaw was any indication. "Hmm. Okay," Terry said. "Well then. Really? Oh, you slimy bastard."

"Everything okay there, Ter?" Jason asked after about three minutes of commentary.

"You were right. He is slippery."

"Is that going to be a problem?" Cassie asked.

Terry glanced over his shoulder long enough for Cassie to see the twinkle in his eye. "Only for him, once I manage to find out who he really is. It'll just take some time. I'll text Jason with an update once I have something significant."

"Let me give you my number," Jason said.

"No need." Terry pulled out his phone, and ten seconds later, Jason's phone chimed to alert him to a new text message. "Hannah gave it to me."

Jason looked down at his phone and back up at Terry, his eyes narrowed. "And you didn't think to reach out? Or even remember that I was stopping by?"

Terry shrugged. "Didn't seem important at the time."

Jason sighed and checked his watch. "We should head back if we want to make lunch, anyway. Hopefully Adelaide made more progress than we did."

"You can see yourselves out," Terry said, without turning around. "Oh, and stick to the path."

Cassie exchanged a look with Jason, and she could tell he was thinking the same thing. Terry might be insane, but he could also be their only hope of tracking down Reed and putting this whole mess with Aguilar to bed once and for all.

That is, if they survived the trek across the yard.

17

HARRIS AND LAURA HAD ALREADY CLAIMED A TABLE IN THE PARK BY THE time Jason and Cassie arrived. Their heads were bent together like they were having a passionate discussion, but when they spotted the others, Laura took an intense interest in her sandwich. Harris' face was impassive, but she didn't meet Cassie's eyes. Was it leftover hostility from their argument, or because she didn't want Cassie to guess what she and Laura had been talking about?

Cassie decided to let it go. If it was about their time together, Laura would come to Cassie when she was ready. There was no point in pressing that topic, even though she didn't want Laura to feel like she had to hide that part of herself. If it was about the argument she'd had with Harris the night before, however, Cassie was happy to leave that on the table for now. And hopefully, it didn't fester in the meantime.

Harris had bought them all sandwiches from the same bistro as before, and everyone dug in like they hadn't eaten a meal in days, let alone a few hours. There was nothing like a good investigation and the constant threat of death to burn away the calories and leave you starving.

"You first," Harris said, when she had scarfed down half her sandwich. "Did you get in touch with your contact? Any luck?"

Jason wiped his mouth with a napkin and took a swig of water before answering. "Terry agreed to help us. If anyone can dig up dirt on Reed, it's him."

Harris eyed him. "It's never that easy."

Jason shrugged. He and Cassie had agreed ahead of time not to mention the shotgun to the face. "He owes me one. Plus, I think he likes the challenge. Doesn't seem to have much going on these days."

Harris glanced at Cassie like she knew there was more to the story, but she must've decided not to press because she switched gears without prompting. "I made a little headway on Reed's old associates."

"The ones Laura found, right?" Jason asked. Cassie had caught him up on everything last night.

"Right. A few of them were duds. One was out of business, another had moved out of state, and a third one was too drunk to even have a conversation with." Harris shook her head like she'd rather not think about that part of her day. "But the last one, Mason Hardy, was right where we thought he was."

"And he talked?"

"Not at first." Harris shrugged, and Cassie had a feeling she was hiding some key details as well. "But he opened up, eventually. Told us Reed had paid him a visit almost as soon as he landed, looking for a place to stay."

Cassie sat up straighter, forgetting her sandwich altogether. "Does he know where Reed is? A hotel, maybe?"

"He has no idea." Harris frowned, like she couldn't believe Cassie was still going on about the hotel. "They hadn't talked in years. Apparently, they had a falling out. I didn't get the details, but it was enough for Mason to be surprised as hell to see him show up on his doorstep like that."

"He must be desperate," Jason added.

"My thoughts exactly."

"What did Reed want?" Cassie asked. "Just a place to lay low for a while? That could mean he wants to stay in the city. He could still be here."

"Not just a place to lay low," Harris answered. Popping the last of her sandwich into her mouth, she leaned back in her chair. A coy smile played around her lips. "Seems he's looking for someone named Natasha Michaelson."

"Who's that?" Cassie asked.

"Mason didn't know, and I believed him."

Cassie wondered what Harris had to do to the man to get his cooperation. "Is any part of this story going to help us at some point?"

"You have no flair for the dramatic, Cassie," Harris said.

"You usually don't either," she shot back.

"What can I say? I'm in a good mood today."

Cassie glanced at Laura, still not meeting her sister's eyes, but before she could say anything to either of them, Jason interrupted. "Okay, I'll bite," he said. "What else did Mason tell you?"

"He said there was only one other person in the entire city who would give Reed the time of day. A woman named Luna Starlight."

"I hate to ask," Jason started, "but what's her, uh, profession?"

Harris looked Cassie dead in the eye. She didn't bother hiding her smile this time. "She's Reed's former lover. And she's a psychic."

Cassie groaned. "You've got to be kidding me."

"Oh, I'm not." Harris was laughing now. "I swung by her place right after I talked to Mason. She doesn't open until two in the afternoon, which means"—she checked her watch—"if we leave now, we'll be her first customers of the day."

"Do you think she's legitimate?" Jason asked.

Cassie glared at him. "With a name like Luna Starlight?"

He shrugged. "Just because she's playing into the stereotype doesn't mean she can't have real abilities."

"I guess." Cassie didn't miss the glint in Harris' eye. "Why do you seem so pleased with yourself?"

"Because there's no way this doesn't work out for us. If she's the real deal, the two of you can crack this wide open."

"And if she's a fraud?" Cassie asked.

"If Reed really did visit her within the last day or two, we'll get information out of her one way or another. Either through good old-fashioned detective work—"

"—or my abilities," Cassie finished. "You know I can't guarantee I'll pick up anything, right?"

Harris stood and tossed her trash away. "I have confidence in you."

Cassie didn't feel comforted, but she had to admit, this was the closest they'd come to Reed so far. If Luna Starlight could even give them one more piece of the puzzle, they might be able to track Reed down before he disappeared altogether.

"I'll text Terry about Natasha Michaelson." Jason took out his phone. "He might be able to find something useful on her."

Cassie turned to her sister. "You're kind of quiet today. Everything okay?"

Laura looked up at her with a smile no one would mistake as genuine. "Yeah, I'm fine. Still hungover."

"Want me to walk you back to work? I'm sure we have a few minutes to spare before—"

"No, that's okay." Laura smiled again, and this time it looked apologetic. "I'll be okay." She glanced at Harris and then away. "Just keep me updated, okay? And don't get into any trouble."

"Us?" Harris said, placing a hand to her chest in mock offense. "Never."

"I'll keep an eye on them," Jason offered.

"You're the only one I trust," Laura said, then laughed when Cassie's mouth dropped open. "You lost that privilege in Chicago."

"What about me?" Harris asked, and this time she did sound mildly offended.

"You lost it the first time I met you. I knew you were trouble when you walked in."

"Did you just quote Taylor Swift at me?"

"Maybe." Laura beamed at Harris, and she looked like herself for the first time that day. "I have to go. Jason, you're in charge."

"Yes, ma'am."

Harris grumbled until Laura was out of earshot, then turned back to Jason. "I gave Laura her car back, so you're driving." She looked him up and down. "And I'm definitely in charge."

Jason dropped his grin. "Yes, ma'am."

Satisfied, Harris turned on her heel and walked out of the park. Cassie and Jason had just enough time to exchange a look before they had to jog to catch up. If nothing else, Cassie hoped meeting Luna Starlight was less dangerous than meeting Terry.

18

It was immediately apparent that Luna Starlight would not help them find Reed.

Because she was dead.

It took them ten minutes to find a parking spot, and another ten to walk several blocks to the crime scene, which was already taped off and heavily guarded by a fleet of police officers. Bystanders gawked from the sidewalk, but it was impossible to see in the shop, no matter how hard they craned their necks.

Jason whispered to Harris under his breath, loud enough for only the two of them to hear. "Didn't you say you drove by here just a couple hours ago?"

Harris nodded, her eyes wide. "It wasn't open. I even looked through the window. No one was in there, and I saw the times on the shop." She checked her watch. "It's only a little after two now."

"She must've gotten here early for the day," Cassie suggested. "Whoever killed her must've known that."

Harris was only half paying attention, standing on her tiptoes trying to see above the crowd. "Is that—" She cut off and held up a hand. "Give me a second."

Harris pushed her way through the crowd, much to the chagrin of the nosy onlookers. As the detective got the attention of one of the officers stationed just on the other side of the tape, a woman turned to see where Harris had come from. A woman with long dark hair and thick black glasses. Cassie recognized her.

"Crap." Cassie turned toward Jason, putting her back to the woman. "Did she see me?"

"Did who see you?"

"Cassie, right?" The woman was right behind her now. "And who's this?"

"Piper." Cassie turned around and pretended like she actually wanted to see the other woman. "This is Jason."

Piper held out her business card by way of greeting. "Do you like podcasts, Jason?"

"Oh, um." He looked down at her card. "Sometimes?"

"I'm trying to convince Cassie here to come onto mine. Think you could put in a good word for me?"

Cassie scowled. "I'm sorry, Piper, but I'm not—"

"This is the second crime scene you've been at in two days," Piper said. She didn't have a microphone out, but Cassie had a feeling she recorded every interaction anyway, probably from her pocket. "Did you know this was going to happen?"

Cassie ducked her head as a few of the onlookers turned toward them. "No, of course not."

Piper didn't look deterred in the slightest. "Is this in any way related to the body you discovered yesterday?"

Cassie opened her mouth—to say what, she didn't know.

She was saved by Harris calling out over the crowd. "Cassie." Harris waved her over. "Come on, let's go."

Cassie tossed Piper an unmeaning apologetic smile and brushed by the other woman, Jason following in her wake. When they got up to the tape, Harris was already on the other side. The officer stationed there lifted it for Cassie to duck under but put up a hand when Jason attempted to follow.

"Just you two," the officer said, gesturing between the two women. "He has to stay."

Jason looked disappointed, but he backed away without argument. When he caught Cassie's expression, he smiled. "It's fine. I'll be here when you're done."

Cassie leaned in close. "Don't say anything to her, okay? Not a word. About me or the case. Or anything."

Jason's eyes filled with questions, but he nodded. Cassie could see Piper eyeing them from a few people back, but Cassie turned before she could snap another picture of her.

Harris was already by the door, impatient and anxious to get inside. "What was that about?"

"I'll tell you later," Cassie whispered, then stepped inside.

The change in atmosphere was immediate. Outside, it was a sunny, beautiful day. Inside, it was dark and stifling. Luna had closed all her windows and covered them in heavy curtains and tapestries. The air conditioning was on, but it was either too old or too low to do any real damage to the heat inside. It didn't help that there were candles lit on almost every surface, and incense burning in every corner of the room. All the lamps had been covered in colored scarves, barely allowing them to give off any light. It certainly added to the ambiance.

The few people taking pictures paid the women no mind as the officer told them to wait while he got Detective Green. A few seconds later, Green stepped out of a back room with a grim look on his face. He glanced between Harris and Cassie as if he didn't know what to make of their presence.

"I realize you're psychic, Ms. Quinn, but out of all the murders in all of Los Angeles, I'm surprised to see you show up to this one."

Cassie didn't like the suspicious look on his face. "We didn't know it was a murder scene when we got here." She paused and cocked her head to one side. "Hang on, you're not a homicide detective. What are you doing here?"

Green sighed, and for the first time, Cassie could see how heavy his shoulders were. "I was the one who called it in. I stopped by to follow up on a lead. Front door was unlocked, but when I stepped inside, no one answered. After a few minutes, I checked the back and found her." He looked at Harris. "Your turn."

"We were also following a lead." She paused, as if weighing her next words. "About Reed. We heard from one of his associates that he might've paid a visit to Ms. Starlight."

"Interesting." He turned back to Cassie. "I'm guessing seeing dead bodies doesn't bother you, considering your line of work."

Cassie wanted to say something about her line of work usually taking place in a museum surrounded by centuries-old artifacts, but it didn't seem worth it to split hairs. "I've seen my fair share."

Green led them into the back room. It was small, clearly used as an office and storage room. Shelving units were full of crystals and ointments and dried herbs. The smell was even stronger back here, and Cassie had to rub her nose to keep from sneezing. In the center of the room, on the floor, lay Luna Starlight. She wore a deep purple dress with a light robe over the top of it, silver jewelry shining from around her neck and on her fingers. Cassie noticed her bare feet and the way her hands were gently folded over her stomach. Her face was covered in a red scarf with gold thread woven throughout.

Standing over her was a woman in sensible pumps, a pencil skirt, and a thin silk blouse. She had jet-black hair and a splash of freckles across her face. Her deep purple lipstick washed out her already pale ivory skin.

"This is my colleague Detective Miranda Song. Homicide." Green nodded at the woman, then gestured to Harris and Cassie. "These are detectives from Savannah." When Song shot him a confused look, he held up a hand. "It's a long story. But they came here to question her about something they're working on."

Cassie wasn't surprised Detective Green didn't mention she was a psychic. That would take even more of an explanation than the fact that they were from Georgia.

Cassie looked back down at Luna. Despite the way the woman was sprawled out on the floor, she looked peaceful. "How was she killed?"

"Strangled," Song said. "Probably with one of her own scarves."

"The killer must've known her," Harris added. "The way her arms are placed and the scarf covering her up. They felt guilty."

"Most likely," Green agreed. "The front door was unlocked, and so was this back room. She either opened up for the killer or he had a key.

There's no sign of a struggle, so he must've surprised her and killed her quickly."

Harris turned to Cassie. "You see anything out of the ordinary?"

Cassie knew Harris wasn't just asking her to look at the crime scene, but to spot something no one else could. The room didn't feel any different. She couldn't see Luna's spirit or feel any one item pulling at her.

Still, Cassie squatted, careful to keep her hands tucked against her body. There wasn't enough room to walk around without disturbing something or someone, but like Green had said, there hadn't been a struggle and the place was still orderly. That meant whoever killed Luna hadn't been after anything in her shop—they'd wanted to kill *her*. But why? To keep her from talking to Detective Green? Or to keep her from talking to Cassie and Harris?

A shiver cascaded down Cassie's spine, and she had to force herself to look at Luna's body. But it was more like looking at a pile of fabric. Directing her next question at Detective Song, she asked, "Have you looked at her face yet?"

Song nodded. "They took pictures of her earlier. Green and I were just about to take a closer look when you arrived."

"May I?" Cassie asked, nodding toward the body.

Song bent down and uncovered Luna's face with gloved hands. The woman looked to be in her late fifties, though it was hard to tell beneath her heavy makeup. Her head was tilted slightly toward the door, her gray eyes open and staring at Cassie now. A blossoming red mark around her neck was turning purple.

When Cassie felt the urge to stand up and back away, she didn't fight it. "I don't see anything," she told Harris. "I need some air. Excuse me."

Harris let Cassie go without a backwards glance, as she and Green bent over the body and discussed the marks in low tones. Cassie tripped over her feet exiting the office and almost bumped into one of the other officers on the site. The man glowered at her, and she mumbled a quick apology. Turning, she made for the exit when a flicker out of the corner of her eye caught her attention.

Standing there, on the other side of the room, was the ghost of Luna Starlight. She was tucked away in the far corner, as though leaning against the wall for support. Her eyes, just as big and gray as they had been in life, stared at Cassie, begging to be noticed.

Cassie looked around the room, but no one paid her any mind now, so she took the opportunity to step closer to the figure. Upon realizing she could be seen, the woman grasped at her throat, clawing at it as though she wanted to speak but couldn't. The killer must've crushed her windpipe. The poor woman wouldn't be able to speak, even if she wanted to.

Keeping her voice low, Cassie whispered to the spirit. "Do you know who did this to you?"

Luna nodded her head, scratching at her throat. Her mouth stretched wide, as though she were screaming. But no sound came out. Her eyes bulged, and a ghostly tear tracked its way down her cheek. Cassie's own throat grew tight, and she had the urge to clear her throat like there was something stuck in it.

"Can you tell me?" Cassie had to choke the words out. "Can you tell me who did it?"

The woman closed her eyes in agony, her mouth stretching wide as though the hinges on her jaw were no longer in place. Cassie caught sight of something sticking out of her trachea, but before she could figure out what it was, someone called her name, and the woman's mouth snapped shut.

"Cassie?" Detective Green asked. "Are you okay?"

Cassie didn't answer right away. Luna's eyes had bulged even more, staring forward as if she had just remembered the rest of the world existed. Whether it was the presence of someone else or the fact that Green had just come out of the room where she'd been killed, Cassie didn't know, but the fear on Luna's face was palpable.

"Cassie?" Green asked again, sounding closer this time. "What is it?"

"Check her throat," Cassie said. She could see Green's eyes pinch in concern. "Something's stuffed inside."

"How do you know that?"

Cassie turned back to Luna, trying to figure out how to explain what she could see, but the woman had disappeared. Instead of the ghostly silhouette of their murder victim, she found herself staring at a large, framed picture hanging on the wall. Cassie hadn't noticed it before, but now it was all she could see.

A large building stood against a clear sky. The image was in black and white, but Cassie recognized the shape from Emily's memory. She remembered the sandy-brown exterior and the bold white lettering written at the top of one of the towers. The words had been out of focus before, when she'd seen Reed and Emily arguing out front, but they were crystal clear now.

Hotel Cecil

Low Daily Weekly Rates

700 Rooms

19

A HAND LANDED ON CASSIE'S SHOULDER. SHE JUMPED AND WHIRLED around.

Green stood there, mouth open, hands raised in the air. "Sorry." He wore a worried look on his face, like he wasn't entirely sure she was in her right mind. "Are you okay?"

"Yes, sorry." Cassie shook herself, still reeling from her realization that she now knew which hotel Reed had been outside of. "Just lost in thought."

"You said something about her throat?" Green asked. He didn't look convinced.

Cassie bobbed her head up and down, welcoming the distraction. "Have you checked yet?" She led Green back to the room. Harris and Song were still inspecting the body. Cassie waited until Song looked up at her. "Her mouth. Can you open it?"

"Why?"

"I think there's something in her throat." Cassie glanced at Harris, who was looking at her with knowing eyes. "Can you check?"

Song looked at Detective Green, who offered no resistance, then back down at the body. Pulling out a toolkit, Song used a thin metal rod about the size of a pen to open the woman's mouth, then shined a light down her throat. When Song went rigid, Cassie knew she had been right. Seconds later, the detective had pulled a piece of crumpled up paper out of Luna's mouth with a pair of tweezers.

Before she unfolded the paper, Song looked up at Cassie. "How did you know that?"

Cassie cast her eyes around the room until they landed on the woman's desk. A ledger was open in the middle of it, and a piece of paper had been torn out of the center. Cassie pointed to it. "Saw that. Took a second for my brain to catch up." Cassie looked at Green. "Figured either someone had stolen the page or used it to make a point."

Green nodded. "Makes sense."

Detective Song either agreed or didn't want to contradict her colleague in front of strangers. She unfolded the piece of paper as gingerly as possible. She scanned it for a moment, then stepped back around the desk to look at the book in the center of it. "Definitely from the ledger. Dates match up too."

Harris stood and placed her hands on her hips. "So, whoever killed her had a stake in her shop? An investor, maybe?"

Cassie let that suggestion hang in the air. Then it clicked. "Most people pay psychics with cash, right? People don't want their loved ones to know they've been wasting money on someone like Luna Starlight."

"Yeah, probably," Harris answered. "What's your point?"

"Luna probably had a cash-only business. Seems like something Reed would invest in, right? We already know he has experience laundering money."

"Reed?" Song asked. "As in Donald Reed?"

"Yeah," Harris said, turning toward her. "Why?"

"His name's in the book. She paid him once a week. All varying amounts."

Harris' eyes lit up, and Green quirked a half smile. For the first time since they'd arrived, he seemed more like himself. "Well, ladies, looks like we're meant to be working together."

"Best news I've heard all day," Harris said. Her energy was tangible, but Cassie couldn't get that poster of the Cecil Hotel out of her head.

"Can I talk to you two for a minute?" Cassie asked Harris and Green, hoping Detective Song didn't take it personally. But the other woman wasn't paying them any attention as she continued to dig through the ledger.

When they were back out in the main room, Cassie led the other two over to the picture on the wall. She pointed to the ground at her feet. "I saw Luna right here. She's the one who told me about the piece of paper."

"She told you?" Green asked, looking alarmed. "You talked to her?"

"Well, no." Cassie grimaced. "She couldn't talk. She kept clawing at her throat, and then I saw the piece of paper wedged in there."

"Sometimes I love that you're psychic," Harris said.

"Only sometimes?" Cassie asked, eyebrow raised.

Harris shrugged. "Sometimes it freaks me out."

Green raised his hand. "Count me in the freaked-out club."

"I'd be a little worried if it didn't freak you out," Cassie said. "But that's not the only thing."

"Please tell me she drew you a map to Reed," Harris begged. "That would be helpful."

"Not quite." Cassie pointed at the poster, and the two detectives looked up at it, blank expressions on their face. "It's the Cecil Hotel."

"Did Luna point to it?" Green asked. "Is that where she said Reed would be?"

"No." Cassie blew out a breath, wishing she had a better answer. "But she was standing in front of it when she appeared."

Green looked at Harris. "Does that mean something?"

"Not that I know of," Harris answered.

"It's the hotel I saw in Emily's memory." Cassie felt like she was moving a thousand times faster than the other two. "It's important. Emily and Reed were arguing outside the Cecil Hotel. And Luna's spirit was standing in front of the poster."

"That hotel is, like, the most infamous hotel in Los Angeles," Harris argued. She pointed to other posters on the walls that Cassie hadn't noticed before. "Look, she's got all sorts of landmarks around the room. Griffith Observatory. The Hollywood sign. Sunset Boulevard. The Chinese Theatre."

"But she was standing here," Cassie pressed.

"I think it was just a coincidence."

Cassie stared at Harris. She didn't want to open up the argument from last night, especially in front of Detective Green, but it was hard not to take Harris by the shoulders and shake her. "What if it's not?"

Harris seemed to consider this. "Where would we even start, Cassie?" She pointed to the poster. "There are *seven hundred rooms.* Did you see a room number? Do you even know what floor to check?" When Cassie didn't answer, Harris' face softened. "We have a much bigger lead working backwards from this ledger. Reed has been in Chicago all this time, which means Luna was either depositing his money for him or sending him checks in the mail. He probably came here for money, and when she wouldn't give it to him, he killed her. It wouldn't be the first time he murdered someone."

Cassie looked to Green for help, but he just gazed back apologetically. "She's got a point."

"I'd bet my badge that most of the businesses on this street have security cams," Harris said. "We can follow his every move, back to wherever he's staying."

Cassie wanted to point out that Harris was suspended and didn't have a badge to bet on, but she bit her tongue. "So then, what now? We wait on a warrant? That could take hours."

Before Green could answer, an officer ducked into the shop and walked up to them. "Sir, there's a man outside who wants to talk to the three of you. He's not taking no for an answer."

"If it's another goddamned reporter, tell him—"

"No, sir." The officer turned to the side and pointed, and Cassie saw Jason practically jumping up and down trying to get their attention. "He says he knows them."

"He's with us," Harris said with a sigh. "Must be important."

Cassie followed the officer back outside, where they had sequestered Jason from the rest of the crowd. There were still plenty of people hovering around, but Cassie only recognized one face from before—Piper McLaren. Didn't she have a podcast to record or something?

Jason was practically vibrating by the time they made it over to him, and the officer keeping tabs was more than happy to step away and let the four of them have some privacy. But when Green stuck around, Jason looked questioningly at Cassie.

"Jason, this is Detective Noah Green. Noah, this is Jason, a friend of Cassie's," Harris answered before Cassie could even open her mouth. "Noah knows everything. What did you find?"

"I had my friend look up Natasha Michaelson," Jason said. Considering the high probability that what Terry did was illegal, Cassie didn't blame him for omitting his name. "Turns out she's been living under a fake name the last couple of years—"

"Norma Mitchell," Green supplied.

All three of them turned to face him, and Jason found his voice first. "How did you know that?"

Harris came in a close second. "The woman from your other missing persons case? The one Ginny is friends with?"

"Who's Ginny?" Jason asked.

"A woman I helped him interview," Harris answered. "She said she saw Norma get into a car with a guy she recognized. Someone she was afraid of." Harris looked up at Green. "Did you find him?"

"Not yet. But wait a second." Green pinched the bridge of his nose. "Why are you looking for Norma?"

"We're not. Or, at least, we didn't know we were. Reed had mentioned he was looking for a woman named Natasha Michaelson. We thought if we could find her, we might find Reed."

"This is beyond strange," Green said, rubbing his temples now. "First, you dig up a woman whose case I worked years ago. Then we both go to talk to the same woman—Luna Starlight—who ends up dead. And now you're telling me you're randomly looking for the same woman I am?"

"Not randomly." Jason's eyes lit up. He wouldn't be able to hide his thrill for the investigation if he tried. "Natasha Michaelson is Emily Washburn's half-sister."

20

GREEN NARROWED HIS EYES AT JASON. "HOW DO YOU KNOW THAT? WHO DID you say this friend of yours was?"

Jason tucked his phone away. "I didn't."

"Wait a second." She turned to Green. "When you had me interview Ginny, you knew Norma Mitchell was Natasha Michaelson. You knew she was Emily Washburn's half-sister."

Green didn't bother denying it. "Yes."

"Why didn't you tell me?"

"Would it have changed anything?" he asked. They all saw by the look on Harris' face it wouldn't have. "Besides, Norma's case is an active investigation. I was already crossing a line by bringing you in. I didn't want to push my luck by revealing her true identity."

"And you wanted to see how I'd react to the Norma Mitchell news," Harris supplied, "in case it looked like I knew more than I was letting on about her connection with Emily."

"Maybe." Green looked drained by the conversation. "Can you blame me? Both women have been missing for years, then you two show up and point us to Emily's body. A day later, I get a report about a woman named Norma who just went missing the day before and looked exactly like Natasha. I needed to know more before I looped you in."

Harris didn't look happy about the turn of events, but there was nothing they could do about it now. And Noah had a point. The fact that they were here on the other side of the police tape looking at a fresh crime scene was a huge privilege.

"Did your friend find anything else about Norma—or, I guess we should start calling her Natasha." Green looked over at Jason, sizing him up. "Any leads on her whereabouts?"

"He's got some contacts at local shelters and hostels. Those tend to be popular with runaways and fugitives. He called around, asking about her. Turns out Natasha was working at Sunset Paradise."

Green pursed his lips. "I know the place. Real shithole."

Jason nodded. "She was working there for free in exchange for a place to live."

"There'd be no records of her. No credit card statements, no bills in her name. It's a good way to stay under the radar."

"Why didn't Ginny know?" Cassie asked. "They were friends, weren't they?"

"Doesn't mean Natasha trusted her," Green answered. "She'd want to keep the list of people who knew where she slept at night to a minimum. It's likely only the owner of the Sunset knew."

"Do we even know why she's been in hiding this long?" Cassie asked. "Three years is a long time to live like that. Why not move to another city? Start over?"

"Her sister was murdered," Green said. "Maybe she didn't want to leave until she figured out who did it."

"Or she knew who did it," Harris said, "and thought she'd be next. Los Angeles is a good place to hide, especially if you have friends who'll take care of you. Much easier than starting fresh in an unfamiliar city." Harris stretched her neck from one side to the other, as though trying to relieve the tension they all felt building. "Reed killed Emily, and Natasha went into hiding. Maybe she was worried she'd be next. Maybe Emily knew something she shouldn't. Something that could help us."

"Only one way to find out." Green looked at Jason. "You got a room number?"

"I do. And the owner will be expecting us. My friend called in a favor."

"Good." Harris walked toward the tape and lifted it up for them. "Let's go."

Cassie hesitated. Something told her they wouldn't find anything at the Sunset Paradise. And another hotel kept calling to her. "You guys go ahead," she said. "I want to check out the Cecil."

Harris frowned. "I don't think we should split up."

"Jason and I can go together. We—"

"We need him to make sure the Sunset owner doesn't try to screw us over. Besides," Harris said, "you don't even know what you're looking for at the Cecil. It could be a huge waste of time."

"So could this." Cassie struggled to keep the frustration out of her voice. "What if you don't find anything?"

"We know this is where she's been staying for a while." Harris guided Cassie under the tape. "If we hit a dead end, we can check out the Cecil."

Cassie bit her tongue and looked to Jason for help. He only gave her an apologetic smile in return. "I think we should stick together," he said. "Reed is dangerous. And who knows who else Aguilar has working for him out here. Four heads are better than two."

Cassie couldn't help the stab of betrayal she felt at Jason's words. When he'd arrived at Laura's doorstep, she thought things would even out. That he'd be on her side. That he'd have her back. She knew he wasn't wrong—they had no idea what Aguilar was up to back home or if he was even aware of what happened in Chicago—but she felt like they were driving in the opposite direction.

Answers lay at the Cecil. She knew it.

But she was outnumbered three to one. She doubted they'd let her go off on her own—Jason because he was worried about Reed, and Harris because she'd want Cassie's gifts on hand. See if she could pick up anything in Natasha's room at the Sunset.

Harris could see when Cassie finally gave in, and she offered a bright smile in return. "Hey, come on. This is a good thing. If we can find Natasha, Reed might come to us. When we find out what he knows, we'll take that back to Savannah and nail Aguilar to the wall. We're so close, I can taste it."

Cassie wished she shared Harris' optimism.

With no other choice, they piled into their respective cars and headed to Sunset Paradise, located in a less than desirable part of town. Cassie could tell it had been abandoned by the city, left to fend for itself. Faded lines in the road and abandoned buildings were the most obvious signs of decay, but she was sure the rot ran deeper than that.

Her thoughts were confirmed when they pulled into a couple of parking spots at Sunset Paradise. What little grass that existed along the edge of the building was either dead or overgrown. Paint peeled from the outside walls, and even a few windows had been boarded up. Somehow, the lot was packed full of cars.

Green must've read the question on her face. "The Sunset Paradise used to be a hotel." He looked up to the building standing four stories high with at least half a dozen windows on this side. "When it shut down, someone bought it and split all the rooms in half, put in pairs of bunkbeds, and started renting it out as a hostel."

Cassie shook her head. "That sounds like a nightmare."

Green shrugged one shoulder. "Probably. But for some people, it's all they need."

"Or all they can afford," Harris said. She cast a glance at Jason. "Ready?"

Jason nodded and led them through the front door. It smelled like stale coffee, cigarette smoke, and mold. The front desk was closed off with bullet-proof glass, and a thin man with a scraggly beard and long, greasy gray hair sat behind the counter. He looked up from his magazine when they walked in. His eyes settled on Green and Harris.

Jason didn't give him time to get spooked. "Al, right? I'm Jason. Terry's friend."

The man scowled. "Don't know anyone named Terry." Jason froze. Silence hung in the air between them. Cassie could feel the tension rising. Then Al barked out a laugh, showing a mouthful of missing teeth. The ones that had survived were yellow and cracked. "Just fuckin' with you, man." He slid a key through the hole along the bottom of the window, and his face turned serious. "You find her, you tell her she owes me. Not runnin' a charity here."

"She's missing," Cassie said, with more bite than she'd intended. "She could be dead."

Al narrowed his eyes in her direction. "I gotta eat, too, lady. I could get four times what I get now for that room. She's lucky I haven't kicked her out yet."

Cassie had some choice words for him, but Harris was already pushing her past the window and down the hall after Jason. "It's not worth it," Harris hissed. "He doesn't care about anyone here. The only thing that matters to him is getting paid."

Jason turned the corner and walked to the end of the hallway, sliding a key into the handle and pushing through the door into Natasha's room. Cassie, Harris, and Green filed in after him, though there wasn't much room to stand.

Natasha's room had been cut in half, but it looked like she got all four bunkbeds to herself. Most of her belongings were in strategically placed boxes—one near the bathroom for her shampoo and cosmetics, one near her bed for books and various odds and ends—as though she wanted to be ready to pack up and leave at any time. The only items she had out were the ones she used regularly, like the phone charger near her bed and the toothbrush in the bathroom. The room was devoid of any decoration except for one framed photo on a small table next to her bottom bunk.

Harris got to it first. "It's Natasha and Emily." She handed it to Cassie. "Anything?"

Cassie took the frame and looked at the photograph. They both looked younger. The picture had been taken around a decade ago. Emily's head was thrown back in a laugh, her eyes closed against the sun in the background. Natasha looked straight into the camera, a wry smile on her face and her long, blonde hair billowing in the wind. The quality wasn't great, like it'd been taken from an old cellphone, but the way the picture was creased and warped around the edges told Cassie that Natasha had carried this picture with her since the day it was taken. Putting it in a frame had been the only way to preserve it.

Other than the warmth that flowed through her chest from seeing these sisters together and happy, Cassie felt nothing when she touched the photograph. She set it back down on the table. "Nothing," she told Harris. "Sorry."

Undeterred, Harris turned back to the room. "There's plenty of stuff to look through here. If we don't find anything, we can start knocking on doors. Maybe some of them have been here for the last week or so. They might've seen her leaving or spoke with her while she cleaned the rooms."

Cassie sighed. It was going to be a long afternoon for all of them.

21

AGUILAR TRIED TO KEEP TO A REGULAR SLEEP SCHEDULE FOR THE SAKE OF his many businesses. Sure, he had plenty of people to do his bidding, but he had learned first-hand that when the cats were away, the mice would play. His reputation did most of the heavy lifting, but Aguilar made it a point to eat at his restaurants, visit his warehouses, and shake hands with his employees. If they never knew when he'd show up, then they were less likely to slack off.

But tonight was worth a celebration. Aguilar checked his watch—his favorite piece, a vintage Rolex gifted by a family friend when he'd turned eighteen—and saw it was a little after one in the morning. He was sitting in his office across from Jasper, sipping on a cabernet and basking in his accomplishments. The last twenty-four hours had been some of the best in his life.

"So, the Bianchis are scrambling," Aguilar said, not trying to keep the pride out of his voice.

Jasper was much too practical to give in to the bait. He sat there, stoic and unmoved, a tablet in his hand. "That's not the word I would use." There was no passion in his voice, but when he saw Aguilar roll his eyes, he quirked a lip into a half-smile. "Essentially, yes. Our informant has told me they're trying to gather muscle from some of the other families.

They want to move against you. So far, no one is willing to step up to the plate."

"Because the other families aren't idiots." Aguilar took another sip of his wine.

There were a few prominent groups in Savannah whom he either did business with or respectfully avoided. Aguilar wasn't inherently greedy. He tried hard not to overstep his boundaries. The other families appreciated that, though it was much more likely they weren't willing to risk their operations to get him out of the way. Aguilar was too embedded in the city's culture. He had his hands in too many pots. Remove him, and everything would come tumbling down.

"The sooner the Bianchis realize they have no leverage, no advantage, the sooner this will be over."

"Still, there are some points of concern." Jasper slid a finger across the tablet and tapped twice, then looked back up at Aguilar. "They have numbers. And weapons. The loss of the restaurant is an issue."

"We have the money and resources to rebuild," Aguilar said, dismissively.

"Even so," Jasper pressed, "if they choose to attack your other businesses, it'll cause unwanted attention. Evidence might surface of your other activities."

"We own half the police force—"

"With Detective Harris gunning for you, I don't think it's wise to push our luck."

Aguilar ground his teeth together. If any other person had cut him off like that, he would've had their tongue. But this was Jasper, and Aguilar had benefitted from listening to him in the past. "What do you advise?"

Jasper was quiet for a moment. Aguilar knew he already had a plan but was going over it once more in his head, looking for any possible holes. There would be none. "It's important for you to stay out of the Bianchi mess. You already killed Pietro, and Nicolas knows it. He'll try to draw you out. You can't let him antagonize you."

Aguilar resented the implication in Jasper's voice, but he didn't argue. "Fine. But we have to be prepared. If he can't draw me out, he'll find another way to get his revenge."

"I think we should kill him."

Aguilar sat up and set his glass down on his desk. "An assassination?" Jasper wasn't usually so bold. "Why?"

Jasper didn't break eye contact. "With Nicolas out of the way, there will be in-fighting. A few more strategic hits within the family, and they'll run back to New Jersey where they belong. If we pay the Straczynski brothers to do it, no one will trace it back to us. They've been itching to remove Nicolas from their board."

"They've been itching to remove *me* from their board," Aguilar said. But he didn't hate the idea. "And you're convinced they'll be reliable?"

"With enough incentive, anyone can be reliable."

"Fair point." Aguilar smiled just as there was a knock at the door. He replaced his amusement with dispassion. "Come in."

One of Jasper's bodyguards entered the room. Aguilar thought his name was Marco or Marcel. Something like that. "Sir," he said, first addressing Aguilar, then Jasper. "The police are here."

Aguilar's dispassion turned into a frown. Jasper spoke first. "Which ones?"

"Crawford and Billings."

Jasper looked to Aguilar, who nodded, then back at the guard. "Bring them in."

Thirty seconds later, two men entered the room. They were both white and middle-aged, though Crawford looked worse for the wear. He had that Old Guard attitude and a chip on his shoulder. Billings, meanwhile, was a little more reserved, though he had a crooked set to his nose which told Aguilar he was no stranger to fighting.

"Officers." Aguilar stood and met them halfway across the room, shaking each hand in turn. "It's good to see you again."

"Likewise, Mr. Aguilar," Crawford said.

Aguilar had met Crawford before. He was arrogant and condescending, but his attitude now was nothing short of polite and reserved. Whether Crawford respected Aguilar or just wanted his money, he didn't know. And it didn't matter. Crawford served a purpose. He was a means to an end. If Crawford thought any differently about their relationship, then he hadn't been paying attention.

"What can I do for you, gentleman?" Aguilar asked. He didn't invite them to sit.

"We have a situation." Crawford glanced at Jasper, as though wondering if Jasper would leave the room. The man should've known better by now. Jasper had earned Aguilar's trust through loyalty, and Crawford would do well to remember that.

"Oh?" It was always better to feign ignorance. "What's that?"

"Nicolas Bianchi is claiming you killed his nephew, Pietro. They found his body yesterday morning. Someone had tortured him before finally putting him out of his misery."

"That's quite a serious accusation."

Crawford smiled. He knew the song and dance. "That's why I told Clementine I'd come down here myself, ask you direct. See if you were involved."

"My hands are clean." Aguilar held up his arms as if to prove his point. "I'm sorry to hear about their loss."

Billings snorted. "The kid was a dick. He was a pain in the ass for all of us."

"Even so," Aguilar said, with all the sincerity he could muster, "a death like that is a blow to a family. Especially one as tight-knit as the Bianchis."

"Do you have an alibi for last night? Around dinnertime?" Crawford asked.

"I was with my associate, Jasper Brown." Aguilar gestured to the man. "One of my restaurants mysteriously burned down. We were going through the appropriate insurance paperwork. In fact, I'm still trying to deal with the repercussions of that terrible accident."

"Checks out to me," Crawford said, not bothering to write any of the information down. "What about you, Billings? Satisfied?"

Aguilar held up a hand. "Before you answer that." He walked behind his desk and to a safe built into the wall, spinning the numbers until the door clicked open. He pulled out two thick envelopes, which he saved for occasions such as this one. When he returned to the group and dropped the cash into the officers' hands, their eyes lit up. "For your trouble."

Billings looked at Crawford with a devil's grin. "I'd say he had a compelling argument."

"With witnesses to corroborate his story," Crawford added.

Aguilar nodded at Jasper and then returned to his desk. By the time he sat down, Jasper had ushered the visitors out of the room. When he shut the doors behind him, they were alone once again.

"Any news from Los Angeles?" Aguilar asked.

Jasper took up his tablet once more and scrolled back through some messages. "Reed is still in the wind. Shepherd is closing in on Emily's sister. She's been living under a false identity. But it should only be a matter of time before he finds her. He's following the investigation as closely as he can without risk of getting caught." Jasper paused. "There's something else."

Aguilar looked up, steepling his fingers in front of him. "What?"

"The other woman, Quinn, mentioned the Cecil."

Aguilar looked up. "Where Emily was hiding when Reed found her." The implications were obvious. "Zbirak searched that room himself. She had no evidence stashed there."

"Shepherd believes the woman knows something. She's been insistent." Jasper waited, but Aguilar didn't say anything. "What if she does find something?"

Aguilar pressed his lips together. Emily had been the last person he'd trusted, besides Jasper. If she had taken evidence with her to California, it would be damning. And if Harris got her hands on it, there'd be no coming back from that. If he was going to make a move, now was the time.

"Tell Shepherd to wait for confirmation of evidence. I don't want this hanging over my head."

Jasper typed away on his tablet. "And after confirmation?"

"I want the whole mess cleaned up. That includes Reed." Aguilar leaned forward and grasped his wine glass, bringing it to his lips. "No witnesses. No survivors."

22

It was after midnight by the time they got back to Laura's house. Harris had insisted Cassie touch each one of Natasha's belongings before giving up. After that, they'd split up in pairs and knocked on every single door, asking questions and, in Harris' case, demanding answers from people who clearly didn't want to talk to the police.

Most people in the building didn't know Natasha. If they did, they only knew her as the woman who cleaned up vomit or knew where to find the extra rolls of toilet paper. Harris had even tried to bully Al, the owner, into giving up information. But it was pretty clear he didn't care about Natasha beyond what she could do to save him a buck. Sure, she got to have four whole beds to herself, but she was also responsible for almost a hundred rooms and four times as many residents constantly cycling in and out of the hostel.

Laura was already in bed by the time they returned, and Harris crashed on the couch without much ceremony. Jason and Cassie piled into bed. She wasn't in the mood to talk, and he was snoring away in under five minutes.

Cassie couldn't sleep. She understood why Harris had to check out Sunset Paradise, since they knew that's where Natasha was staying. The detective wouldn't have done her due diligence if she hadn't. A lot of people didn't realize that real-life investigations weren't like the movies. There was a lot more legwork and a lot of dead ends. The hostel was one of many they had already run into.

But Cassie couldn't stop thinking about the Cecil. Out of all of Emily's memories, why had the one where she'd argued with Reed outside the hotel floated to the surface? Out of all the posters hanging in Luna Starlight's parlor, why had she been standing in front of the Cecil's?

Harris was already talking about going back to Sunset Paradise in the morning to see if they could find anyone new to talk to. Or revisiting Mason Hardy, Reed's old associate, to see if he had anything else to say. As much as Cassie argued it, Harris saw no point in wasting time at the Cecil if they didn't know which room number to visit. But Cassie's abilities weren't always consistent or straightforward. It could be a ghost or a vision or a feeling that led her in the right direction, but she'd never find out which if she didn't go to the hotel.

Before Cassie's brain caught up with her body, she was slipping out of bed and changing back into her clothes from earlier in the day. They were still damp with sweat, and she probably needed to put on more deodorant, but it would've taken too long and there was too high a chance Jason would've woken up and asked her what she was doing.

She opened the door, squeezed through the crack, and closed it again without disturbing anyone, but escaping her room was the least of her worries. Harris was on the couch, and Cassie had a feeling she didn't sleep as deeply as Jason.

He'd tossed the keys to the rental car on the dining room table, and Cassie had to tip-toe around the couch to get to them. She used all her remaining stealth and patience to lift them from the surface as slowly as she could, making sure the metal didn't jingle. Harris shifted in her sleep, and Cassie froze with one foot hovering an inch above the floor, but the detective just pulled her blanket up over her head. Cassie breathed a sigh of relief and placed her foot down as gently as possible, doing her best to avoid any creaking floorboards.

Thankfully, the front door opened silently, and Cassie slipped out into the cool night air without any more trouble. She took a moment to let her eyes adjust, then shut the door behind her and tiptoed across the driveway, as though Laura would be able to sense any disturbance outside the house.

It was only when Cassie was settled into the front seat of the vehicle that she realized she'd forgotten her phone inside. But it was too late now. The car had a built-in GPS unit, which would have to be good enough. Hopefully, Cassie would be back before anyone noticed she was gone.

Turning the key in the ignition, Cassie cut the lights as soon as the engine roared to life and eased out of the driveway. She didn't turn them back on until she was halfway down the street. Luckily, it was late enough that hardly anyone was on the road in Laura's neighborhood.

That changed as soon as Cassie left Inglewood and got on the highway. It was almost one in the morning, but this was Los Angeles. Maybe it wasn't the City That Never Sleeps, but it wasn't exactly known for being a sleepy town. Plenty of people were on the road, and it took a good half hour to get back downtown. It was easy enough to find parking, but Cassie didn't enjoy navigating the streets on her own. She kept her head down and walked at a brisk pace until the building loomed in front of her.

It looked different than it had in her vision—or even in the poster at Luna Starlight's. The building's framework was the same, and Cassie hated to admit that maybe Harris was right about it being too big to tackle without more information. But everything else looked slightly different. The huge words detailing the rates and number of rooms that had once been stenciled onto one of its towers had been covered in white paint. The historic sign out front had been replaced with a bright orange one that read Stay on Main.

During their downtime earlier that day, Cassie had looked up the hotel's history. The building had seen a lot of tragedy since it'd opened in 1924. It may have started off as an opulent hotel, but the Great Depression had done plenty of damage across the country. The nearby Skid Row didn't have good standing either. Over the years, the Cecil had fallen into decline.

It wasn't just the sketchy neighborhood that had caused issues. The hotel had gained a reputation for violence. It had only taken three years after the opening for the first suicide to occur. The hotel had become notorious for prostitution and drug activity. In the '80s, infamous serial killer Richard Ramirez, the Night Stalker, stayed at the Cecil while he went on his murder spree.

There were others, of course, but Cassie had read enough. Of all the suicides and murders and violence that were known, there were plenty more that went unsolved. With that much history, a building like the Cecil would hang onto that energy. It would come alive in a way that some might feel and even fewer could see.

It wouldn't have been her first choice to show up at the hotel by herself in the middle of the night, but if she were honest, the Cecil would've been just as haunted during the day. Steeling herself for the onslaught she was about to encounter, Cassie stalked forward and wrenched open the front door.

The temperature dropped by a few degrees, and an army of goose-bumps raced up her arms. The lobby was beautiful, with white floors and a stunning stained-glass window in the center of the ceiling. Pillars and arches gave the hotel an old-world feel, and the hanging lanterns kept the place dim and atmospheric.

But that's not what stole Cassie's attention. While there was no one behind the front desk—maybe they were in a back room—flickers of light and shadow shifted from the corners. She could feel the spirits turning toward her, wondering who she was and what kind of power she had. They could tell the moment she sensed their presence, and while some sank further into the dark, a few stepped out, longing for any kind of connection.

Cassie had practiced tuning them out. It wasn't like it had been before, when she had ignored them, hoping they would go away. Now, it was more like a barrier she set around herself. A window. They could see her and she could see them, but she kept the spirits separate. She had her boundaries, and they were forced to respect them.

Still, she wasn't sure why she was at the Cecil. She had hoped she'd feel a pull toward a certain level or a certain room, but right now all she could feel was the overwhelming presence of tragedy. It was easier not to get pulled under than it had been last time she'd been in a situation like this—back at the hospital in New Orleans—but there was a weight that dragged at her feet and made her want to turn around and head home.

But she was here now, and Cassie knew she couldn't leave, as much as she wanted to. If Harris found out she'd been to the Cecil and didn't find anything, she'd feel even more assured in her decision not to go to the hotel. Cassie might never get another chance. She had to take the opportunity she'd made for herself.

Turning toward a staircase to the second floor, Cassie walked with purpose. There was no one in the lobby, but the hotel was far from quiet. She'd read somewhere that Stay on Main was now an affordable housing complex, so these residents were more permanent. What that meant for her destination, if she ever found out which room that was, she wasn't sure.

Upstairs, the hallway was just as lush as the lobby, though she could tell everything was old. Maybe it was to keep the history of the hotel alive, but it gave off a worn and dilapidated feel. The edges of picture frames were cracked and broken. The rug was worn and nearly threadbare in the center. Dust lingered in the crevices.

Cassie avoided the elevators, instead opting for the back staircases leading up to each level. If she had to step out onto each floor and feel her way forward, she'd find the room she was looking for. Even if it took all night.

But as she drew closer to the door to the stairwell, a dark presence peeled away from the wall, blocking her path. She could've stepped through him, but she'd rather know what she was dealing with first. Even if this spirit couldn't physically harm her like a living person might, they could still affect her if they were strong enough. She'd had evil entities affect her emotions before, even try to burn her up from the inside out. Back then, David had been there to help her. Now, she was alone. It wasn't worth taking chances.

The presence coalesced in front of her, growing more solid by the second. She could make out some of his features—long greasy hair, an unshaven face, and dark eyes that nearly pinned her to the wall—but he was hazy around the outside, not quite fully formed. Was he too weak, or simply conserving energy? Right now, the only feelings she could sense coming off him were curiosity, accompanied by a dark, predatory tinge.

Casting her gaze anywhere but at the ghost, Cassie gave him a wide berth as she moved toward the door. She shouldered it open and had crossed halfway over the threshold when a tendril of heat wrapped around her wrist and squeezed. The burning sensation was so sharp and sudden, she couldn't stop her scream as it echoed up the stairwell.

23

GHOSTLY FINGERS ENCIRCLED HER WRIST LIKE HOT IRON CUFFS, SEARING HER skin. The pain encompassing Cassie's wrist was so white-hot that her vision began to fade. She could barely breathe or think. Instinct took over. She moved to shake off the steely grip on her arm.

The figure had somehow pushed through her invisible barrier without her knowledge. The pain only grew hotter. He wouldn't let go. Out of sheer panic and terror, Cassie did the one thing she had tried to avoid.

She looked him in the eye.

Everything she had thought she'd known about him had been wrong. He wasn't an old or a weak spirit—his clothes told her he had died maybe twenty or thirty years ago. Plaid button-down shirt and jeans, a large belt buckle. A longhorn skull pressed into the metal, and the word TEXAS stamped in the middle. She met his soulless eyes again. The fire around her wrist blazed hotter.

She refused to cry out.

A few months ago, she wouldn't have been strong enough to defend herself like this. She knew better now. She knew what she had been put here to do. And she wasn't afraid of this man, even if every fiber of his being screamed murder and bloodshed.

Sweating from the exertion, Cassie didn't look away from his black eyes. She forced every ounce of her energy into forming a barrier over her skin, starting at the top of her head. It moved down her neck and chest, to her arms, and eventually her legs. Then her hands and feet. His white-hot touch cooled, and Cassie could think straight again.

Whoever this man was, he liked to inflict pain for no reason except that he could. This was the type of spirit who left marks on unsuspecting victims or broke lights and vases. He enjoyed terrorizing people. He fed off of it.

But he wasn't going to feed off of her. She would outlast him at every turn. Something clicked in her mind, and her heart rate slowed. The adrenaline receded. She stood taller. This man couldn't do anything worse to her than she'd already survived.

The moment the shield snuck its way under the ghost's fingers, he let go in surprise. It was all the opening she needed. With all her remaining strength, she pushed the barrier against him. He stumbled and regained his balance. She pushed harder, driving him farther away, back out the door, into the lobby, and out the entrance. He'd be weaker out there, farther from his source of power. His energy would drain. Even if he managed to get back inside, he'd be a shade of what he once was.

Cassie let herself relax. Her own energy plummeted from her body, and she stumbled to the stairs. The cool air brushed against her skin, giving her some relief. She shook with giddy victory.

Most people weren't as affected by spirits because they couldn't see them. The energy exchange between the spirits and Cassie was stronger because they operated on a similar plane of existence. They could touch her. Talk to her. Hurt her.

But she could hurt them right back.

A shuffling noise caught Cassie's attention, and she turned to see a sliver of light emanating from the shadows. A slender young woman peered out from the corner. She looked scared, but curious. Cassie smiled, and the other woman's eyes grew wide with wonder.

"It's okay," Cassie said, her voice still breathless. "I won't hurt you."

The girl shuffled forward again, revealing more of her form. Even against her translucent body, Cassie could see the large welt on her wrist.

Cassie held up her own, where a nasty red mark lingered from the other spirit's touch.

"Did he hurt you too?" Cassie asked.

The girl looked to the door, her face pinched in pain, then back at Cassie. She nodded.

"He's gone now," she assured the girl. "He'll be weak for a while. Are there others here who can keep him outside?"

The young woman nodded and stepped forward again. She was wafer-thin, and Cassie found herself holding back tears. How did she die, and at nineteen or twenty years old? Was it a tragic accident, or murder? Was it someone she knew, or had she been in the wrong place at the wrong time? Was it the man from Texas? What a hell that would be, trapped forever in the afterlife with the person who killed you.

Cassie looked up at the stairwell. Any ability to sense where she needed to go next was gone. She was too drained. Had this whole trip been for nothing? Finished before it even started?

Then she looked back down at the girl. Her eyes were sharp with intelligence. She wore her hair long and in pigtails, and her dress was from the seventies. Had she been trapped here that long? Cassie could barely comprehend everything this young girl must've seen. All the people she'd watched from the shadows over the years.

"I'm looking for someone," Cassie said, her voice still quiet. "Someone's room. I don't know why, but I think it's important. Do you think you could help me?"

The girl tilted her head to the side, then walked forward until the two of them were only inches apart. Holding up her hand, she held it just shy of Cassie's face. It took her a moment to understand what the spirit wanted. When it clicked into place, her eyes widened. Ghosts had shared their thoughts and memories with Cassie in a number of ways. Like Emily, some of them had shown her what they wanted through a series of pictures and visions. There was no reason why that energy exchange couldn't go both ways.

Leaning forward, Cassie pressed her face into the girl's hand and closed her eyes. She pictured Emily in her mind, just as she'd seen her with Reed. That would be about the right time. Windblown hair. Worry lines on her face. But a strength that came from deep inside. The same strength that had propelled her halfway across the country so she could tell Cassie her story.

A cool sensation slid down the side of Cassie's face. Goosebumps lit up across her shoulders and neck, but not from the darkness she had felt when she'd stepped into the lobby. This was a different kind of chill, the kind that only accompanied the knowledge that a being from the other side was sifting through her memories. Seeing what she could see. In the same way Emily had shared her life with Cassie, Cassie was now sharing Emily's life with this young woman.

After a few more seconds, the coolness faded, and Cassie blinked open her eyes. She was alone, and for a moment, she worried she'd scared the girl or hurt her somehow. Then a shuffling sound came from somewhere above her.

Getting to her feet, Cassie ascended the stairs, finding the girl peering over the railing a few floors up. It took longer than it should have in her weakened state, but Cassie finally made it to the fifth floor. The girl passed through the door to the other side like it was made of air. Wrenching it open after her, Cassie had just enough time to see her disappear around the corner. Hurrying to catch up, she found her standing outside a room halfway down the hall. As soon as Cassie approached, the girl once again drifted through the door.

Cassie stood there, not knowing what to do. These weren't just hotel rooms anymore. People lived here. She couldn't knock on the door and wake them up in the middle of the night. What would she say if she did? *Sorry to bother you, folks, but a ghost led me to your room. I'm looking for something a dead woman might've left here three years ago. Mind if I look around?*

As Cassie contemplated her next move, she felt a gentle tugging in the pit of her stomach. She'd felt it plenty of times before, but most recently downstairs with the man from Texas. For a second, she thought maybe he'd returned to drain more of her energy, but then she realized the sensation wasn't quite the same. It felt like someone asking permission. Realizing her spirit guide on the other side of the door was still trying to help her, Cassie opened herself up to the young girl, giving her what she'd politely asked for.

The transition of energy was far less painful when it was freely given instead of stolen, and a few seconds later, there was a sliding noise, like a lock turning, and then a click. The young girl had used Cassie to coalesce enough to open the door for her. Against her better judgment, Cassie twisted the handle and pushed. The door swung open, and she stood in the hallway for a moment while her eyes adjusted to the darkness inside.

Before she could talk herself out of it, she stepped over the threshold.

If someone lived here, they hadn't been back in a few days. The air was stale and smelled like old socks. Thank goodness it was just a single room, otherwise the whole place would've stunk worse. Cassie hoped whoever lived here was doing okay—and that they wouldn't return home in the next hour or so.

She looked around for the young woman, but she had apparently served her purpose and disappeared. Cassie whispered a thank you to the open room, and a slight breeze brushed by her cheek. It didn't do anything to help the sweat rolling down her back, but it was acknowledgement enough.

There was no point in ransacking the room. Emily hadn't been here in years. Cassie trusted the young woman had led her to the right place, but why was she here? What was she looking for? Had Emily hidden evidence against Aguilar? Had she left something behind for her sister? Was there any proof that Reed and Zbirak had been the ones to kill her? Looking for something as normal as fingerprints or hair would be useless this many years later. But maybe Cassie could find something else.

Standing as still as possible, she closed her eyes. Tried to hold a bit of Emily close to her, thinking of what the other woman would've done three years ago if she had been worried her time was coming to a close. If she had something to hide, where would she have hidden it?

Breathing slowly and steadily, Cassie searched the room with her mind, traveling across the floor, under the bed, around the chair, and up the walls. She thought of Emily's spirit, of her presence. Something tugged at her when she reached the ceiling, pulling her to the corner of the room and setting off distant alarm bells in her head.

When she opened her eyes, Cassie noticed a grate in the corner of the room, like the kind you would use to heat or cool the building. Grabbing an antique sitting room chair a foot away, Cassie dragged it over and carefully climbed up until she was balanced on the back, precariously clinging to the wall and hoping one wrong move wouldn't send her tumbling to the ground.

Using Jason's car keys to unscrew the grate, Cassie pulled it free and stood on the tips of her toes to peer inside. She could just about peek over the lip of the opening, but it was dark.

Cassie cursed herself for leaving her phone behind and shifted to the side, tilting and then regaining her balance. She stuck her arm into the vent, trying not to recoil from the number of spiderwebs her hand passed through. But other than a thin layer of dust, there was nothing there.

Maybe if she knew what she was looking for, it would be easier. Something was here—she knew it—but how big was it? A hidden note or a bloody knife? It felt hopeless, and Cassie couldn't believe she had come all this way just to run into a dead end.

Something skittered over her fingers, making her jump and then yelp when she almost lost her footing. Her reflexes took over, and she gripped the wall until she was steady again. With a deep breath to calm her nerves, she inched her hand back inside the duct. When she'd shaken off whatever had crawled over her hand, she'd hit loose one of the metal panels inside. Someone had installed a false wall.

Hesitating for only a fraction of a second, Cassie reached up and found that the ventilation system extended above her as much as it did out in front. Fighting against the urge to get her hopes back up, Cassie felt along the sides of the duct. When her fingers brushed over an uneven surface, she almost jumped back in surprise again, thinking maybe it was another creepy crawly.

But it was hard and plastic. She traced the outline with her fingers, coming across the rough edges of duct tape holding the treasure in place. Holding her breath, Cassie peeled away the adhesive and let the plastic contraption fall into the palm of her hand. Barely daring to let her mind run wild, she withdrew her hand and looked down at her discovery.

She was holding a sleek black external hard drive, and taped to the front was a handwritten note addressed to Natasha.

24

CASSIE CUT THE CAR'S HEADLIGHTS BEFORE SHE PULLED INTO THE DRIVEWAY, but it didn't matter. If the illuminated lamps in the living room were any indication, everyone in Laura's house was awake, anyway. Cassie winced as she got out of the car, a strange mixture of adrenaline and fatigue coursing through her system. She wondered how long they'd been worried about her being gone and who'd noticed first—Harris or Jason?

Not bothering to be quiet as she got out of the car, by the time she made it to Laura's front door, it was already wide open. Three people stared at her with an array of different facial expressions. Laura was wiping tears from her cheeks. Jason looked relieved and confused. Harris looked pissed.

Before Cassie could shut the door behind her, Harris snapped, "Where the hell have you been?"

"The Cecil." Cassie answered her like she'd just run to the grocery store to pick up milk and bread. "I'm sorry if I worried you—"

"*If?*" Harris asked, letting out a bitter laugh. "Cassie, you snuck out in the middle of the night. The car was gone. We had no idea where you went. We called you a million times until we realized you'd left your phone behind."

Jason held up Cassie's cell as proof, and Cassie took it from him without meeting his eyes. "I didn't do that on purpose. I forgot."

"Why would you go there by yourself?" Jason asked, sounding more hurt than angry. "I would've gone with you in the morning. Hell, if you'd woken me up—"

"Because you would've talked me out of it." Now it was Cassie's turn to get mad. "I told you guys I had a feeling there was something going on at the Cecil. And I was right." Cassie held up the hard drive and waved it around. "Something was driving me there, and you kept shrugging it off. Saying it wasn't worth it." She looked right at Harris. "I know you've been a detective for a long time, and I know you have your own instincts to go on. But there was nothing at the Sunset Paradise. I told you there wouldn't be. And I found this at the Cecil."

"What is it?" Jason asked.

"A hard drive. And a note to Natasha with it."

No one stepped forward to take it from her. Laura cleared her throat, but her voice was still watery. "I was really scared, Cassie. You can't just run off like that in the middle of the night. Los Angeles is a big place. You could've gotten lost or something could've happened. And the Cecil isn't in the best neighborhood."

Before Cassie could respond, Jason pointed to her arm. "What happened to your wrist?"

Holding it up, the red ring was shiny, like she'd been burned. "A pissed off ghost that didn't like the fact I was in his territory. And I took care of it." Cassie took a deep breath before looking at all three of them in turn. "Look, I'm sorry that I worried you. I shouldn't have run off like that. The last thing I wanted to do was worry you." She looked at Laura when she said that last part. After everything Cassie had been through, Laura had good reason to be afraid. "But I'm not going to apologize for going to the Cecil. I followed my instincts," she continued, meeting Harris' gaze, "and I found something. That's why I'm here. I don't need you guys to shelter me from every bad thing that could happen to me in this world. I've survived everything the universe has thrown at me, and I'm not afraid anymore." A thrum of pleasure coursed through her body as she realized how true those words were. "I'm stronger now than I was before. And I understand my abilities better. It's taken me a long time to get to this point, and I'm not going to sit back and let the world dictate how I feel anymore. I wanted to do this *with* you. All of you. We need to start getting on the same page so we can find Reed and nail Aguilar to the wall. So we can demand justice for David."

Silence filled the room except for Laura's occasional sniffles.

Much to Cassie's surprise, Harris was the first to speak. "You're right."

Cassie couldn't help the grin that spread over her face. "I'm sorry, can you say that again?"

Harris rolled her eyes, but she smiled now too. "I said you're right. I'm not gonna say it a third time."

"Just wanted to make sure." Cassie sobered a little bit. "Thank you. And I'm sorry. Really."

Laura stepped forward and embraced her.

When she let go, Jason replaced her, squeezing Cassie until she squeaked in protest. "I'm glad you're safe," he said. "I don't know if supernatural ghost burns are anything like real-life burns, but I did bring a first-aid kit with me."

Cassie laughed. "Best we can do is try."

"Okay, enough of this." Harris held out her hand for the hard drive. "Let's see what we're working with."

Cassie passed the device over while Jason went to get cream for her arm. She held on to the note. Though she'd been itching to read it, her antics earlier in the night had gotten the attention of the other spirits in the hotel. It was better to just get home.

"How did you find this, anyway?" Laura asked.

"A lot of luck," Cassie answered. "And a little help from the other side."

"What's the note say?" Harris asked, pulling out her computer and plugging the hard drive into a port.

Jason returned with his first aid kit, and Cassie held out her wrist to him, using her other hand to peel open the dusty note and read it out loud.

"Dear Nat," she began. "It sounds so cliché to start a letter with 'If you're reading this, it means I'm dead,' but it's the only way you'll ever find this. I'm sorry about...everything. You knew who Francisco was the minute you laid eyes on him, and I didn't want to believe it. Then, when I started to see the truth, I was too scared to leave. I know you don't trust Detective Klein either"—Cassie's voice faltered, and Jason's hand stilled against her wrist—"but I have to believe he's one of the good guys. He's not going to be happy I left, but I have to keep this evidence hidden until he can build a case against Francisco. Once he does that, I'm going back to Savannah. I know that's the last thing you want me to do, but I want to look Francisco in the eyes when I testify against him. I want him to know it was me who gathered the evidence. I want to cause him as much pain as he's caused me. And I don't want him to be able to hurt anyone else ever again. After that, I hope you and I get to grow old together like we always imagined, with our husbands and dozens of dogs and a big swimming pool. But if not, I need you to do one last favor for me. Give this drive to Detective Klein. ONLY Detective Klein. I'm trusting you on this, Nat. You're the only one who'll know the password. This is what I want. Emily."

Jason had finished wrapping Cassie's wrist and was now inspecting the hard drive attached to Harris' computer. "This was definitely a brand-new model about three years ago when Emily disappeared. There are better ones now, but this one is still going to be hard to crack without a password. I know some people who can do it, but it'll take time."

Harris gestured to the computer screen. There was a window open and a blinking cursor. "It'd be faster with the password."

"We need to find Natasha," Cassie said, looking back down at the letter. "Emily was working with David. They were trying to get dirt on Aguilar for years."

"That's why both of them are dead," Harris said. Her eyes were dark but determined. "He wasn't working with Aguilar because he wanted to. He was trying to help Emily build a case against one of the most dangerous men in Savannah."

Laura looked around at the three of them, her face scrunched up as though she were in pain. "Aren't you guys scared?"

"Terrified," Cassie answered. "But this is what we're good at." She exchanged a look with Harris, who gave her a sharp nod. "And this time it's going to stick. Aguilar is going down."

Laura looked down at her phone. "It's almost four. We won't be able to do anything for at least a couple hours. Let's get some sleep. Then we'll come up with a plan."

Cassie looked back down at the letter, zeroing in on Emily's tight, looping handwriting. On David's name. Cassie never doubted David's intentions, but it was still a relief to see that he was the same man she had thought he was all along. She just wished he'd been able to reach out to her or Adelaide. To confide in him. Maybe things would be different.

But she couldn't change the past. All she could do was tackle the future.

25

It was almost noon by the time Cassie and the others pried themselves from their beds. It was amazing how quickly she had gotten used to sleeping next to Jason. In fact, she had found out he was the reason why everyone knew she was missing. He'd woken up a few minutes after she left and realized she'd snuck out. A warm feeling flooded her chest whenever she thought of him. She couldn't wait to go home and figure out what came next.

With plenty of caffeine running through their systems, the four of them piled into Jason's rental, ready to tackle what was left of the day. Cassie must've spent her sleeping hours thinking about their problem at hand because when she woke up, she'd realized their next step: Talk to Natasha's friend Ginny, the one Harris had already interviewed on behalf of Detective Green.

Harris hadn't loved the idea of talking to Green's witness without him around, but she'd seen the determination in Cassie's eyes. They all realized how close they were getting to real answers. This was not the time to fight amongst themselves. If they were going to take Aguilar down, they had to stand as a unit.

Jason drove them to the small café where Ginny worked. She had just walked out the door, ready to grab something to eat on her lunch break, when Harris approached her. Ginny seemed just as nervous as Harris had said she'd been that first day she met her. Cassie hung back and waited for Harris to introduce her while Jason and Laura went inside to get some more coffee. The pair of them had agreed to hang back until they were needed.

After about a minute, Harris motioned for Cassie to join them. Ginny was looking at her with apprehension, her lips pressed firmly in a straight line. She had a severe bob of jet-black hair, cut to just below her ears. It was hard to tell under the heavy makeup that was a few shades too dark for her pale skin, but Ginny looked younger than Cassie thought she'd be. Maybe early twenties. A pang of heartbreak shot through Cassie's chest. This girl was just a kid, but she'd seen so much. And she was possibly the only person who could help them find Natasha.

Cassie smiled, going for somewhere between shy and friendly. The last thing she wanted to do was spook the woman. "Hello," she said, giving a polite wave. That morning, she'd realized her wound from the night before had healed, and she was glad she was no longer wearing the wrap Jason had tied to her wrist. "Thanks for talking to us."

"I don't have much time." Ginny's voice was curt, but not rude. "I only get a half hour."

"We'll be quick, I promise." Harris motioned to an empty table where all three of them sat down. "I just want to follow up with you on Norma."

Ginny looked like she was ready to bolt at any second, but she stayed in her chair. "Where's Detective Green?"

"He couldn't be with us today." Harris moved the conversation forward as quickly as she could. "Did you know Norma's real name was Natasha?"

Ginny hesitated for a moment, then nodded. "She said I was the only one she ever told. She didn't trust anyone else."

"Natasha got into a car with a man you were afraid of," Harris said, recounting what she'd learned the day before. "I know you already talked to me about that a little bit, but I was hoping you could tell my colleague what you said."

Ginny took a deep breath, reciting the information like she's already been through it a dozen times. "His name is Dominick Lindholm. You go to him if you can't find a job or need money quick. Mostly women. He always finds them something. Either as strippers or waitresses in a nightclub. Sometimes something worse."

"Worse how?" Harris asked, not unkindly.

"Hookers. Escorts. And not the high-end kind." She shook her head. "He's a sleazebag. Takes fifty percent of their earnings. They either end up working for him forever, or they're never seen again."

"Does he hurt them?" Cassie asked, thinking of Natasha.

"Some of them for sure." Ginny's eyes kept darting around, not landing on either Harris or Cassie for long. "A few of them save up enough to leave. A lot more stay behind. At least it's steady work, you know? But everyone knows what kind of risk you're taking by getting into bed with Dom. Literally and metaphorically."

"Do you have any idea what happens to the girls who go missing?" Harris asked. This isn't the problem they came here to solve, but Cassie could tell Ginny's words bothered the detective. "Are they sent somewhere else?"

"I really don't know. A few of them turned up dead. Overdose or beaten, stuff like that. Some just never come back. I try to think maybe they found their way somewhere better." Ginny looked directly at Harris now. "I thought you wanted to know about Natasha?"

"Why did she get into contact with this guy?" Harris asked. "She was already working at Sunset Paradise."

Ginny's eyes lit up. "Was she? I didn't know that. Guess she needed more money then. Maybe she was trying to leave. Wish she would've told me." Ginny sighed and slouched back in her chair. "I would've gone with her."

"Did she tell you why she wanted to leave?" Cassie asked. "Did she mention a guy named Don Reed?"

Ginny shook her head. "Doesn't sound familiar, but we didn't really talk about that kind of stuff. Guys we were seeing, you know?"

"This wouldn't have been a guy she was seeing," Cassie clarified. "It'd be someone she was trying to get away from."

Ginny barked out a laugh. "In my experience, those are usually one and the same."

"Did she ever mention her sister, Emily?" Harris asked.

Ginny's face grew wistful. "Yeah, all the time. Nat said she disappeared three years ago. The way she talked about her, I think she knew Em was dead. Kept talking about getting revenge on the guy who killed her. His name was Francisco."

Cassie and Harris exchanged a look. "But she never mentioned Reed?" Harris asked. "He worked for Francisco."

"No." Ginny looked down at her phone. "Look, I only have twenty minutes left, and I have a double today."

Harris pulled out a wad of cash and pushed it into Ginny's hand. "A few more questions, and then you can go get something good for lunch, okay?"

Ginny slipped the money into her pocket and nodded. "What else do you need to know?"

"Do you know where Natasha would go once she had enough money saved up?"

"Savannah, probably. She was always talking about going there. I think that's where her sister lived before she moved back home." Ginny tilted her head up and closed her eyes against the sun. "We talked about a lot of other places, too. Washington. North Carolina. Paris and Amsterdam." She looked back down at them, a wry smile on her face. "If we won the lottery, at least."

"And you have no idea where she'd be working? If she's still with Dominick?"

"Like I told you the other day," Ginny said, her voice sad, "she hasn't contacted me at all. I saw her get into his car, and they drove off together. Natasha was always smart. I was surprised to see her leave with him. When her phone died and she didn't come back, I called the cops."

"You reported her missing?" Cassie asked.

Ginny looked down at her hands, where she began to pick at her fingernails. "Like I said, Nat was smart. We always said if we ever went to work for Dom, we'd text each other once a day. Just to make sure everything was okay. I waited a couple days, but I had a bad feeling. That's why I filed the report. I know she wanted to stay off the radar, but I couldn't let something happen to her. She's the only friend I've got left. I've lost everyone else."

Cassie's heart broke for the woman, but something she said sparked an idea. "Did he ever try to recruit women? Instead of waiting for them to go to him?"

"Oh yeah. He had business cards made up and everything. Pretended to be a modeling agency. That's how he covered up what he was doing and found new girls."

"He ever try to recruit you?" Harris asked.

Ginny looked away and nodded. When she turned back, there were tears gathering at the corners of her eyes. "Almost went over there one day. Natasha talked me out of it, thank God."

"Went over where?" Harris' voice was gentle, but there was a forced steadiness to it. "I thought you didn't know where he lived?"

Ginny blushed and looked back down at her hands. "I didn't want to get in trouble. If Dom knew I'd sent the cops over there—"

"It's okay." Cassie laid a hand on Ginny's forearm and waited until the other woman looked up at her. "I'm not a cop, and you're not going to get in trouble. We just want to find Natasha. Help get justice for Emily. The same person who killed Natasha's sister killed our friend. We have evidence against him. Stuff that Emily put together three years ago. But we need Natasha's help. We need your help."

Ginny looked Cassie in the eyes, searching for the answer to a question she was too afraid to ask. Could she trust these strangers? Cassie looked back at her with as much vulnerability and empathy as she could muster. She knew Ginny was afraid, but they couldn't help Natasha without her. They couldn't get justice for Emily or David without a new lead. This was their only hope.

The woman must've seen something she could trust in Cassie's eyes because she reached into her purse and pulled out a worn and faded business card. It was off-white with gold lettering that peeled at the corners. She offered it to Cassie, who held her breath as she took it.

No sooner had Cassie touched the card than a flood of images passed through her mind's eye. Natasha getting into Dominick's car. Him introducing her to the bouncer at a nightclub. Her going back to his apartment because she was too scared to go home. Him sitting too close to her on the couch, and her pushing him away.

Cassie looked down at the card, at Dominick Lindholm's name and address, then back up at Harris. Flashing the card at the detective, she gave her a look she hoped Harris could read by now. One that said she'd had a vision. That she knew what she was talking about. That Harris had to trust her.

"Natasha is staying at Dominick Lindholm's apartment," Cassie said. "And she's in trouble."

26

With lunchtime traffic, it took them forty-five minutes to get to Dominick Lindholm's apartment just a few miles away. Harris felt like the scenery was crawling by at a snail's pace.

Harris didn't know Natasha, but it was hard to not feel protective of her. Her sister had died, and she'd been hiding out ever since. That wasn't an easy life to live in a city as unforgiving as Los Angeles. They might not have been able to do anything for Emily, but she'd be damned if she let anything happen to Natasha.

The second Jason parked the car, Harris jumped out of the passenger seat and ran up the front steps to the building. It was a small complex, but infinitely nicer than Sunset Paradise. This building didn't have a name, but it did have a manicured lawn, sweeping gardens, and more than one Mercedes in the parking lot.

That made Harris even angrier. Dominick Lindholm earned his money by extorting women. He got half their paychecks just by finding them a job, and that was just the work she knew about. What else was he capable of? Thoughts like that should've stopped her in her tracks, but she found herself storming through the entrance, racing up the steps to the second level, and pounding on the man's door.

Lindholm wrenched it open, a baseball bat in one hand and a beer bottle in the other. There was a sneer on his face, but when he caught sight of Harris, he hesitated. The way he looked her up and down made it feel like he was appraising her, trying to figure out exactly how he could make use of her.

She did the same to him, though something told her it didn't have the same effect. The man was only a few inches taller than her, with a dark combover and stubble along his face. He wasn't wearing a shirt. Lindholm wasn't overweight, but his muscles weren't defined. He was soft, and the shape of his gut told her he went heavy on the beer. The stench emanating from his apartment told her he went heavy on the cigarettes too.

But what really caught Harris' attention was his bloody nose and black eye. They were both fresh, and Harris wondered who had given them to him. Was it Natasha, or someone else? Was the person still inside? How did they look in comparison?

Lindholm lowered the bat but kept his sneer in place. "Who the fuck are you?"

Harris ignored him. "Where's Natasha?"

"I said, who the fu—"

Cassie, Jason, and Laura came bounding up the stairs behind her, but Harris didn't let Lindholm get distracted for long. "Where's Natasha Michaelson?" Harris repeated. When it got no reaction, she corrected herself. "Norma Mitchell?"

"What is it, her birthday today or something? Why is everyone looking for this chick?"

Harris stepped forward. "Who else is looking for her?"

"You ask a lot of questions." There was a tinge of weariness to his gaze now. "What's it to you?"

"We're her friends," Cassie said from behind Jason. "We just want to know she's safe."

"She ain't here." Lindholm tried to close the door, but Harris slapped a hand out and stopped him. He seemed shocked by the force of the blow. "That's not a smart move."

"Neither is ignoring my questions," Harris said, her voice low. Dangerous. "Where is she?"

"Hell if I know. But if you find her, tell her she owes me two grand."

"Two grand?" Harris didn't let up the pressure on Lindholm's door. "Why?"

"Bitch stole it from me." He pointed to his nose. "Said she needed cash quick. Tried to get her a job at one of my clubs. Not as a dancer, either. All she had to do was take drink orders and play nice with the customers. Apparently, that isn't in her skillset."

"You picked her up a couple days ago," Harris pressed, going off of what Cassie had told her. "She's been staying here, hasn't she?"

"What can I say?" Lindholm's lips curled up into a disgusting smile. "I'm a generous man."

"Did she do that to you?" Harris asked, pointing to his face. The man's silence was answer enough. "Doesn't look like she appreciated your brand of hospitality."

Lindholm's smile dropped. "That bitch will get what's coming to her. If she isn't dead already."

Harris didn't give him any warning. She drove her shoulder into the door, making him stumble back, and sending his beer bottle crashing to the floor. Glass and booze sprayed everywhere, but Harris stalked forward all the same. Lindholm raised the bat, but the detective was quicker. She stopped his swing before it even got started, ripping the bat from his grasp and flinging it across the room. She didn't even feel the sting of the wood against the palm of her hand.

"What the hell do you think you're doing?" Lindholm spat. "Get the hell out of my apartment. I can have the cops in here in less than two minutes."

Harris threw her head back and laughed. She sounded unhinged, even to her own ears. Good. Let Lindholm wonder what she was capable of. "You're the last person who wants the cops sniffing around your shit. I know who you are. I know what you do to the women you hire." Harris backed Lindholm against the opposite wall and threw a forearm against his throat. All he could do was sputter. "Did you know Natasha's been reported missing? I'm sure the LAPD will be interested in the fact that she was last seen getting into your car."

Lindholm's eyes narrowed. "You don't have any proof."

"Actually, we do." Harris didn't let up on the man's throat, and his face turned red. "We have a witness. And you have a reputation. It's not hard to put two and two together."

Lindholm took several deep breaths. Finally, he said, "What do you want?"

"Answers." Harris eased up a bit. "And no bullshit. If you think you can manage that, we'll get out of your hair." Harris glanced up at the top of his head. "What's left of it, anyway."

The man looked like he wanted to argue, but it was four against one. Even if he got out from under Harris' grasp, there'd be no way he could escape all of them. Not to mention everyone in that room knew the cops would probably take any excuse they could to lock him up. Or at least drag him downtown. He growled out his answer. "Ask your goddamned questions and then get out."

Harris dropped her arm but didn't step back. "What'd she need the money for?"

"I don't know." Before Harris could choke him out again, he put his hands up. "I don't ask, and they don't tell. Not my problem."

"I guess that means you don't know where she was going then, do you?"

"Like I said, not my problem."

Jason stepped forward. "You said someone else was looking for her. Who?"

"Hell if I know. Some asshole. Didn't give me his name. Said he was her lawyer and needed to find her."

Harris looked back at Cassie, and they spoke at the same time. "Reed."

Cassie locked eyes with Lindholm. "What happened next?"

"Nothing. Told him the same thing I told you. Bitch owes me two grand. Then he took off."

"Does he know something we don't?" Jason asked, looking between Harris and Cassie. "There are too many bus stations in L.A. to know which one she would go to. We could start at the closest and circle out from there."

Harris felt as hopeless as he sounded. "That's still too many. They both have a head start on us."

Cassie's sharp inhalation had everyone looking in her direction. "There was a picture of Emily on Natasha's nightstand. She wouldn't leave town without it. She'd go back to her room before she hopped on a bus anywhere."

"You're sure?" Harris asked, searching Cassie's face.

Cassie looked at her one and only sister, and Harris felt like she could read her mind. If all she had of Laura was a wrinkled photograph, Cassie wouldn't leave town without it. Natasha had already lost so much. It was a stupid and sentimental thing to do, but humans are emotional creatures.

"I'm sure," Cassie said. "She's going back to the hostel."

Harris looked Lindholm up and down. Without warning, she reared back and punched him in the eye. He dropped to the floor in a howl of pain. "There," Harris said. "Now you've got a matching set."

Cassie was already halfway out the door, and Harris took off after her. She was trying to do the math in her head—how long ago had Natasha left Lindholm's apartment, and how long had it been since Reed had gone after her? It had taken them almost an hour to get to the apartment from the café Ginny worked at. Where were they now in relation to Sunset Paradise? Harris cursed herself for not paying better attention on the drive over.

Her head was still spinning as the group emerged back into the sunlight, temporarily blinded by the afternoon sun. Before Harris' eyes could adjust, however, she heard the sound of a police siren from only a couple dozen feet away. A door slammed shut, and then a voice rang out.

"Freeze. Hands where I can see them."

27

As Cassie blinked away the sun, Detective Green came into focus. Standing a few feet from his car, he blocked the sidewalk leading to the parking lot, and he had his gun lifted at a forty-five-degree angle. Not pointing it right at them, but wanting them to know it was serious. Cassie believed him. Lifting her hands in surrender, she watched as the others did the same.

Harris was the last to put her hands up. "What the hell are you doing?"

"I'd like to ask you the same thing." Green kept a steady eye on her. "Why are you here?"

"Something tells me you already know."

Green narrowed his eyes. "You talked to my witness without me."

"Yes, I did." Harris didn't exactly sound sorry. "We didn't want to waste any time."

"I can see why you got suspended." Green stared at her in silence for another few seconds and then his stance relaxed. Pointing his gun at the ground, he didn't put it away. "You crossed a line, Adelaide. Ginny didn't want to talk to us in the first place. You could've set us back in our investigation."

"With all due respect." Harris lowered her arms. "But she didn't want to talk to *you*. She doesn't trust men, and she's got good reason not to. She didn't mind talking to me, and she didn't mind talking to Cassie. We found out a lot more about Dominick Lindholm."

Green looked at the building behind them. "This is his apartment complex." It wasn't a question.

"You know who he is," Harris said. That wasn't a question either. "What kind of business he runs."

"Of all people, you should know these situations aren't always cut and dry. Sometimes you gotta use the smaller fish to catch the bigger ones."

"Lindholm doesn't seem like a small fish to me," Cassie chimed in, thinking of all the women whose money he stole. All the women who disappeared because they decided to make a deal with the devil. "He's hurt people. And you're just standing by, doing nothing?"

Green ground his teeth together, and Cassie could've sworn his hand holding the gun moved up a couple inches. "With all due respect," he said, throwing Harris' words back at them, "you don't know what the situation is here. You shouldn't have talked to my witness without me. I've done you plenty of favors while you've been here. Brought you along when I could've iced you out. I don't think asking for a little trust is out of line."

"You're right." Harris' voice was passive now. Calming. It sounded forced to Cassie, but they didn't have a choice. "And I'm sorry about that. I am. I know how it feels to have someone else come in and step on your toes. It won't happen again."

Green eyed them all in turn, then nodded curtly and holstered his gun. "You found something, didn't you?"

"Lindholm has a black eye and a bloody nose, compliments of Ms. Michaelson." Harris smiled when Green's eyebrows shot up into his hairline. "He said she stole two grand from him and left. He also said Reed showed up at his door not long after, then chased after her."

"She's got money now." Green shook his head. "She could be anywhere."

"Cassie thinks she's going back to Sunset Paradise." Harris nodded in Cassie's direction. "She thinks she'll go back for Emily's picture before she skips town."

"What are we waiting for then?" Green jogged back to his car, then gestured to Harris. "You're riding with me."

Harris didn't protest, and Cassie had no interest in arguing. With a police escort, they made it there in a fraction of the time. Green cut the lights and the siren as he approached. The last thing they wanted to do was spook Natasha when they were this close. Cassie couldn't stop her heart from pounding in her chest. Everything they had been working for was now within reach.

Green and Harris were out of their vehicle first, sprinting toward the front entrance. Cassie didn't wait until Jason put the rental in park. As soon as it was moving slow enough, she pushed open the door and jumped out. Laura and Jason yelled after her, but Cassie ignored them. A tugging sensation in her chest told her they were close.

The Sunset Paradise looked the same as it had the night before, except Al, the owner, was nowhere to be seen. Had he taken a break or retreated into a back office as soon as he saw Green run inside, guns blazing? Cassie found she didn't much care.

Pounding footsteps from behind her told Cassie that Jason and Laura were on her tail. Without slowing down, she turned the corner and spotted Green shouldering his way through the door with Harris on his heels. A few seconds later, she was crossing the threshold and the entire scene unfolded before her as if in slow motion.

In the middle of the floor, Reed lay on top of Natasha. He was out of breath and sweating profusely, but he still had the upper hand. A knife was between them, and each had a grip on the handle, doing their best to gain control and be the one to come out on top. So far, Natasha was losing.

Cassie had seen Natasha in Emily's memories, but they had all been from years ago, when her hair was long and blonde. Now, it had been cut to her shoulders and dyed black. She wore shorts and a tank top, and Cassie couldn't help but think how easy it would be for Reed to tear into her skin with that knife. Like a flash, it brought back memories of Cassie's own night of terror. The night when Novak tore his way through her own skin.

Green froze just inside the door, his weapon already out and pointing down at the twisting bodies on the floor. "Police." His voice boomed, making Cassie jump. "Freeze."

Whether the two didn't hear him or ignored the command altogether, Cassie couldn't tell. They kept fighting. Natasha wore a pair of heavy boots, and she attempted to kick Reed off her. Other than a small grunt of pain, however, he kept his hand on the knife. The blade was pointed sideways, the sharp side toward his face. While he was shorter than her, he was considerably heavier. Still, Natasha wouldn't let up.

"Drop your weapon." Green stepped forward. His voice was even louder now. "Hands where I can see them."

Natasha must've heard them this time because she gasped and looked at the intruders. It was enough of a distraction for Reed to wrench the knife free of her grasp. He held it out to his side, tip down, and examined it in triumph. Then his weight shifted. For a split second, it looked to Cassie like he was about to get off Natasha.

But Green didn't wait around to confirm. He'd given them a warning. Twice. Reed hadn't dropped the weapon, and if he waited any longer, a young woman would die. Cassie heard Green's sharp inhalation right before he pulled the trigger, letting loose two bullets that found their way into Reed's flesh.

The man dropped to the ground with a thud, the blade clattering against the floor a second later.

28

Cassie sat close to Natasha in the hospital waiting room, partly to make her feel safe and partly because she was worried the woman would bolt at any second. Natasha's eyes kept roaming the room, locking on the exit doors and appraising each new person who arrived. She was shaking, but Cassie couldn't tell if it was from fear or the adrenaline still coursing through her system.

Detective Green had shot Reed twice in the shoulder. When the man started howling and clutching his arm, it only took them a second or two to realize that while he was seriously injured, he wasn't in any immediate danger of dying.

Still, they called an ambulance and followed the vehicle to the hospital. Harris had ridden with Green, while Laura kept Natasha company in the back seat of Jason's rental. The woman hadn't wanted to go with them until Cassie mentioned she had a letter from her sister. After that, Natasha was compliant, if a little quiet.

The hospital staff had rolled Reed straight into surgery while the rest of the group sat in the waiting room. Cassie's energy was rebuilding after her night in the Cecil, and she was able to make sure she wasn't distracted by any of the spirits who lingered in the waiting room for them. Mostly, the ghosts just watched, occasionally testing her limits by pushing against her barrier.

As for the living, Jason and Green kept their distance, though Cassie could tell the L.A. detective wanted nothing more than to question Natasha. Harris and Laura sat on the other side of Cassie, so Natasha wouldn't feel like she was trapped, though none of them had any intention of letting her out of their sight.

They had checked Natasha over, but she had no physical injuries. Then again, that didn't mean she was okay.

"Can I get you anything?" Cassie asked.

Natasha laughed a little, but it was dark and humorless. "Answers would be nice."

"I'm not sure I'll have everything you're looking for, but I'll do my best."

The other woman sized her up, then glanced beyond her to the others sitting in the waiting room. "Who are you?"

"My name is Cassie Quinn." There hadn't been much time for introductions between the ambulance arriving and the ride to the hospital. "This is Detective Adelaide Harris, from Savannah, Georgia." Natasha's eyes lit up in recognition of Aguilar's base of operations. "You've already met my sister, Laura, and over there are Jason and Detective Noah Green. He's with the LAPD."

"Savannah," Natasha said, her gaze landing on Harris. "Did you know Detective Klein?"

"I did," Harris said. "David was a good man."

"I heard about his murder," Natasha said. "I keep an eye on everything going on down there. I thought it was over when he was killed. I figured he was the only one trying to bring Aguilar down."

Harris' eyes blazed with determination. "Not the only one."

"That's why we're here," Cassie said. "David was our friend. My best friend. When he was murdered, we were pretty sure we knew who did it—"

"Aguilar," Natasha said.

Cassie nodded. "He gave the order, but he didn't pull the trigger. We tracked down a man named Joseph Zbirak in Chicago. He was the one who did it. That's also where we found Reed."

Now Natasha's eyes blazed with something angrier than determination. "He killed my sister."

"We followed him here from Chicago. He knows exactly what happened to Emily. And to David. We want to get him to talk. To turn on Aguilar. To be a star witness. The reason Aguilar finally ends up in a jail cell."

"He deserves a grave," Natasha spat. "That man is evil, through and through. I don't know what my sister ever saw in him."

"How did that happen?" Cassie asked. Natasha was angry, but it was nice to finally talk to her. To fill in the blanks. "How did she get mixed up in all of this?"

"They met while he was out here on business. It felt like something you'd read in a romance novel. Hot rich guy picks out totally normal woman from the crowd. Falls madly in love." Natasha rolled her eyes. "We were so naïve."

"How did she end up in Savannah?"

"He would come to L.A. once a month for about a year. It wasn't enough for them. He asked her to move in with him, and she didn't hesitate. I didn't want her to go. He gave me the wrong vibe, you know?" Natasha shook her head. "I thought he was controlling, but she loved him so much. Neither one of us had any idea what he was really mixed up with."

"When did Emily figure it out?"

"Probably after another year. We talked almost every night in the beginning. Francisco didn't love that, and she started calling less often. But we found ways to stay in touch. I could tell there was something she didn't want to tell me. Eventually, she opened up about it. Said he ran businesses that weren't exactly legal. I thought he was just a drug dealer, but she said it was so much more than that."

"Do you have any of these messages?" Harris asked. "Anything she wrote down, detailing what she'd seen or heard?"

Natasha shook her head. "I should've recorded our calls, but I wasn't even thinking about getting him arrested. I just wanted my sister to come home."

"Eventually, she did," Cassie offered. "She saw who he really was."

"It took a few years, yeah. I was so happy. We both thought that was the end of it." A tear fell down her cheek, but she didn't bother to wipe it away. "I should've known it wouldn't be that easy. That he wouldn't let her go."

Cassie wanted to know what happened next, but she didn't want to push Natasha. "You don't have to talk about it right now. I know it's a lot."

"It feels good, actually. To talk about it, I mean." Drawing in a deep, shaky breath, she looked a little lighter, a little more centered, after letting it out. "The day Emily disappeared, I knew Aguilar was behind it. I didn't have any proof, of course, but he'd been calling her. Asking her to come back. When she refused, he threatened her. Said no one would ever find her. She was scared, but we figured if we stayed under the radar, stuck together, he'd eventually give up. Men like that always move on to the next shiny thing, you know?"

"Except he didn't," Cassie suggested.

Natasha shook her head. "She went out grocery shopping. I was supposed to go with her, but I had a shift. They made me stay late. I got home, and she wasn't answering her phone. I talked to the police, but they said they couldn't do anything for another day or two. By that time, I knew she was dead. It was just like Aguilar had said. No one would find her." Natasha looked up. "Except you did. How?"

Cassie didn't know what to say. Did she tell this woman the truth, and risk Natasha thinking she was a crazy person? Harris saved her from answering. "We ran into Zbirak in Chicago. Cassie discovered some vital details." Not a lie, at least. "By the time we got here, we knew where she was. I only wish we could've found her sooner."

"Thank you," Natasha said, looking first at Harris and then at Cassie. "For finding her. I hope she's in a better place now."

"She is," Cassie assured her. Cassie had to believe that. "But what about you? You've been hiding for three years. This all must be a lot for you."

"It is," Natasha confirmed. "But I didn't trust Francisco to stop at

Emily. I was in touch with David for a while. He was convinced Emily had evidence with her when she went back to California. That's why Aguilar wanted her dead so badly. But Em never told me about that. I had a hard time believing it was real. And when he died? I gave up hope."

Cassie pulled Emily's note from her purse and handed it to Natasha. "This is addressed to you. From your sister. I'm not sure when she wrote it, but I think she'd been anticipating a day like this for a long time."

Natasha stared down at the letter. "You read it?"

"Yes." Cassie felt a small surge of shame, as though she'd been witness to a private moment. But Emily had shared part of herself with Cassie. There was a kinship there that Natasha wouldn't understand, if she could believe it at all. But that didn't make it right. "I'm sorry."

"What does it say?"

Cassie heard the pain in the other woman's voice. "She says she's sorry for everything." Cassie was holding back tears now, too. "She says she loves you. And she asks you for a favor."

Natasha looked down at the letter. Steeling herself, she unfolded it and began reading. Cassie tracked the movement of her eyes, the way she slowly inhaled each letter, each word, until she was ready to move on to the next. It took several moments, and by the time she was done, tears were pouring down Natasha's face. Cassie had to wipe her own away, too.

When Natasha found her voice again, she asked, "You have the evidence?"

Cassie pulled out the hard drive. "She said you're the only one with the password."

Natasha bobbed her head. "We had a shared password. It's what she would've used if she wanted me to get into it. No one else would know."

"Will you help us?"

Natasha took the hard drive and turned it over in her hands. It looked so benign, so simple. But the answer to all their problems, the justice for all of Aguilar's victims, was on there. Or so they hoped. Cassie could see that hope in Natasha's eyes, too.

"Yes." There was no hesitation in her voice. "It's what Emily wanted. I'm tired of running. Aguilar needs to pay for what he did to my sister. To Detective Klein. To everyone else he's ever hurt."

A surge of pride and excitement filled Cassie to capacity. The tips of her fingers tingled in anticipation of what was to come. They weren't there yet, but this was the closest they'd gotten so far. They only needed to jump one more hurdle.

As if on cue, a doctor emerged from one of the doors on the other end of the room and strode over to them. He was a tall, thin Black man with short-cropped hair and large glasses. "I'm looking for Detective Green?"

Green stood up. "That's me. You have news about Reed?"

"He's going to be just fine," the doctor said. "The bullets didn't hit anything major. He's in some pain, but he's asking to talk to some of you." The doctor looked around at the large group. "Specifically, Detective Harris and Cassie Quinn?"

Cassie stood up and looked at Harris. "What's he up to?"

"Only one way to find out," Harris replied. "Lead the way, Doc."

29

"HE'S ON PAIN MEDS, SO HE MIGHT BE A LITTLE OUT OF IT," THE DOCTOR said, leading Cassie and Harris to Reed's recovery room. "Try not to press him too hard. There will be time for interrogating later." When he got a nod of confirmation from both women, he turned to leave. "I'm going to talk to Detective Green about getting some security on his room. I don't love having to put armed guards on my patients, but I understand Reed is a suspect for multiple crimes." Pausing at the end of the hallway, he turned back to them. "You two are going to behave yourselves, right?"

"Scout's honor," Harris replied, a little too enthusiastically.

As soon as he rounded the corner, Harris pushed through the door and stood over Reed's bed with a scowl on her face. The man had his eyes closed, and his breathing was deep and rhythmic. Sleeping. Cassie couldn't help but notice how at peace he looked. After everything they'd been through, everything he'd done, she hated that he could rest like that.

Harris must've had the same thought because she gripped his good shoulder and jerked him awake. Reed sputtered and looked around as though he'd forgotten where he was and how he'd wound up there. When he looked up at Harris, he tried to scoot away from her, but when he locked eyes with Cassie, he relaxed.

"You have a lot of nerve asking to talk to us," Harris said. "If you think you're going to talk your way out of a jail cell, you're going to be disappointed."

"It's better than a grave," Reed said, his voice low and gravelly. He sounded exhausted and in pain. Dressed in nothing but a hospital gown and with an IV in his arm, he looked small and weak. This was a far cry from the man they had met in Chicago last week. "Lesser of two evils and all of that."

"That's hilarious." Harris leaned in conspiratorially. "You know *we're* the good guys, right?"

Reed blinked, and he was so slow to open his eyelids again, Cassie thought he might have fallen back asleep. When he looked back up at them, he was weary, but determined. "Is Natasha okay?"

Harris clenched her fists at her side. "Don't you talk about her. Don't even think about her. What you did to her sister—"

There was a spike in the beeping associated with Reed's heartbeat, and Cassie had to force Harris to take a step back. "He asked us here for a reason," she said. Cassie wasn't sympathetic to Reed's current predicament, but she was curious. "Let's hear what he has to say."

"Is she?" Reed asked again, looking to Cassie this time. "She's not hurt, right?"

"Natasha's fine. Not a scratch."

"You must be disappointed," Harris spat.

"I wasn't trying to hurt her." Reed tried to sit up a little, as though he didn't like the way they stood over him. "She's the one who came at me with the knife. I was trying to get it away from her. Talk to her."

Harris snorted. "Bullshit."

Cassie's curiosity piqued even more. "What did you want to talk to her about?"

"I know Emily had evidence against Aguilar. I thought maybe Natasha would know where it was. So I—so we could use it."

"You mean so you could trade it," Harris said. The sneer on her face didn't hide her thoughts. "You want to hand the evidence over in exchange for immunity."

"Look." Reed shifted again, sounding like his old self. Curt. Grating.

Slimy. "I'd be an idiot not to try, right? Zbirak's dead. Aguilar's not going to be too happy about that. He's trying to clean up all his loose ends, and I might be useful, but I also know too much. He wanted Rose Sherman dead, and he didn't manage that. He wants Natasha dead because he figures she knows what Emily knew. Now you guys have her. I can see the tide shifting, and I don't want to drown."

"You're a piece of shit," Harris said.

"I'm a survivor," Reed countered. "And you wouldn't be here if you didn't want to hear what I have to say."

"We have the evidence," Cassie said, but there was no bite to her words. "We don't need you."

Reed's eyes widened in surprise, and then narrowed in disappointment. Cassie could see the gears working in his head, and by the time he opened his mouth to speak, he already had a new angle. "I can tell you about Detective Klein. Clear his name."

"His name doesn't need to be cleared," Harris hissed. "David wasn't working for Aguilar willingly."

"I know that, and you know that, but will the rest of the force see it that way? Will the media or the general public?" He let those words sink in. "I was there from the beginning. I dealt with a lot of Aguilar's issues, a lot of his books and payments. If not directly, then I knew the people who did. Emily's evidence will be enough to bring Aguilar down, but it's not going to be the whole picture. And a live witness is better than a dead one."

Cassie had to hold Harris back this time. As much as she wanted to see the detective swing at the man before them, it wasn't in their best interest.

"Let's hear what you have to say." Cassie kept her voice as neutral as possible. "If it sounds like you're useful enough to our case, then we'll consider your offer."

Reed laughed, though it was more like a strained chuckle in his current circumstance. "No offense, sweetheart, but you don't exactly have the authority to offer me that." Pointing to Harris, "I want to hear her say it."

Harris ground her teeth together. Cassie knew it was the last thing she wanted to do, but they needed to know once and for all the truth behind David's story. "Fine," Harris spat. "We'll consider it."

The smile on Reed's face was wicked, but there was relief in his eyes. "Aguilar is in the habit of keeping an eye out for desperate people. That's all David was to him—desperate and useful."

"Less commentary," Harris growled, "more facts."

"Do you remember when you killed Luca White's kid?" Reed asked.

Harris froze, and Cassie's heart dropped into her stomach. When Harris didn't answer right away, Cassie stepped forward. "That was in self-defense."

"I never said it wasn't. The good detective here wanted facts, and I'm giving them to her." Reed seemed to relish in the moment a little too long. "The fact is, self-defense or not, Detective Adelaide Harris shot and killed Luca White's one and only son, the heir to his criminal empire. As you can imagine, Luca wasn't too happy about that. He spent several months stomping around Savannah, causing all sorts of trouble."

"Causing trouble?" Harris had finally found her voice. "Those months were the worst of my life. I was practically on house arrest. I couldn't go anywhere without an escort."

Cassie was dizzy with the revelation. Over the last few weeks, she had learned more about Harris and David than she would've thought possible this time last year. She'd known David for ten years, and yet he'd harbored a dark secret she had no inkling ever existed. Cassie had known Harris for far less time, but they had been through so much. That kind of trauma bonded you, and yet here was a significant, traumatic part of the detective's life that Cassie was just learning about for the first time.

"Maybe you would've been safe for a while," Reed said, "but White would've gotten to you sooner or later. He had a few of your guys on the payroll. It was only a matter of time. I think David knew that."

"How do *you* know that?" Cassie asked. "I can't imagine you and David swapping information over drinks. And weren't you in Chicago?"

"I was wherever Aguilar needed me," Reed said, turning haughty. "I'm very good at my job."

"Screwing people over?" Harris snapped.

"Finding loopholes," Reed clarified.

"Same thing."

Reed shrugged. "Either way, I traveled a lot between Chicago and Savannah back then. Aguilar liked to wine and dine, and I'm not one to pass up a good meal."

Aguilar loved his restaurants, and he wasn't shy about eating at them. There was usually a private room reserved for him, though he sometimes sat with the public. He loved his adoring fans, it seemed, and there were plenty of men and women willing to get into bed with him one way or another if it meant they came out on top.

"But why did Aguilar care?" Cassie asked. That's the part she didn't understand. Who was White to him? For that matter, who was David? "Why was this even on his radar?"

"Aguilar was just an upstart back then. He had plenty of charisma and money, but not as much power as he'd like." Reed winced in pain. When he closed his eyes, it looked like he had to fight to open them again. Whatever drugs were coursing through his system were good, but it seemed like he wanted to tell this story as much as they wanted to hear it. "White had something he wanted, simple as that. Aguilar is smart— smarter than a lot of people give him credit for—and he was studying White. He had people on the inside. There was nothing White could do that Aguilar didn't know about."

"Plus the media ran with the story about his son being shot and killed," Harris said, bitterness infusing every word. "It's not like he wouldn't have known about it."

"True." Reed's eyes were distant now, as though he'd been transported back in time. "It was the perfect opportunity to shake things up. Aguilar knew it. David knew it. They had common ground."

Harris' shoulders tensed. "David had nothing in common with that man."

Reed didn't even look like he was trying to rub it in their faces anymore. "They had one thing in common. Both of them wanted White out of the picture."

"David wouldn't—" Harris broke off, trying to regain her composure and failing. "He wouldn't."

"Look, it doesn't benefit me to lie to you. I need your help." Reed's face was pained, but this time, it didn't look to be from his physical injuries. "I know Aguilar better than anyone. I was there from the beginning. I saw who he was before he became King of Savannah. I helped him build that empire."

"And you're willing to throw that all away?" Cassie asked. She couldn't believe it. Not from someone like Reed, who always seemed to find a way to slip out the back door.

"Like I said, I know him." Reed licked his lips, like his mouth was suddenly dry. Was it from the stale hospital air, or from fear? "Aguilar hates loose ends. That's why he hired Zbirak to kill Officer Warren and David and Rose Sherman."

That revelation snapped Harris out of her daze. "Zbirak killed Warren?"

"Warren was getting too close to the truth. He and David were working together. Aguilar found out and had him killed. That was David's first warning." Reed shook his head, then leaned back. This conversation was taking a toll on him. Looking weaker than when they had first walked in, he wouldn't be able to fight the meds much longer. "Aguilar hates loose ends," he repeated. "And I'm one of them. The walls are closing in on all of us. Aguilar will cut away any rot before it has time to spread. He's in the hot seat. You're close to taking him down. I know that. He knows that. And he knows I'm not going to let him drag me down with him."

Cassie couldn't argue with that. She hadn't known Reed for long, and she certainly didn't know him well, but it wasn't hard to see what kind of person he was. They could trust him because this was in his best interest. The truth in exchange for immunity. It was a win-win for everyone except Aguilar.

"You think David wanted to put a hit out on White," Cassie said. "That's what you meant by wanting him out of the picture."

Reed shrugged before he remembered he shouldn't move his shoulder and then swore under his breath. "If it was anyone else but David, you'd say he was putting a hit out on him too." Reed thought for a minute. "White was the type of man who cared about his family above all else. His wife had died a few years ago—cancer or some shit—and he was left to raise his son, his only child, on his own. He wasn't going to stop until Harris was dead. Everyone who knew White didn't question that."

Silence filled the room, and Cassie wondered if Harris felt the same way she did. Trepidation for what came next, mixed with a sort of eagerness to finally—*finally*—get to the truth.

"David knew Aguilar. He'd been a person of interest in a few cases, and a detective like David had enough experience to know Aguilar was someone to keep an eye on. He also knew Aguilar and White didn't get along. They'd had a few territory disputes in the past. Bodies left on the street. White came out on top, every time. David knew Aguilar would be interested in learning some vital information about the man."

"How did David have this vital information?" Harris asked. Even though Cassie was getting on board with all of this, the detective still sounded skeptical. "If Aguilar had men planted within White's operation, how did David know something Aguilar didn't?"

"David caught another cop heading back from White with information. I don't know what it was, but I assume it had something to do with your location or movements. Either way, David was in control now. He knew where White would be—thinking he'd have the chance to put a bullet in *your* head—and he knew Aguilar would appreciate knowing that exact location."

"David told Aguilar this," Cassie said slowly, "knowing Aguilar would kill White?"

Reed's eyes drooped, and the women waited until he shook himself awake. He blinked a few times, then picked up like nothing had happened. "Look, I didn't know David that well. I assume he was a good cop. My guess is his back was to the wall. They couldn't get White on any charges, so they had to wait for him to make a move. That would've endangered your life," Reed said, looking at Harris, "and my guess is he didn't want to risk it. So, he got proactive about it."

For the first time since they'd entered the room, Harris looked defeated. She took a step back. Then another. Until she sank into a chair against the wall. Cassie's knees were shaking, but she forced herself to keep standing. To keep processing what Reed was telling them.

David had gone to Aguilar knowing the other man would take the opportunity to wipe White from the board. As a cop and a detective, going outside the law like that went against everything David believed in. But Cassie knew him, knew how much this would have weighed on him. He must not have seen any other way forward. This had been his only option to keep Harris alive.

Sometimes doing the wrong thing for the right reason was the only way to keep your friends safe. David might've carried the guilt of this moment in his soul until the day he died, but he never would've regretted it.

"How did Aguilar keep him on board?" Cassie asked. She needed to know everything, the whole story.

"Aguilar recorded that first conversation with David and used it to blackmail him." Reed's eyes were getting heavier. His words were slurring a little. Every time he took a breath, it sounded like half a snore. "Aguilar didn't press at first, just kept it over his head. Then he'd ask him for small favors. A piece of information. A person's name. Over time, those favors built up. David probably felt trapped. Aguilar started pushing for more. From my understanding, David always pushed back. He was a good man." Reed chuckled, but Cassie didn't know what was so funny about that. "Aguilar respected him, but he enjoyed taking him down a peg. Getting him to do things he didn't want to do. Eventually, it got to be too much. He started looking for ways out. Ways to take Aguilar down. Even if it meant going down with him."

It was starting to make sense now. Everything was becoming clear. Cassie felt a pang in her gut, but she pushed it down. She could deal with her feelings about all of this later. "That's where Emily comes in?"

Reed nodded, his eyes closing more often now. "Aguilar's girlfriend. Good girl. Didn't deserve that life. One of the few people I actually felt sorry for." Laughing again, a tear slipped out of the corner of his eye. "Once she got a good look at Aguilar, a real look at who he was, she started recording everything. Video, audio, you name it. Took pictures on her phone. Everything. She and David were gonna hand it over. Aguilar found out. Emily ran away, back to California to her sister. David was punished. Not sure how." Cassie could hear the weariness in every word. "I told Aguilar not to trust him, but he thought David was useful. That maybe he could get him to bring in new recruits. Decided to punish Emily instead. Sent me after her."

"And you killed her," Harris said from her chair. She sounded tired, too.

"I killed her." A sob escaped Reed's throat, but he didn't bother to hide it. Didn't bother to wipe away the tears steadily flowing down his face. "Couldn't even finish the job. Had to call in Zbirak. Only time I ever saw that man with regret on his face. Emily was too good for this world. She didn't deserve any of that."

Silence hung heavy in the air between them. Cassie was a tornado of emotions. Anger, despair, disgust, and hope. The same emotions flitted across Reed's and Harris' faces, too. They were all crying. The truth wasn't easy to accept, but Cassie found she was relieved, nonetheless.

"I want to help," Reed said, breaking the silence. "I don't want to go to jail, but Aguilar will put me in the ground unless I make the first move. And if he does that, well, I know where I'm going. If God is real, I don't think he'd let me walk through those pearly gates without letting the Devil take a pound of flesh. I want to do something right before that happens."

"I'm holding you to that," Harris said, looking at Reed. "We've got the evidence. We've got Rose Sherman. And now you're on our side too. There's no way Aguilar is getting out of this one."

"I hope not," Reed said, drowsily. "For all our sakes."

30

THEY WENT HOME AFTER THAT. THERE WAS NOTHING LEFT FOR THEM TO DO. Detective Green posted an officer outside Reed's door in case the man decided to make a break for it, but Cassie didn't think he would. Their conversation hadn't been easy, but it had been honest. If she could trust Reed on one thing, it was that he'd prioritize his own interests. And right now, they both wanted the same thing.

Natasha had nowhere else to go. With money in one pocket and the picture of her sister in the other, she was more of a flight risk than Reed. But she also didn't want to let the evidence out of her sight. Emily had worked so hard to gather it, and Natasha had made it clear she'd do what her sister had wanted.

It was time to take Aguilar down.

Laura had offered Natasha the couch. After everything the woman had been through, Cassie wished they could offer her more, but this way they could keep an eye on her. She still seemed spooked, but she had taken to Laura and looked at Cassie and Harris like they were water in the middle of a desert. Maybe it wasn't much, but it was all they needed for now.

Harris had been quiet on the way home from the hospital. Cassie couldn't blame her—she'd been lost in her own thoughts, too. It was difficult to process everything Reed had said about David, but at the end of the day, it didn't change anything. At least for Cassie. David had done what he thought was best, both when he approached Aguilar to protect Harris and when he continued to work inside the man's organization to take him down. A small part of Cassie wanted to know what he'd had to do to stay on Aguilar's good side, but the larger part was still dealing with everything she'd learned.

In another reality, maybe David got a happy ending. But in this one, he'd died trying to protect his loved ones.

For Harris, it was different. She had been the reason David had gone to Aguilar in the first place. Cassie couldn't tell if Harris felt guilty or angry or sad. There had been enough pain written on Harris' face when she'd told her story about Luca White's son that Cassie knew it still weighed heavily on her shoulders. There was no way she wasn't blaming herself for what had happened to David.

Cassie wanted to say something—anything—to relieve the tension in Harris' body, but words wouldn't be enough. The only way to make any of this better, to make sure David hadn't died in vain, was to finish what he'd started. Emily's evidence would see to that.

The group was silent as they walked through the front door. Laura gave Natasha a little tour, making sure she knew she was welcome to make herself at home. After living at Sunset Paradise for so long, Laura's place probably felt like a mansion. It was crowded now with all five of them there, but Cassie liked the comfort of having everyone within arm's reach.

Jason helped Laura make dinner while Harris plugged the hard drive into her laptop. Cassie's heart pounded against her chest like a caged animal trying to tear through its bars, but she forced her breath to even out. It was as much from fear as anticipation. There was no telling what was on the drive, but it had been worth Emily's life.

A window popped up on the screen, and Harris clicked on the folder icon for the drive. Another window opened, prompting them to put in the password.

Harris moved out of the way, and Natasha leaned over the keyboard, fingers poised. The ghost of a smile flickered across her features. "It's a stupid password. Probably not even that secure, but we've had it since we were kids." In practiced strokes, her fingers flew over the keys. "Rogue-Storm1992. We were obsessed with that X-Men cartoon from the nineties. Our favorite characters."

Natasha exhaled before bringing a single finger down on the enter key. Without delay, the dialog box disappeared, and they were granted access to the drive. All three women leaned closer, trying to see the device's contents.

Harris' voice was quiet. "It's separated into the different file types. Pictures. Video. Audio." She turned to Natasha. "Where do you want to start?"

Natasha's eyes were already shining with tears, and Cassie could feel her own emotion rising in her throat. "Pictures. I don't know if I can—" Natasha's voice wavered, and she had to clear her throat before she moved on. "I think I need a minute before I hear Emily's voice again. Before I see everything Aguilar did."

Harris looked like she understood. Dragging a fingertip across the laptop's touchpad, she directed the mouse to the appropriate folder and double-clicked. Inside, there were even more folders. Hundreds of them. All labeled with dates and names. Cassie didn't recognize most of them, but Harris' quiet gasp told her this was everything they had been hoping for and more.

"Who are they?" Cassie asked. "People you know?"

"Some," Harris said. She scrolled through the list slowly, her gaze dragging back and forth across the page and her eyes widening each time. "Politicians. Cops. Local community leaders."

Cassie was focusing on the dates. "There must be a couple years' worth of evidence here. Emily spent so long collecting this."

"Risking her life," Natasha said, and Cassie couldn't tell if it was in awe or anger. "Doing what she thought was right."

As Harris reached the bottom of the page, she gasped. It didn't take more than a second for Cassie to realize why. The last folder was labeled *Zbirak*, and it was right before Emily had disappeared three years ago.

With a look to Natasha for approval—and a subsequent nod from the other woman—Harris double-clicked on the folder. There were about a dozen photos, but there was no hiding Aguilar and Zbirak bent over a meal, talking as though in low voices so they couldn't be overheard. The pictures were a little grainy, and Cassie was certain they had been taken on a cellphone. But in a court of law, there would be no denying Aguilar's close relationship with the assassin.

Harris backed out of the folder and scrolled back up, clicking on them at random, though Cassie was sure she had recognized most of the names. Reed had his own folder filled with hundreds of pictures. Most were of lunch or dinner meetings, but a few were in a home that Cassie assumed was Aguilar's. In some cases, Emily had gotten close enough to snap pictures of the paperwork they were pouring over, but it would take time to decipher everything and uncover its true importance.

While Cassie might not have recognized the names on the other folders Harris had chosen, it was clear why she had picked them. They were almost always cops in uniform, either casually chatting with Aguilar or receiving an envelope that could only be stuffed with cash. Most of the pictures were from an obvious hiding place, but others were close up, as though Emily had been invited to the meeting.

Each time Harris opened one of these folders, she hissed in frustration. Cassie had to wonder if she was surprised by any of the people who had been on Aguilar's payroll, or if it confirmed how she had already felt about them. Either way, the evidence was damning. Between these photographs and Reed's confession, no one would be able to deny their relationship with the so-called King of Savannah.

And there was so much left to uncover. Natasha must've been thinking the same thing because she gulped and squared her shoulders. "I want to listen to some of the audio."

Harris looked up at her, searching the other woman's face. "Are you sure? You can't take back anything you hear. It might not be worth it. We have people who can go through this. You don't have to be the one to—"

"I'm sure," Natasha said, looking Detective Harris in the eye. "I want to make sure this is everything we need."

Harris waited a beat to see if she could sense any hesitation in the other woman, but she must not have seen a shred of doubt. Backing out of the folder of pictures, she clicked on the one labeled *Audio*.

There weren't nearly as many folders as the ones that contained pictures, and these seemed to be newer. Like Emily had started by taking photographs and worked her way up to the audio files.

Cassie held her breath as she leaned forward, looking more closely at all the labels. They seemed to range from phone calls and meetings to just casual conversations. Most of them featured Emily and Aguilar, but a few were between Aguilar and someone else. Only three of them were of Emily and David.

The three women exchanged a look and came to the same conclusion. Cassie was aware of Laura and Jason cooking in the background, listening to but never joining their conversation. The silence before Harris hit the first clip was resounding.

The audio was laced with static. It didn't make it hard to hear the conversation, but it was obvious it had been recorded from a cellphone. Emily spoke first, after a brief hesitation.

"Hello?"

"You need to be more careful."

Cassie had anticipated hearing David's voice, yet she was wholly unprepared for the emotion that built up in her chest and came out in a heavy sob. It felt like he was right there in the room with them, like nothing had ever happened. For a moment, Cassie allowed herself to pretend he was still alive, even though she knew it would hurt more in the end.

"I don't know what you're talking about," Emily said. Her voice was light and airy. She sounded young. Cassie could hear her innocence. It held a sharp defiance, softened by the breathy quality of her words.

"Emily, please." David's voice was strained, and Cassie had no trouble envisioning the pinch of his forehead and the frown on his lips. Cassie had witnessed that face many times over the years. "I'm serious. If Aguilar catches on, he's going to hurt you. Or worse."

"I'm not afraid of him," Emily said, and Cassie almost believed it. "He should be afraid of me."

Silence stretched on so long that Cassie was starting to believe David had hung up. Finally, he sighed into the receiver. "He found your camera in his office. Asked me about it. I told him I wasn't stupid enough to leave it in the open like that. I convinced him he's got a mole. One of his men. He's going to be more vigilant from now on. You need to be smart about this."

Cassie didn't know Emily well enough to gauge her reaction, and she was surprised to hear the woman wilt a little. "I'm sorry about that. I don't want you to get into trouble."

"I know that. I know you didn't do it on purpose. But you have to be smarter."

"Teach me." The way Emily spoke told Cassie this was not the first time they had discussed the matter. "Help me. Together, we could find enough to bring his whole operation down. We could do more than just put him in jail."

This time when David sighed, he sounded tired. It was hard to imagine that this was a time when Cassie had worked with David, had spent a significant amount of time with him. And yet, she never knew he was under this kind of pressure. She had always thought the weariness of his expression was just from the job. But there was so much more going on.

"If I help you, there are going to be rules." A sharp intake of breath told Cassie that Emily was listening to every word. "You've been taking too many risks. I'm not going to let you put yourself in danger. Stings like this require patience. We have all the time in the world. We need to be smart about it."

"I promise." Emily sounded like she wanted to jump for joy. "No unnecessary risks. You're the boss."

"We'll talk more later," David said.

"Thank you, Detective Klein." There was a smile in Emily's voice. "I mean that."

"Don't thank me yet," David replied. And then he hung up.

Tears were running down Harris' cheeks when she turned to Cassie. "Proof he was helping Emily. That they were working together. This is it."

She smiled, even though she was still crying. "This is how we nail Aguilar. This is how we prove David was trying to take him down from the inside."

"Then it's time to go home," Cassie said, tears streaking her own face. "And finish this."

31

Cassie had a hard time falling asleep that night. Her thoughts were filled with David's voice and possible scenarios where he had put his life on the line playing a double agent under Aguilar's gaze. When she thought back on the last few years of their friendship, she couldn't help but wonder which days had been the toughest for him. When he'd been late to lunch or looked more tired than normal, had that been from his unsanctioned undercover operation trying to take down Savannah's kingpin?

When Cassie had exhausted herself enough to sleep, it felt like she had only just closed her eyes before Harris was shaking her awake. Cassie groaned in protest, but the urgency in the detective's voice had her sitting up in bed as though the room were on fire.

"What is it?" Cassie asked, looking up into Harris' face. Jason was awake now, too. "What's wrong?"

"The hospital just called." Harris' hair was sticking up out of her ponytail, and she looked like she'd just rolled out of bed, too. "Reed is dead."

"What?" Cassie couldn't process the words. "What do you mean, he's dead? They said he had the all clear. The bullets didn't hit anything major."

"He was poisoned. They don't know how or who did it yet." Harris was already backing out of the room, her car keys in hand. "Get dressed. We need to go."

The next half hour was a whirlwind of movement. Cassie and Jason threw on whatever clothes they could find. Laura tried to comfort a pacing Natasha, but the other woman was anxious about the development. She kept taking out the wad of cash she'd stolen from Dominick Lindholm and looking at it like it was her last hope.

Harris took Laura aside and told her not to let Natasha out of her sight, no matter what, not even for a few seconds. Laura, wide-eyed and shaking, nodded in agreement. Harris gave her a quick kiss on the cheek before strolling out of the house, Jason and Cassie in tow. They had no time to waste.

Cassie wasn't sure of the time, but dawn was just breaking over the horizon. The orange glow of the sun pushed the dark of the night back by the minute. Soon, it would be another perfect California day.

Having beaten the morning traffic by an hour, the hospital was bustling as they walked in, both with doctors and patients. And of course, the ghosts of the recently departed. Cassie wondered if she'd see Reed here, or if he had already left this world behind.

Harris led them through the waiting room, into the elevators, and up to Reed's floor. There were two cops and a doctor outside the room, and a few nurses inside.

The conversation broke off as soon as the three of them approached.

"Can I help you?" one of the cops said. Older, with the kind of tan and weathered face you'd find on a farmer, he wore a uniform a size too small and shifted from foot to foot like it hurt too much to stand in one place for too long.

"Detective Adelaide Harris, from Savannah." Harris stuck her hand out and shook the two officers' and the doctor's hands in turn. "Reed was a witness to a crime back home. We were hoping to transport him back to Savannah soon." Harris' words were succinct and clipped. She was pissed, but polite. "How did this happen?"

The younger cop—who had brown skin, a wispy mustache, and looked to be several decades younger than the other—opened his mouth to answer, but the older officer cut him off. "We're still looking into that. When we have more details, we'll—"

Harris turned to the doctor, an Indian woman with long dark hair twisted up into a tight bun. "What can you tell me?"

The doctor looked between the older officer and Harris before deciding she'd rather piss off the older guy than this new detective. "As far as we can tell, Mr. Reed was poisoned. We're still not sure what was used, but early signs are clear. A rash along the skin, his lips and tongue are blue, and his temperature was elevated."

"Didn't the machines catch the change?" Harris asked.

"It did, but by that time, it was too late. The poison worked its way through his system. We couldn't bring him back."

Cassie leaned back to peek into the room. A few nurses going over every inch of Reed's body, looking for any clues or signs of injection, though they likely wouldn't need that with an IV in his arm. She couldn't see Reed's spirit.

Jason must've been thinking the same thing because he leaned in and whispered in Cassie's ear. "See him?"

Cassie shook her head. "If he was going to stick around, he'd still be here."

Harris, oblivious to the exchange, was now questioning the cop. "How did this happen? He was supposed to have a guard on duty all night."

"He did." The older officer puffed himself up to his full height, though Harris didn't look at all intimidated. "We had a schedule, and my guys stuck to their schedule. Something else must've happened. Maybe one of the nurses slipped him something."

The doctor frowned and looked to Harris. "I can get you a list of names of everyone who was on duty." Her gaze flicked to the officer. "Though I've worked with everyone on my team for years. I'd be surprised if one of them had a connection to Mr. Reed or wished to do him harm."

"I'd appreciate that," Harris said. The doctor nodded in response and walked off to gather the list. Meanwhile, the detective turned back to the two officers. "Who was on duty while this happened?"

The older officer tipped his head to the younger one. "Morales here was on duty. Reed crashed soon after he took over."

Harris turned her attention to Morales, who seemed unsure whether to wilt or stand up straighter under her gaze. "Who did you relieve when you came on duty this morning?"

The older officer answered before Morales could even open his mouth. "You have no jurisdiction here. I don't need to tell you shit."

Harris took a step forward and jabbed a finger into the older man's chest. "This has nothing to do with jurisdiction. Our witness is dead, and I need to know what happened and who was behind it. This is so much bigger than the LAPD, and if you pulled your head out of your ass, you'd realize that." While the officer stuttered and stammered in anger and shock, Harris looked up and down the hallway. "There are cameras everywhere. I've got friends on the LAPD, too. We'll get access to the tapes. Find out what happened."

In the midst of the older officer's sputtering, Morales took his opportunity to speak. "They've been wiped." When everyone turned their attention to him, he blushed and cleared his throat. But his voice was still strong. "All the tapes from overnight have been deleted. We don't know how."

Harris eyed him. "Who did you relieve?"

"Officer Sanchez." Morales looked at the glower on his superior officer's face, but he must've decided it was worth being insubordinate. "But he wasn't here when I arrived."

"Why not? Where was he?"

"Not sure. Must've left his post early. We haven't gotten a chance to find him." Morales pulled out his phone, as though hoping he could deliver good news. But they had no such luck. "He might've gone straight home to sleep. He was pulling a double."

"We need someone to go to his house," Harris told the older officer. "That should've been your first move."

"You don't get to tell me—"

"Ma'am?" Morales interrupted. "My shift started at three in the morning. Sanchez wasn't here, but I did pass Detective Green on my way in. I don't think he noticed me. I came in before my shift to get a cup of coffee.

I was going to let Sanchez off a few minutes early, but he was already gone."

"Detective Green?" Harris asked. She sounded as stunned as Cassie felt. "Noah Green?"

Morales nodded. "I don't think he saw me. Seemed like he was in a hurry."

Cassie looked at Harris but found no answers on the other woman's face. "Why would he be here in the middle of the night?"

"He could've had the tapes wiped. Could've let Sanchez off early. He didn't expect Morales to show up before his shift started." Harris sounded like she was putting the puzzle pieces together in real time. "Reed had the knife, but I could've sworn it looked like he was going to get off Natasha. And Reed told us he didn't want to hurt her. That she attacked him first."

"Which means Green shot Reed on purpose," Cassie supplied.

"He wanted to kill Reed," Jason added. "But the shots were clean. He put two bullets in him, but he didn't finish the job. We got him to the hospital too quick."

"Noah came back to finish what he'd started." Harris looked at Cassie with pain in her eyes. "You were right. We shouldn't have trusted him. He's working with Aguilar."

Cassie didn't care about being right. Didn't need the credit. She just needed people to be safe. And that's when it hit her.

"He's going after Natasha," she said, already spinning on her heels and running down the hallway. "He knows she's staying at Laura's house."

The sound of the other two running after her was no reassurance at all.

32

CASSIE COULDN'T THINK STRAIGHT, GOING THROUGH THE VARIOUS scenarios they'd walk into. Laura wasn't picking up her phone, and they didn't have a number for Natasha. A very small part of her thought maybe they were watching TV, trying to keep their minds off everything going on. But a bigger part heard alarm bells going off in the back of her mind.

Traffic picked up as they moved through Los Angeles. Jason dialed the police and explained the situation as best he could. At first, it sounded like they didn't believe him, especially when he mentioned Detective Green by name. But after some shouting and cursing, he took a more neutral tone and gave them as much information as he could muster in the time it took them to pull into Laura's driveway.

The house looked quiet. Pleasant, even. There were a few lights on inside, but they couldn't see through the windows. A gentle breeze ruffled the plants out front, and Cassie caught sight of a baby bunny darting under a bush as soon as the car pulled up. Only one part of the scene didn't belong there.

Green's car was in the driveway, parked next to Laura's vehicle like he was a guest who had been invited over for an early breakfast.

Harris threw her door open and ran out onto the dawn, and Cassie scrambled after her, grabbing onto the detective's arm and holding her back. When Harris whipped around to face her, her face was written with anger, annoyance, and sheer panic.

"Stop," Cassie begged her. "Just stop. You can't go in there."

"He's going to kill Natasha." There was no doubt in Harris' voice. "And then Laura will be next."

Cassie tried to ignore the mental image those words created. "You don't even have a gun. He will."

Jason rounded the vehicle and came to stand next to Cassie. "She's right. It's too dangerous."

"We have no other choice." Harris shook free of Cassie's grasp but didn't make another move toward the house. "Besides, there's five of us, and only one of him."

"But he has plenty of bullets," Cassie argued.

"We delay him. Until the cops get here. We just have to be smart about it." She hesitated, and Cassie saw how scared she really was. "If you see anything—get any visions or talk to any ghosts—use it. Anything we can to prolong this, okay? Once the cops get here, he'll have nowhere to go."

Jason and Cassie exchanged a look, but neither of them had a better plan. If they didn't go in now, there was a chance Natasha and Laura wouldn't make it out of this alive. Their best bet—their only bet—was to keep Green talking long enough for the police to show up.

Not hearing an argument from either one of them, Harris turned back toward the house and stalked forward with more determination and courage than Cassie had seen a second ago. Jason followed in her wake, making sure he was between Cassie and whatever came next. For her part, Cassie tried to open her mind's eye to whatever they were about to walk into. But she felt no spiritual presence or tugs on her consciousness. She was walking into the house as weaponless as Harris.

They paused outside the door, all three of them leaning in close. Cassie could hear voices on the other side—one male and one female—which seemed like a good sign. But she couldn't tell if it was Laura or Natasha. Was one of them just being quiet, or were they injured—or worse?

"I'm going to open the door," Harris said, her hand hovering above the knob, "and go in first, with my hands up. You two follow me and do the same. Then we're going to spread out. Don't make him feel like he's being surrounded. Just enough that we're not all clumped together as one target."

"Shouldn't one of us go around back?" Jason asked.

Harris shook her head. "The door's probably locked. I don't want him to feel like he's getting jumped. Our best bet is to waste time."

With one final shared look between the three of them, Harris squared her shoulders and twisted the doorknob, pushing her way through the entrance and raising her arms in surrender. Jason walked through and did the same. Then Cassie.

Cassie wasn't sure what she had expected when she walked through the door. Maybe they had misconstrued the entire scenario. Maybe Detective Green was there to protect Natasha, not hurt her. They could've been sitting on the couch, waiting for the others to return, while Laura made them all breakfast.

On the other end of the spectrum, Cassie imagined walking into a bloodbath. She'd seen enough horror—and lived through her fair share—to know that humans could be barbaric. Would Green kill Natasha slowly, or would he just want it over with? Would Laura have a chance to fight back, or would she be dead as quickly as Emily's sister? And what about Green himself? Would he be standing there, triumphant in his victory, or would he shoot his way out of the house and escape before the cops arrived?

What Cassie walked into wasn't that extreme. Both Natasha and Laura were sitting comfortably on the couch. At least, as comfortably as they could with their hands and legs bound by duct tape. Green was standing by the dining room table, gun raised in Harris' direction, staring daggers at the newcomers.

"It's over, Noah," Harris said, moving to the center of the room. Jason and Cassie fanned out beside her. "We know everything."

"That's far enough," Green said, shifting the gun from Harris to Laura. Cassie came to a sudden halt and saw the other two did the same. "Don't make me do something I'll regret."

"You don't regret killing Reed?" Harris asked. "You're okay with murdering someone?"

"Reed was a monster," Green sneered. "He deserved to die."

Harris kept her voice as even as she could. "You don't get to make that call."

"I think you'll find that I do." Green's gaze traveled from Harris' face to Jason's and then finally settled on Cassie's. "You didn't see this coming? Really? All that time we were together, and you had no idea?"

Cassie wanted to spit in his face, but she had to play nice. "I didn't want to trust you, at least not right away. You played your cards right, though. We helped you find Reed."

"Thanks for that."

"Why?" Cassie thought she knew the answer, but she still couldn't connect all the dots. "Who was Reed to you?"

"No one. I mean, not really." Green shrugged. He looked calm and casual, and the gun in his hand was steady as he kept it pointed at Laura's head. "Aguilar wanted him dead, and I owed him a favor. Simple as that."

"How do you know Aguilar?" Harris asked.

"We have mutual friends. Maybe you've heard of them?"

Cassie didn't need him to finish the thought. "Apex?" It always came back to Apex. Ever since her trip to North Carolina, the company was around every corner. From the outside, they ran publicity for celebrities and politicians. But Cassie knew it was a different story behind closed doors.

"Bingo." As soon as the word was out of his mouth, a ding sounded from behind him. Green's grin widened. "I'm not stupid, you know. I'm sure you called the cops as soon as you saw my car in the driveway. But you're not the only one who wanted to waste time."

He stepped to the side, and Cassie got a look at what had made the sound behind him. Harris' laptop was open on the dining room table, and the hard drive with all the evidence was still plugged into it. A window was open with a dialog box, and even though Cassie couldn't read it from across the screen, she knew what it said.

"Deleted," Green informed them. "All of it."

Natasha sobbed, but it sounded as angry as it did devastated. Cassie felt like the floor had fallen out from under her as her legs threatened to buckle. Even Harris looked shocked and at a loss for words. Laura sat as still as she possibly could, and Cassie had an urge to go to her, to wrap her arms around her. To fling herself in front of her sister and tackle Green to the ground.

"So, what now?" Harris asked. "There's five of us, and only one of you."

"I've got a gun," Green said, waving it in front of him. Cassie saw Laura shudder.

"Even if you kill one or two of us, the rest of us will take you down." Harris' voice remained steady, and Cassie had newfound appreciation for the detective's nerves of steel. "No way you're getting out of this."

Green eyed her, as though finally seeing the woman he'd spent the last few days working with. "Unless? It sounds like you have an alternative plan."

"Let Natasha and Laura go. Leave now. We won't stop you. Walk away from this. And we'll go our separate ways."

"I won't have a life to go back to." Green looked down at Natasha, contempt written across his face. "I have a different idea." Swinging the gun to point at Natasha's head now. "How about I kill all of you, and stage a crime scene. Just like I did at the psychic's shop."

"You killed Luna?" Cassie asked. She thought the woman's spirit had disappeared as soon as Detective Green approached because she was disoriented and easily scared, but it was because he'd been the one to kill her. "Why?"

"She wouldn't cooperate. Plus, I was hoping it would flush Reed out of hiding. It was easy enough to take her out, then get rid of any surveillance footage."

"Just like you did at the hospital," Harris added.

"What can I say, I have friends in high places." Green swung his gun toward Jason. "Come on, man. Don't be stupid. It's not worth it. You don't have to be involved in this."

Jason had inched his way around the couch. He was closer to Laura now, almost within arm's reach. He'd been so quiet, Cassie had almost forgotten he was there. But Jason had used that time to his advantage. He was close enough to Laura now that he might be able to shield her if Green started shooting.

But Green had other plans. He grabbed Natasha by the arm and yanked her up off the couch and slammed her into his body, spinning her around and using her as a human shield. He held the gun to her temple and forced her forward, toward the door, which was difficult given her legs were still taped together.

"The evidence is gone," Green said. "Natasha doesn't need to die. But she will if you follow me. I'm driving away from here. I'll leave her on the side of the road, no harm done, as long as I don't see you in my rearview."

"Leave her here," Cassie said. "Take me instead."

Everyone in the room protested, but Green just laughed. "You're an interesting one, Cassie Quinn. Everyone's talking about you. But once Apex gets their claws into you, they're not giving you up easily. Trust me, I'm doing you a favor."

"Why?" Cassie was desperate to keep him talking. "Why do me any favors at all? You hardly know me."

He shrugged, finally backed up to the door. "Because as far as I'm concerned, this has nothing to do with you. Believe it or not, I used to be a good cop." He laughed, but it was bordering on hysterical. "Now look at me."

"You can still be a good cop, Noah." Cassie wasn't above begging and pleading. "But please don't hurt Natasha. Turn yourself in. Testify against Aguilar." She couldn't help the hope blossoming in her chest. "We were going to offer Reed a deal. Immunity in exchange for his testimony. You can have that same deal."

"Reed turned on Aguilar and look what happened to him." Green sounded sad when he said it, like there was no hope at the end of the tunnel for him. "This is my only way out." He used one hand to reach back and open the door, then pulled Natasha tighter against his chest as he backed out into the morning air. "She'll be fine, as long as you don't follow me."

Cassie kept her mouth shut because she saw what Green hadn't noticed yet. Outside, parked in the driveway and on the front lawn and all along the street, was an army of cop cars. They had just arrived, no lights and no sirens, so as not to tip off their suspect. Green turned just as several of them climbed out of their cars and drew their guns on him. He stilled.

"Freeze! Hands up!" one cop shouted.

Another one, a softer voice, said, "Noah, let's talk about this. It's not over for you yet. We can still work this out."

The entire world sat on the edge of a precipice. Cassie could see straight out the door, count the expressions on every cop's face, from confused to horrified or downright pissed off. The sun was above the horizon now, and the orange glow had turned bright yellow, shining down on them all like a beacon of hope.

But it must not have looked like that to Detective Green. He was surrounded, held at gunpoint by his fellow officers. He'd just confessed to two murders, and all his witnesses were still alive. Sure, he could take out Natasha, but he'd be riddled with bullets as soon as he squeezed the trigger. And if he gave up, what then? Where would he go? Everyone knew cops never made it far in prison. Too many enemies around every corner.

"Hands up," someone repeated. "Let her go."

Green complied. He pulled the gun away from Natasha's head and released her. As soon as she felt his grip leave her arm, she hobbled to the side, toward one of the cops, and hunkered down behind an open car door.

"Drop your weapon," that same officer shouted.

Green looked like he was considering it. For a brief second, Cassie thought the morning wouldn't end in tragedy. Turned out, you could be wrong even if you had psychic abilities. There was no love lost between her and Detective Green, but too many people had already died because of Aguilar. She didn't want him to claim another body.

Green must've disagreed.

He kept one arm held high in the air while he moved his other hand to his temple, putting the barrel of the gun flush to his head. There was no hesitation, no second thoughts. As soon as he lined up his shot, he pulled the trigger.

The last thing Cassie saw before she twisted away was Green's body dropping to the ground.

33

AGUILAR'S SKIN PRICKLED WITH SATISFACTION AND PLEASURE. HE DIDN'T believe in luck—only hard work—but the events of the last twenty-four hours might have been enough to change his mind. As he leaned back in his office chair, cup of coffee in hand, he couldn't help but bask in his own good fortune.

As Jasper had predicted, the Straczynski brothers were all too happy to temporarily align themselves with Aguilar. The Straczynskis ran a successful construction business. They were expensive, but they did good work. Aguilar had reluctantly commissioned them to build a few of his shipping facilities.

The Bianchi family had made enemies of the Poles early on in their settlement of Savannah when they brought in an outside contractor for one of their projects. Someone they knew from back home in New Jersey. The Straczynskis had confronted them, and while there had been no bloodshed, a line had been drawn in the sand. Petty retaliation had been the game ever since, but only because taking out such a large family would've meant the loss of other allies along the way. Some battles weren't worth fighting.

Which is why Jasper had made it worth the Straczynski brothers' time. Times had been tough the last few years, and money was the way to their heart. Or at least, the way to their weapons. For a nominal fee, they had agreed to take out Nicolas Bianchi and a few other members of his family. They'd even agreed to keep quiet about their benefactor, but Aguilar wasn't naïve enough to believe that would hold forever.

Then there was the issue of one less family standing between him and the Straczynskis themselves. One day they'd play their hand, and Aguilar would be ready. He had nothing personal against the Straczynskis, other than the fact that they liked to test their limits with him. But they were smart, and for now, Aguilar was still on top.

Of course, the entire plan hadn't gone off without a few setbacks. Taking a sip of coffee, Aguilar relished in the burn of the hot liquid down the back of his throat. He'd sent the Straczynskis after Nicolas Bianchi, and the man had somehow managed to escape. Aguilar wasn't convinced Nicolas hadn't talked his way out of the situation, but the Straczynski brothers had been adamant he'd cut and run.

Not that it mattered. The Bianchi family was gone—at least, the ones in Savannah. The Straczynskis had taken their men to the half dozen properties owned by the Italians and hit them each at the same time. Nicolas and a few of his men were the only ones to escape. By now, he was probably halfway back to New Jersey. At least, he would be if he were smart.

Aguilar had told Jasper to keep an eye on movements from the Northeast. There were plenty of Bianchis left to hold a grudge, but they lacked the capital to do anything about it. That's why Nicolas had begged for money to take back home. He'd tried to swindle Aguilar and had paid the price. Hopefully he'd tuck and run, and Aguilar wouldn't ever have to see or hear from him again.

But it wasn't just the destruction of the Bianchi family that had Aguilar in high spirits. Earlier that morning, they'd received a message from Jasper's contact, Shepherd, who had been following Harris around Los Angeles, trying to gain her trust and get to Emily's evidence before she did. Aguilar hadn't been sure about the man—all the information about him had been secondhand—but Jasper seemed to trust him.

Detective Harris had proven a capable opponent, as well as her companion, Cassie Quinn. The psychic had known exactly where

Emily had hidden the evidence and had even gone to the trouble of retrieving it for them. Despite the mishap at the hostel in which Shepherd had failed to kill Reed, he'd rectified his mistake and finished the deed.

But what had really sent a jolt of excitement coursing through Aguilar's body was the fact that Shepherd had destroyed all of Emily's evidence. Deleted it straight off the hard drive. For the first time in years, Aguilar felt a weight lift from his shoulders. Emily had been dead a long time, but she'd betrayed him from the shadows of his own home, and it had haunted him ever since.

Good riddance.

A soft knock sounded on the door, and Jasper slipped inside. He had his ever-present tablet in one hand and his phone in the other. A frown marred his face, and Aguilar's excited heart slowed to a more reasonable pace. He knew that look—it was nothing good.

"I've been trying to reach Shepherd for a couple hours." Jasper shook his head. "Nothing."

"Should we be concerned?" Aguilar asked. The evidence was destroyed, so why did it matter?

"Normally, I'd say no." Jasper handed over the tablet. "Then this popped up in my alerts."

Aguilar looked down at the screen. It was a headline from a local Los Angeles paper about a detective who had attempted to kidnap two women, failed, and shot himself rather than go to jail.

Aguilar found the man's name and looked back up at Jasper. "Detective Noah Green?"

"Shepherd," Jasper confirmed with a curt nod of his head. "I'm still getting some of the details from a few of our other contacts, but it looks like the two women he attempted to kidnap were Natasha Michaelson and Laura Quinn."

"Emily's sister." Aguilar knew the name well. The two had been close. "And Cassie Quinn's sister?"

Another curt nod. "Looks like he'd blown his cover killing Reed."

Aguilar handed back the tablet with a slow shrug of his shoulder. "Reed is dead. The evidence is destroyed. Even if Emily had confided in

Natasha, the woman doesn't have any proof. And Detective Harris won't be able to tie Shepherd back to us, correct?"

"Correct."

"Then as far as I'm concerned," Aguilar said, leaning back in his chair and clasping his hands behind his head, "this is just one more loose end we don't have to worry about."

34

THERE WAS NOTHING KEEPING CASSIE, HARRIS, AND JASON IN LOS ANGELES now. With both Reed and Detective Green dead, two of their major connections to Aguilar had been severed. Natasha was more nervous than ever and refusing to fly back to Savannah without viable evidence. Jason tried to convince her that not all hope was lost, but she was too scared. At least she'd taken a burner phone from Harris, in case they could recover the hard drive. Then there was nothing left to do but fly back home.

Cassie had been gone for less than two weeks, but it felt strange to return to Savannah. The air was hotter and more humid than in California, but there was a warmth and comfort to it. This was home, as much as the city had given Cassie trouble over the years. This was where she'd decided to take root.

Apollo and Bear had been beside themselves to see her, and they had demanded a full hour of cuddling on the couch before they let her back up again. Jason had used that time to reach out to yet another one of his endless military contacts—someone who could help them recover the evidence Green had deleted from the hard drive.

After a tearful goodbye and baleful howls from Bear, Cassie slipped out of her house and joined Jason on his drive downtown to his contact's apartment. Harris had already left to put eyes on Aguilar, although Cassie wished Harris hadn't gone alone.

"Do you think it's smart?" Cassie asked Jason. "Letting Harris go off on her own like this? When we're so close?"

"I don't think she'll do anything to disrupt the investigation. Not now." They both looked down at the hard drive between them. It didn't need to be said out loud for both of them to know it was their only hope. "Besides, it would've driven her nuts to sit around waiting for someone to recover everything inside that thing."

Jason had a point, so Cassie cast it from her mind. She and Harris still carried some baggage between them, and they hadn't had a chance to talk properly. All three of them had been scattered throughout the plane on the flight home, and the detective had peeled off from the group as soon as she could. Part of Cassie couldn't blame her for wanting their target in sight, but the other part wished Harris had stayed.

The apartment building downtown was nondescript. It was in a good neighborhood, and the structure looked modern without being over the top. Jason buzzed his way inside, and Cassie caught the nameplate attached to the apartment number: Carmen Moreno.

A short elevator ride later, they knocked on Carmen's door and a woman answered it with a wide smile full of straight, white teeth. Her skin was a rich brown, and her eyes a stunning hazel. Thick, jet-black hair fell to her waist, and she'd pulled it back with a red bow that matched her pantsuit. Cassie had no idea what she did for a living, but she looked like a lawyer or a real estate agent. Someone who always seemed put together.

Carmen stepped back to let them in, then shut the door behind them. Taking Jason's hands, she kissed him on the cheek. "The first time you call me in over a year, and it's to ask for a favor?" She had the slightest hint of an accent that told Cassie Spanish had been her first language. "I thought you were a Duke, not a scoundrel."

Jason had the wherewithal to look sheepish. "Sorry."

The woman waved him off, then took Cassie's hands in her own, leaning forward to place a kiss on her cheek as well. She smelled like vanilla and cinnamon, a sweet and spicy scent that seemed to match her personality. "And you must be Cassie Quinn. So nice to meet you!"

"Nice to meet you, too."

Cassie looked to Jason with an eyebrow raised, but Carmen answered before he could. "Duke didn't tell you anything about me, did he?"

Jason blew out a breath of air that sounded a bit like a chuckle. "I honestly didn't know where to start."

Carmen led them into the kitchen. "Coffee? Wine?" Checking the clock on the microwave, it was almost six in the evening now. "Something stronger?"

"Coffee," Cassie said. The events of the last twenty-four hours—let alone the last week or so—were starting to catch up with her. "Thank you."

"Same," Jason said, when Carmen looked to him.

Carmen flitted around the kitchen, pulling out mugs and preparing the coffee while she talked. "Duke and I met when he first got to base. I'd already been there for a few years, and someone thought it was a good idea to stick me with some fresh meat."

"It was a good idea." Jason was grinning, and Cassie wished she could experience the memories he was reliving right now. "For me, at least."

Carmen looked at Cassie and dramatically rolled her eyes. "I was at the top of my class, but I was angry and bitter and didn't care about getting to know anyone. Duke brought me out of my shell, and I taught him everything he knows."

"Everything?" Cassie asked. She wasn't jealous, but a part of her was mournful that she would never know that version of Jason.

"Almost everything." Carmen winked. "We kept it professional over the years, if that's what you're wondering."

Cassie stuttered. "I wasn't—I didn't mean—"

Carmen tilted her head back and laughed, and Jason saved Cassie from any further embarrassment. "She became a cyber security expert," he said. "She and Terry worked together for a time. Both of them helped me on a few investigations over the years."

"How is Terry these days?" Carmen asked, pouring coffee into three mugs and setting out sugar and creamer. "Still as *passionate* as ever?"

"More, probably." Jason took a sip of his coffee and sighed with pleasure. "You'll be happy to know, he's moved into the digital business."

Carmen quirked an eyebrow. "Mr. I-Like-Doing-It-The-Hard-Way? Fascinating."

Cassie picked up her own mug and cradled it between her hands, blowing across the top to help it cool faster. "What do you do for work?"

"I work for the government." Carmen winked again. "But if I tell you, I'll have to—"

"Kill me?" Cassie finished.

"God no!" The woman laughed, and Cassie luxuriated in the warmth of it. "Probably make you sign an NDA and put a digital boot on all your devices." She laughed again. "Kill you? You've been watching too many movies."

"My life feels like a movie sometimes," Cassie supplied.

Carmen looked between the two of them. "What's going on here? Are you in trouble?"

Jason hesitated. They'd had a discussion before arriving about whether they should loop Carmen in on everything. Jason trusted her, but it wasn't just about that. Every time a new person found out about their investigation into Aguilar, the danger increased. The kingpin already knew they were after him, so he'd be watching their every move. Just coming to Carmen's apartment was a risk.

"We can't say much, but Cassie is working with the Savannah PD to take down a pretty big criminal organization." He shook the hard drive, bringing their attention back to the device. "We had all the evidence on here that we need, but someone deleted it before we could stop him. Do you think you could recover it for us?"

Carmen took the drive and examined the underside. "How was it deleted? Did he use a program to do it, or hit the delete button?"

"My guess is just hit the delete button," Jason said.

"Should be easy enough, then." Carmen held the drive in one hand, and her coffee mug in the other. "You stay here, make yourself comfortable. Bathroom is through the back. I'll let you know when I'm done."

A wave of relief flooded through Cassie's body. "Thank you. This means a lot to us."

"Just be careful," Carmen said, retreating into another room. Pausing long enough to look over her shoulder, she gestured to Jason. "This one knows how to get into trouble."

Cassie and Jason waited until she shut the door behind her before collapsing onto the couch in the living room. They sat close enough to touch, and Cassie appreciated his warm and solid presence. Although it wasn't enough to turn off her brain, it helped slow it down.

"I like her," Cassie said after a moment of silence.

"Carmen's great." Jason had his head tilted back and his eyes closed. When he chuckled, it rumbled throughout his chest. "You wouldn't know it to look at her, but she could kick my ass in seven seconds flat."

"Really?" Cassie laughed, too. "That makes me like her even more."

"I thought it might."

Cassie felt a soft rustling in the air that stirred a few strands of her hair. She sat up and looked around, but nothing was there. Was the chill creeping along her skin from the winter air, or was it something else?

"What's wrong?" Jason asked. His eyes were open now, peering down at her with concern.

"Nothing." Cassie internally shook herself, trying to break free of the feeling. "I just hope she can recover that evidence."

"She will. She's the best at what she does."

Cassie's gaze slid sideways to him. "You know a lot of people," she prompted.

"I've made a few friends over the years, yeah."

"And you seem to like investigating. You're really good at it."

Jason narrowed his eyes. "You're up to something."

"I'm not up to anything," Cassie said innocently. "Just pointing out the facts."

"It's suspicious."

The idea had been floating in the back of her mind for a few days now. She wasn't sure if she should bring it up to Jason, but something about the way his eyes lit up whenever they got closer to their goal told her he wouldn't be totally averse to it. "Have you thought any more about becoming a private investigator?"

Jason didn't say anything for a few seconds. Then he let out a puff of air. "Yeah, actually, I have."

"Really?" Cassie blinked up at him. That was easier than she thought it'd be. "Why haven't you?"

"Fear, mostly. I've seen a lot of bad things happen to good people. I'm not exactly excited to jump back into that life."

"That's fair." If anyone knew the horrors of the world, it was Cassie. "But you love helping people."

"I do." Jason shifted, like he was uncomfortable baring his soul like this. "But it wasn't just fear of what I'd see. It's been a while, you know? Would I be any good at it? I've made mistakes in the past. Big ones. I don't want to repeat them."

Cassie had to bite her tongue before asking what kind of mistakes he'd made. She had to trust that he'd tell her in time. "You've been instrumental in helping us protect Rose Sherman and track down Natasha. You're the reason we even have a chance at recovering the evidence Detective Green deleted."

At the mention of Green's name, the air shimmered, and a chill crept down Cassie's back. But Jason didn't seem to notice. "I appreciate you saying that. But my own business? How could I afford that? How would I find clients? Do I need employees? I'm not sure I'm ready for that."

Cassie tried to ignore the growing dread in the pit of her stomach that had nothing to do with the topic at hand. "I could help you get it off the ground. I've got some extra money I could invest."

Jason looked at her with a slack jaw. "You mean, like, become partners?"

Cassie shrugged, battling the heat in her face and the chill in her spine. "If that's something you'd want to try, yeah." She rushed on. "Clients would be easy. Between social media and my uncanny ability to find my own kind of trouble, I'm sure we'd have plenty to work with. Plus, we have Adelaide. I bet she'd throw us some work now and then. As for employees," Cassie continued, finally taking a breath, "we could call in some favors to start with, and once we make some money, we could start paying them as independent contractors. It wouldn't be a glamorous lifestyle, but I think you'd find it more satisfying than working at the museum."

"And you'd want to do that? With me?" Jason asked. The vulnerability in his eyes would've made Cassie weak in the knees if she'd been standing.

"I would. Yes." Her voice came out breathy and quiet, but there was no hesitation. "I know everything has been intense the last few weeks, and we haven't really had a chance to talk or explore what's going on between us, but once Aguilar is arrested, I'd like to get to know you better."

Jason's lips quirked up into a smile. "So, you want to be my girl-friend?" he asked. "And my business partner?" His voice was quiet and playful. "That doesn't always work out for most people."

Cassie shrugged. "We aren't most people."

"That's for sure." Jason stared at her for a long moment before leaning forward and pressing a soft kiss to her lips. They stayed like that for what felt like several moments, forgetting about anything and everything else.

A sharp gust of arctic air made Cassie gasp and pull away. Pushing off the couch, she stood, facing the outline of a spirit. At first, it looked like it was made of smoke and static, but once Cassie locked eyes with it, the spirit solidified.

"What is it?" Jason asked. He was standing now, too. "What's going on?"

Cassie couldn't breathe. She recognized those eyes. That hair. The face. It was the last person on the planet she wanted to see right now, and she had no idea what it meant for them or their final move against Francisco Aguilar.

"It's Detective Green," Cassie told Jason, never breaking eye contact with the spirit. "He followed us home."

35

HARRIS TRIED TO FOCUS ON HER MISSION, BUT IT WAS HARD NOT TO WONDER if Cassie and Jason were having any luck recovering the evidence. She didn't know anything about Jason's contact, but he'd insisted they were the best of the best. Harris had to trust it was being taken care of.

She snorted at that thought. Not too long ago, the only person she'd trusted was David. Then that circle expanded to Cassie. And now it included Jason. Not knowing much about him other than a few key details, over the last few days, Harris felt like she'd gotten a good look at the kind of person he was. If nothing else, he was fiercely protective of Cassie, and that made Harris feel better about leaving her side for a couple of hours.

All the evidence in the world wouldn't do them any good if they couldn't find Francisco Aguilar. But he wasn't exactly hiding. She'd followed his car from his house—more like a small mansion—to one of his restaurants. Not his usual haunt, which surprised her, but he was still out in the open, moving around like he didn't have a care in the world.

That would change soon enough.

No, Harris was more concerned about the comings and goings of Jasper Brown, Aguilar's right-hand man. They'd known about him for a while, but he was slippery. Aguilar wasn't hard to track down most of the time, but Brown had a tendency to disappear for days at a time. If anyone was doing the dirty work, it would be him. If they could recover the evidence, there was no way Aguilar was getting away. He'd be in prison for the rest of his life. But what about Brown? As far as she knew, they had nothing on him, and he might be able to walk free. What was stopping him from taking over Aguilar's operations?

With that in mind, Harris followed her gut and tailed Brown's car when he left the restaurant, leaving Aguilar behind. She wanted to know what he—and therefore Aguilar—was up to, and whether they knew the police were closing in on them. Intel like that could keep them going steady or force their hand. Either way, Harris wasn't going to take any risks. Aguilar was going down, one way or another.

Brown had driven outside the city, to a small residential area filled with middle-income houses. Most of them had white picket fences and above ground swimming pools—empty now, in the winter—and at least two cars in the driveway. Harris was careful to keep her distance as Brown pulled up to a house with a for sale sign in the front yard. After a moment's hesitation, he climbed out of his car, produced a key, and walked inside.

Harris parked her car one street over. It would be difficult to see as the sun faded from view. For now, though, she could look between the houses and keep an eye on Brown's. All the lights were off, which made her wonder if he was dropping something off or picking it up. It didn't seem like he had met anyone there—unless they had yet to arrive.

Harris decided to give herself an hour to follow Brown around, either sitting here until something happened or following him to his next location. It was dinnertime, so Aguilar was probably meeting one of his associates at the restaurant. He likely wouldn't leave before the hour was up, so Harris had plenty of time to get back to his location. With a bit of luck, maybe she'd catch Brown in the act of something criminal. It'd be the perfect cherry on top of what was looking to be a decadent dessert.

A vibration from her cupholder made Harris jump, and she snatched up her phone before it could make the sound again. Looking down at the screen, she frowned at Chief Clementine's name. They'd only been back in Savannah for about an hour. Why was she calling now?

Harris answered on the third ring. "Hello?"

"Adelaide," Clementine said, by way of greeting. "Glad to see you made it home in one piece."

Harris furrowed her brow. "How did you know?"

Clementine chuckled. It was a low, rich sound that made Harris' own lips quirk upwards in response. "I have my ways. There are still some officers I can trust, though fewer than I'd like."

"Well, you can trust me," Harris said. Although she'd messed up a few times, maybe gone off the deep end once or twice, she was loyal. She wouldn't turn her back on Clementine, not for a second.

"I know." The woman on the other end of the line blew out a breath, and it sounded weary. Exhausted. "When I suspended you, I knew you wouldn't stop looking for answers. I hope you found them."

"I did. *We* did," she clarified. There was no telling if this line was secure, so she kept her information vague. "There's a lot to unpack. A lot I didn't know."

"I'm sure." Clementine paused, as though she was weighing her next questions, debating if she wanted to know the answer. "Where are you right now?"

"Not home, if that's what you're asking."

"Figured as much." Another pause. "Be smart, okay? This situation has gotten a lot more complicated since you left."

Harris didn't like feeling out of the loop. "How so?"

"For one, Nicolas Bianchi's nephew was killed a few days ago."

Harris sucked in a breath. The Bianchi family wasn't as powerful or connected as Aguilar, but they weren't the kind of people you wanted to mess with. "Who do you think did it?"

"Aguilar."

"I thought they got along?" It'd be a stretch to call them friends, but Aguilar and the head of the Bianchi family were often seen dining together. "Why would he do that?"

"Your guess is as good as mine. Someone burnt his restaurant down. The Brazilian steakhouse. Then a day later, the kid was dead. He'd been tortured. It was bloody and brutal."

"That explains why Aguilar didn't go there for dinner tonight. He usually takes meetings at the steakhouse."

"I should've known you'd be following him. Is that what you're doing right now?"

Harris winced. "No, not right now. I'm hoping he stays put for a little while longer. I'm following another lead."

"You're not going to tell me what it is, are you?" When Harris didn't answer, Clementine sighed again. "Didn't think so." Her voice hardened. "Look, it's gotten worse than that. Someone tried to take out the entire Bianchi family."

Harris blanched, and for a second, she couldn't find her voice. "What? You've got to be kidding."

"I wish I was. It wasn't Aguilar. We had eyes on him. He wasn't laying low. Which means—"

"He paid someone else to do it. Who?"

"We're not sure right now. It was efficient. This wasn't about teaching them a lesson. This was about wiping them out."

Harris swore. Something nagged at the back of her mind. "You said someone *tried* to take out the entire family. Who'd they miss?"

"Nicolas Bianchi." There was the creak of a chair in the background, and Harris imagined Clementine leaning back, stretching out. "Since his body wasn't on the scene, I can only assume he got out alive. Not that it matters. His family is gone. Either he's going to do something stupid, or he's going back to Jersey."

"For backup?" Harris asked, imagining worst-case scenarios.

"Maybe."

"That could mean a war on the streets of Savannah. We don't need that."

"You're telling me." The chair creaked again, and this time Clementine grunted softly, like she stood up. "Look, I called to tell you to be careful. I'm ready to move on Aguilar whenever we can, but we need evidence. Once you have it, you let me do the heavy lifting. Technically, you're still suspended."

"Damn. You don't have to rub salt in the wound, Chief."

"I mean it, Harris." Clementine's words were sharp, like a slap to the face. "This might be our one chance to get this right. I know you want justice for David, but we have to do this one by the book. Got it?"

Harris forced her jaw to relax so her words would come out normal. "Got it."

"Good. Now, get that evidence to me as soon as you've got it. I've got a judge on standby. He'll sign the warrant, and we'll be on our way."

Another car had pulled into the driveway of the house Brown had gone into, and Harris had to force the excitement out of her voice. "Copy that," she told Clementine. "See you soon."

"I'm holding you to that," Clementine responded, before hanging up.

Harris had no intention of leaving Brown behind, especially now that it looked like something was happening. Two men emerged from the car, but they kept their back turned to her, so she couldn't see their faces. There was something vaguely familiar about the one on the left. He was shorter than the other and considerably heavier, but it was all about the way he carried himself. She recognized his swagger.

The detective debated pulling her car around the corner for a better vantage point, but the risk of being seen was too high. Then again, as soon as the door closed behind the two men, she had to fight the urge to walk up to the house on foot. She was much safer in the car, not only from weapons, but also because it gave her a quick getaway. There was no telling if anyone else in one of the surrounding houses was working as a lookout for Brown and his men.

Sixty seconds passed before the decision was made for her by the sound of two gunshots from the house. A dog started barking, and a neighbor's lights switched on. More than likely, they'd call the police, but what if Brown or the other men got away in the meantime?

As soon as the thought formed in her head, Harris made her move. She pulled her gun from the glovebox. It felt good to have it back in her hands, especially in a situation like this where she had no idea what she was getting herself into. Then she shouldered open her car door and hit the ground running, leaving her vehicle unlocked in case she needed to retreat quickly. Cutting through several yards, she hopped a fence until she was sneaking up alongside Brown's house.

Crouching low to the ground, she waited for another sound, a third crack of a gunshot or the door banging open as someone tried to escape. She strained her ears to hear anything—a cry of pain or a muffled shout of surprise. But there was nothing.

Nothing, that is, until a third and fourth shot rang out in the air. Another neighbor's light flipped on, but Harris was already on the move. Quick and steady, she ran up the front porch, staying as low as she could. Without another second to spare, Harris planted one foot on the ground and lifted the other to aim a kick right above the door handle. It only took one shot for the wood to splinter and the door to swing open.

Harris moved to the right, using the outside of the house as cover. But no bullets sped by, and there were no sounds of movement. Leaning forward to peek inside, it was dark, but her eyes were already adjusting. The living room, empty of any furniture or décor, was clear. Stepping inside, she placed her feet carefully and hoped the floor wouldn't give away her position.

Not that it mattered. They'd been waiting for her.

One man emerged from her right, out of the kitchen, while the second emerged from the door in front of her. Both held guns raised to her chest. She froze. There was no way she'd be able to take them both down without one of them getting a shot off first.

Harris focused on the face of the man in front of her. He only took a few steps forward before she cursed herself for being so stupid. Now she knew why she'd recognized his swagger. It was Crawford, one of her least favorite people at the precinct. David hadn't liked the man while he was alive, either.

Crawford sneered, looking pleased with himself, but he wasn't the first one to speak. Neither was the man on Harris' right—Billings, if memory served correctly. No, the one to speak was the man descending the creaky stairs. He also had a gun, hanging lazily by his side like he didn't think Harris was a credible threat. The shots she'd heard had been the bait, and she'd fallen for it, hook, line, and sinker.

"Detective Harris," Jasper Brown drawled. "I'm so glad you could join us."

36

"WHAT DO YOU MEAN, DETECTIVE GREEN FOLLOWED US HOME?" JASON hissed.

Carmen was still in the other room, behind closed doors, working on the hard drive, but Cassie appreciated him whispering all the same. Having just met the woman, there was nothing quite like revealing you could talk to ghosts within minutes of making a new acquaintance. Those situations usually went in one of two directions. Either there were a lot of questions, or a lot of prayers and crossing of one's person. Neither was ideal for Cassie.

"I mean," Cassie said through clenched teeth, "I can see him. Right now. In front of me."

Green wore what he'd worn in death—a button up shirt and slacks. His hair was styled the same, and his face was identical to what it had been in life. If you could get past the hole in his head where he'd shot himself, that was.

Like most spirits, his color was faded, and he was transparent. But the fire in his eyes was still there. Cassie had seen that with people who had killed themselves. It was such a desperate, agonizing, emotional act that it left a stronger imprint than murder. Detective Green would not be an easy ghost to dispel.

As if on cue, Green's eyes locked on Cassie's. His mouth drew back in a snarl, the whites of his teeth now a dull gray, and an inhuman sound escaped his throat. That sound caused goosebumps to erupt up and down her arms. She'd likely never get used to it. Not that she wanted to.

If the spirit world ever stopped surprising her, she knew she was in trouble. It wasn't natural to get used to those kinds of sights and sounds.

"What's he doing?" Jason asked. His gaze was locked on an area to the right of Green.

Green's mouth opened, and another deep, grating sound escaped, barely forming the word, "Where?" Then his jaw snapped shut, like he was confused that he had produced the noise. Spirits didn't always talk directly to Cassie—not in words anyway—and sometimes she was grateful for that. They had to use energy instead of vocal cords to speak, and it didn't produce the same result.

"He's asking me where he is," Cassie said, never dropping her gaze from Green's face. Then, speaking to him in a low voice, she said, "You're in Savannah, Georgia. You followed me home from Los Angeles. Do you remember that?"

His image flickered, and Cassie got the sense he was confused. When he opened his mouth again, the sound was clearer, but just as disconcerting. "Why?"

"You killed yourself, Detective Green. Do you remember?" Cassie was hedging her bets here. It wasn't always smart to remind the dead that they weren't alive. Sometimes they went off the deep end. But in this case, she didn't have a choice. The sooner she could get rid of Green, the better. "Outside my sister's house. You were surrounded by the police. You raised your gun to your temple and pulled the trigger."

Green hissed and took a step forward like he wanted to attack her, but in that same moment, the door to the back bedroom opened and Carmen emerged. Green looked up in surprise and then blinked out of existence. One minute he was there, and the next he wasn't. The air grew a degree warmer, and the lights flickered momentarily before steadying themselves again.

"That was weird," Carmen said, looking at the lamp next to the couch. "What was that?"

"Not sure," Cassie said. Then, more for Jason's benefit, "But I think it's okay now."

"Don't tell me you're done already?" Jason asked, looking at the drive in Carmen's hand.

"Of course I am." She sounded mildly offended. "Don't you know me better than that?"

"That quickly?" Cassie asked. "And it's all there?"

"It's all there." She frowned. "What have you gotten yourselves into?"

It was risky enough that they'd come here in the first place. Cassie didn't want to make matters worse by telling Carmen too much. "We don't want you to get into trouble. It's better—"

"I know who Francisco Aguilar is." Carmen handed Cassie the drive. "He's no joke. What you have on that drive is enough to put him away for a long time. He deserves worse than that, but that's not my call." She looked at Jason. "Are you being careful?"

"As careful as we can be," Jason said. "We're working with a detective. Someone we trust."

"Aguilar's gotten out of tighter spots before," Carmen supplied. For the first time, Cassie got the impression that Carmen knew a lot more than she was letting on. "Let's hope this one sticks."

"It will," Cassie promised. "It has to."

The look on Carmen's face told Cassie the other woman knew at least a fraction of the pain she was going through. Had Carmen lost someone too? Or had her work with the government put her in opposition to Aguilar in the past? She wanted to ask, but something told her this wasn't the time or place.

A gentle vibration had Cassie reaching for her phone, tucked into the side of her purse. It was Harris. "Speak of the Devil." Cassie answered and didn't even wait for Harris to speak. "Hey, we got the drive. All the evidence has been recovered. Can you meet us?"

"Of course," a male voice purred. "But can you come to me? I'm tied up with a guest right now, and I don't want her to think I'm playing favorites."

Aguilar.

A sudden release of adrenaline had Cassie swaying on her feet. "Where's Harris? What did you do to her?"

"She's here, with me," Aguilar supplied. His voice was calm. Playful. "She's unharmed. For now."

"What do you want?"

"You're smarter than that, Cassie Quinn. You know what I want."

Cassie looked down at the drive in her hand.

"I want you to meet me at a private location. I'll text you the address. I assume Mr. Broussard is with you?"

Cassie locked eyes with Jason. "Yes."

"You may bring him, but no one else." Aguilar's voice turned hard. "Do not involve the police. I will know if you do."

"If I bring you the evidence," Cassie said, "you let Harris go?"

"That's the deal." Aguilar clicked his tongue. "I'm choosing to trust you, Cassie. Can I do that?"

How else was she supposed to answer that? "Yes."

"Good. Do not make any copies. If you have already, delete them. Do you understand?"

"Yes."

"If I find out you've lied to me," Aguilar continued, "I will kill everyone you care about. Detective Harris. Jason Broussard. Your sister, Laura. Your parents in North Carolina. Even those cute pets of yours." His voice took on a sick quality. "Detective Klein was lucky. He died quickly. The others will not. Have I made myself clear?"

Cassie couldn't decide if she wanted to scream or cry. "Yes."

"Good. I expect you within the next half hour."

Aguilar hung up without another word, but Cassie didn't lower the phone from her ear. She needed the extra few seconds to pull herself together, to make sure her voice wouldn't waver when she spoke again. Somehow, she forced the tears gathering in her eyes not to fall.

When she finally pulled the phone away from her head, she looked at Jason, now standing by her side. "Aguilar has Harris." Her voice cracked, and she took another few seconds to get her emotions back under control. "He'll trade her for the evidence."

"I could make copies," Carmen suggested.

Cassie shook her head. "If there's even a hint at the possibility that we made copies, he's—" She broke off. She couldn't do it. Couldn't say it out loud.

"We'll figure it out," Jason said, laying a hand on her arm.

Cassie's phone vibrated again, and a text message from Harris showed on the screen. It was the address for the meeting. "We have half an hour."

"At least let me call the cops," Carmen suggested, pulling out her own phone.

"No." It came out sharper than Cassie intended. Drawing a deep breath, she let it out slowly. "No. Please. He'll know. He has too many men on his side. We just have to make the exchange. We don't have another choice."

Carmen looked pained, but not surprised. Her gaze flicked to Jason's face. "Call me as soon as you're both safe, okay? I expect to hear from you tonight. Don't leave me hanging, Duke."

Jason nodded. "Yes, ma'am." Taking Cassie's hand, he led her to the door. "We'll be fine." Whether he said that for Carmen's benefit, Cassie's, or his own, she didn't know. "We'll figure it out. Aguilar's not getting away again."

In a daze, Cassie let Jason lead her into the elevator, through the lobby, and back out onto the sidewalk. The chilly winter air wasn't enough to clear her head—which was full of images of a bloody and broken Detective Harris—but the way Jason's body tensed with apprehension snapped her out of it.

Looking up, Cassie saw a man leaning against Jason's car. He wore slacks and a button-down shirt, and even though they were well-fitted, Cassie could tell the man was a little overweight. In his fifties, gold jewelry shone on his neck and wrists. A pair of sunglasses hid his eyes, but Cassie could tell the moment he locked onto her.

Jason stepped in front of Cassie and looked the man up and down. "Who are you?"

"Nicolas Bianchi."

37

Bianchi held out his hand, but when Jason didn't approach to shake it, he let it drop with a shrug, like he'd expected as much. "I'm here to talk to Ms. Quinn."

"I don't think so." Jason squared up with him. "Leave. Now."

"Afraid I can't do that." He said it like he was a gangster in an old mob movie. The effect was still terrifying.

"Aguilar already got in touch with us. We don't need an escort."

Bianchi snorted and pushed off the car but didn't approach. "Trust me, I'm not here to escort you. I'm here to help you."

"Why?" Cassie didn't know much about this man, but she knew enough to be careful. "Why would you want to help us?"

Nicolas drew himself up to his full height and pulled the sunglasses from his face. For the first time, Cassie noticed the bruises around his eyes and along his cheeks. "Because he murdered my family."

Cassie felt the cold stir around her again, and even though she couldn't see him, she knew Detective Green was starting to manifest. No one else seemed to notice, and she hoped Green would stay away long enough for her to focus on the man in front of her. She could only handle one dangerous entity at a time.

"I'm sorry to hear that," Jason said, keeping his voice even. "But we can't help you."

"Let me lay this out for you, okay?" Bianchi took another step forward, still keeping a distance. "Aguilar knows you've got evidence against him. He took something of yours in exchange. I'm guessing it's the detective, right? She's been a pain in his ass for too long, anyway." Bianchi took their silence for confirmation. "That's what I thought. So, he got in touch with you. Told you he'd give you back your detective if he gets the evidence. Probably made some threat about not making copies or he'd wipe out everyone you've ever loved. Sound familiar?"

Cassie couldn't help answering. "Yes."

"That son of a bitch has more men on the force than I ever did, which means you can't call the cops. He wants the two of you to come alone and deliver the goods." Bianchi's gazed flicked to the drive in Cassie's hand, and she gripped it tighter in response. "Only, when you hand over the drive, he's going to put a bullet in the detective's brain."

"You don't know that," Cassie said, but it sounded feeble.

"It's what I would do," Bianchi said, shrugging. "No evidence. No annoying cop. You two would be next. Problem solved. He's gotten away with murder before, and he'll do it again."

Silence hung in the air, and Cassie became aware of a presence off to her right. She looked in that direction and saw Detective Green. Dusk was approaching, and Cassie could now see his figure had a faint glow. It made him look even more ethereal. And menacing.

Green locked eyes with her. "Liar," he hissed. His voice was more fully formed. Less scratchy. Was he gaining power? If he realized what he was capable of, he could ruin everything. Cassie suddenly felt tired enough to sit down right there on the sidewalk. Concern for Harris' wellbeing was the only thing that kept her standing.

Cassie had the sudden urge to laugh. The hysterical sound bubbled up from her throat, but she clamped down on it, killing the noise before it could escape. She had no idea who to trust—the gangster relaying her worst fears back to her, or the man who had manipulated her in life and was trying to do the same in death.

"Why should we trust you?" Cassie asked, if only to say something to break the spell Green's presence had on her.

Bianchi looked at her like she was stupid. "Because you don't have another choice. Either we plan this together, or I follow you there. I want Aguilar dead. Retribution for my family. I don't give a shit about you or your boyfriend. Or even the cop. Give me this, and you'll never see me again."

"Unlike you," Jason ground out, "we're not in the business of murdering people."

"If you go in there alone, you'll die." He leveled a look at Jason. "She'll die."

Cassie felt Green get closer. The movement caused a chilly gust of wind, and she wondered if Jason and Bianchi could feel it as sharply as she could. Against her better judgement, Cassie looked Green in the eyes. They were wide with manic glee. Any confusion over his death and subsequent afterlife had been wiped away. The detective was becoming more sure-footed. "Liar," he hissed again.

Cassie shook her head to clear away Green's poisonous words, but when her eyes refocused, he was closer than ever. Against her better judgement and instincts, she turned away from the spirit and faced Bianchi. She didn't want to work with him, but much like Reed, he had no reason to lie. If Cassie and Jason met with Aguilar alone, there was little chance they would walk out of there alive once Aguilar got his hands on the hard drive.

What other choice did she have but to work with the man in front of her? It might be the only way for her to get Harris out alive. But just because she would use the help he offered, didn't mean she'd let him kill someone else right in front of her. Aguilar deserved to pay for his crimes, but if she could do it the right way—by arresting him and letting him rot in jail—then she'd do everything in her power to get it done.

But Bianchi didn't need to know that. And maybe she could kill two birds with one stone.

"All right," she finally said, feeling Green's presence fading at her back. "We'll go together. For Harris' sake."

38

Cassie and Jason sat outside the address Aguilar had texted from Harris' phone. It was another one of his restaurants—more like an upscale cantina, really. Cassie had always wanted to eat there, but it hadn't met her budget. A bitter taste formed in her mouth at the thought of first stepping in there to trade a piece of vital evidence for her friend's life. None of this was fair.

She watched as Jason surveyed their surroundings. He was taking in every shadow, every flicker of movement, looking for hidden figures and possible getaway routes. Even though the car was in park, he gripped the wheel with enough ferocity that she wouldn't have been surprised if he ripped the whole thing off the dashboard.

"Thank you," Cassie whispered, before she could talk herself out of this conversation. "For coming with me, I mean."

Jason startled a little at her voice, like he'd been so hyper-focused on what was outside the car, he'd forgotten she was sitting there next to him. "Of course." He looked over at her, his eyebrows pinched together. "I wouldn't leave you to do this on your own."

Part of her wished he wasn't so good a person. The guilt pooling in her stomach reminded her he wouldn't have been in this mess if it wasn't for her. He'd be home right now, getting ready for bed so he could wake up early the next day and make it to work on time. Instead, this could be the last thing either of them ever did. What a way to start a relationship.

"This isn't a good idea," Cassie whispered. She didn't like voicing her fears—giving them a weight in the real world instead of letting them swirl around in an anxious cloud of thought inside her head—but it was easier to admit the truth around Jason. He had this uncanny ability to put her at ease with one look.

Except this time felt different.

"Is that your fear talking?" Jason asked. He was trying to be playful, but she could tell it was a serious question. "Or something else?"

She'd heard various forms of that question over the years. People always wondering whether she was having one of her infamous *feelings*. Cassie dug deep, trying to decipher the truth. Part of it was her fear. She knew Aguilar wouldn't play by the rules, but this was something more. She felt caged in, with no other option than to do what he asked of them.

But what about that other part screaming out at her from somewhere deep in her gut? Was it her supernatural instinct warning her to look at this from another perspective? To find an alternative solution? It's funny how those feelings always told you when you were in danger but never seemed to solve the problem in the moment, the bastards.

Before she could answer Jason's question, Cassie's phone chimed. Their half hour was up. It was time to head inside.

They hadn't seen Bianchi arrive, but Cassie assumed he was hidden in the shadows somewhere. It was probably a good thing if Jason hadn't spotted him because that meant Aguilar and his men wouldn't either. They just had to hope Bianchi would fulfill his end of the bargain, preferably before she and Jason got themselves killed.

Aguilar had provided specific instructions. Arrive at the restaurant and enter when the half hour was up. Not a minute before or after. Walk around the back and use the rear entrance. It would lead them to a private room separate from the main part of the cantina. It would be safe and secure—for Aguilar, at least.

As she slipped out of the car, Cassie took in the restaurant. It wasn't large, but it had that classic feel to it, with the brick walls and hand-painted signs. Given what she'd read about the quality of food, it was in high demand. The small space lent itself to a cozy atmosphere—one reserved for the elite. Well, those who wanted to pretend they were the elite for a night.

Now, the cantina's windows were dark. Aguilar had shut down the restaurant for the evening. There were no other cars in the parking lot save for a pair of black sedans. The windows were tinted enough that they couldn't see inside, but a prickling feeling along the back of Cassie's neck told her someone was keeping an eye out, relaying their movements to Aguilar.

Warmth spread throughout Cassie's hand and up her arm, and she looked down to see that Jason had interlaced his fingers with hers. The entire situation had her senses going haywire, but the feel of his hand grounded her, at least enough to get her head back on straight.

"It's going to be okay," Jason whispered, as though there were people around who might overhear. Maybe there were. "Whatever happens, your life is more important than that evidence, okay? We'll figure something out. We still have Natasha and Rose Sherman on our side. We can still build a case."

It was nice to hear those reassurances, but they both knew it would be a lot harder to put Aguilar away without the hard drive gripped in her other hand. Cassie's heart beat faster as she looked up into Jason's face. "The same goes for you," she said. "Don't take any risks. Not on my account. Not even on Harris'." She hated saying those words, but Jason sacrificing himself for Harris would be no victory at all. "All three of us are getting out of there alive. With the evidence."

She wished her words had come out more confidently, but she saw the determination in Jason's eyes. Even though Aguilar had the upper hand, she and Jason had a secret weapon.

Before she was ready, the pair of them stopped in front of the door leading into the back room of the restaurant. Jason looked down at her and waited for her resolute nod before he knocked twice, sharp and quick. Only a second went by before someone pulled open the door in response.

The air inside was warm and held remnants of the dinnertime rush.

Cassie didn't recognize the man who had come to the door, but her gaze slipped past him and landed on Francisco Aguilar.

The King of Savannah leaned against a table in a plum suit with a smirk across his face. His lips might lie, but his eyes couldn't—they were cold and sharp as a knife. He was angry, and Cassie felt the full weight of his stare as she met his gaze.

"Miss Quinn." His tone was measured. He glanced at Jason. "Mr. Broussard." But before she got a second's relief, he was staring at her again. "I'm glad you made it on time."

The man at the door gestured for them to enter, and with no other option, they both complied. Now that she had a better view, Cassie took in the rest of the space. Even though it was a private room in a high-end cantina, the area was plain. The walls were a dark, forest green. The trim was done in gold, with a few pieces of décor here and there to match—a small oval mirror on one wall and a large, framed landscape on the other. Somewhere in the back of her mind, she recognized it, but her brain didn't care to solve that particular puzzle right then and there.

One door sat on the opposite wall and another one on the wall to her right. Cassie figured they led to the main bar area and the kitchen. Or maybe one was a storage closet. Either way, she only had one reliable exit, and it was the guarded door behind her.

Two other men occupied the room, neither of whom she recognized. Both were bigger than Aguilar, covered in tattoos and sporting long beards. Each wore a suit with the jackets unbuttoned so she could see the gun holsters hanging at their sides. Cassie hadn't expected Aguilar to come unarmed, but the open display of hostility took her aback. Did Aguilar consider her that dangerous?

As if on cue, she felt a cold wind at her back and knew Detective Green's spirit wasn't far away. He seemed to appear when she was stressed or when her fear got the better of her. Was he feeding off of it? Could it make him stronger? His voice had been clearer the last time she heard him speak. That couldn't bode well for her. But what was he up to? It was bad enough she had to deal with the machinations of the man before her, let alone anticipate the plans of those from beyond the grave.

Forcing herself back to the present, Cassie met Aguilar's eyes. "I want to see Adelaide," she demanded. "Where is she?"

Aguilar's lips stretched into a full, genuine grin. "I'm afraid Detective Harris couldn't make it."

Cassie's heart dropped into the pit of her stomach like a ball of ice. They had talked about this—Aguilar's potential betrayal—but she had been holding onto the hope that he'd keep his word. It was bad enough for them to lose the evidence. Cassie thought maybe Aguilar would throw them a bone.

No such luck.

Detective Green's spirit coalesced over the other man's shoulder, though no one else in the room seemed to notice. Was it her eyes deceiving her, or did he look marginally less transparent? When their gaze locked, she saw his mouth turn up into an animalistic grin. Whatever kind of person Green had truly been in life, he had become twisted and warped in death.

Cassie had to work to pull her eyes from Green's visage, once again focusing on Aguilar. "That wasn't the deal," she said, forcing her voice to come out strong. "No Harris, no evidence."

Aguilar tipped his head back and laughed, then gestured to the men surrounding her. "Maybe you haven't noticed, Ms. Quinn, but you're not in a position to negotiate." His smile widened. "In fact, you've become almost as troublesome as your friend. I haven't gotten as far as I have without being cautious. Maybe I should wipe you from the board, as well."

Cassie's heart threatened to beat out of her chest now, and she felt Jason shift next to her, getting ready to throw himself in front of her if it came to that. She had to think fast, to figure out what to say to Aguilar that would stretch this meeting out long enough for Bianchi to storm through the door.

Green's spirit moved closer, sensing Cassie's elevated heartbeat. He seemed to take in a deep breath, and his pale eyes gleamed in the low lighting of the back room. Cassie curled her hands into fists. She needed all her faculties to deal with Aguilar. Green's distractions on top of that were almost too much to bear.

Then something shifted in the back of her mind. A connection she hadn't made before. Everything that had happened to her in the last few months kept coming back to one thing—not Aguilar, but Apex. After visiting her parents in North Carolina, they had found her in New Orleans, Zbirak had mentioned them when he kidnapped her in Chicago, and Detective Green had brought them up when she and the others had confronted him at Laura's house.

"How would Apex feel about that?" Cassie asked.

Seeing the grin wiped from Aguilar's face was worth his ire. His eyes flared, and he took a menacing step forward. "Apex doesn't control me. They don't dictate what I can and can't do. If I decide to kill you, it's my choice."

"Something tells me you don't believe that," Cassie said. Maybe it was all the posturing that looked more like fear than anger. "Apex has been after me for months. Probably longer. They'd be disappointed to learn you took a resource away from them without asking." As Aguilar gritted his teeth in frustration, Cassie pushed forward. "How much of this do you owe to them, anyway? I heard you were a self-made startup, but that's not true, is it?"

Aguilar took two more steps forward and wrapped his hand around Cassie's throat. Jason moved to throw the man off her, but the guard behind them wrapped a meaty arm around his neck and practically hauled Jason off his feet. It took everything in Cassie not to struggle against the fingers digging into the sides of her neck. Standing still, she refused to look away from Aguilar, aware that the two other men in the room had put their hands on their weapons.

"Everything I've ever received, I earned. I pried money and power and influence out of the cold, dead hands of my enemies. I am the King of Savannah because I'm more ruthless and cunning than all my opponents combined. Apex came to *me*," he spat, spraying Cassie's face with angry spittle. "They wanted *me*. It was a business transaction, like all my other dealings."

"Not all of them." Cassie struggled to take in enough air to talk. The Apex angle had gotten a reaction out of him, had prolonged their conversation, but it hadn't given her the upper hand. "Your relationship with Emily was real."

Aguilar stilled, looking deep into Cassie's eyes. The grip around her neck tightened before he shoved her back. "Don't talk about her like you knew her."

"I did know her." Cassie rubbed at her throat. Easier to speak now, but her voice came out raspy. "You know who I am. What I'm capable of." It was a guess, but a solid one. Cassie waited for Aguilar to deny it. He didn't. "She traveled halfway across the country to contact me. Spent every last ounce of energy making sure I knew where she was buried and where she'd hidden the evidence."

Aguilar adjusted the cufflinks on his shirt and nodded at one of the two men standing to Cassie's left. The closest one stepped forward and snatched the hard drive out of her hand, handing it over to Aguilar before stepping back into position.

"And look what good it's done you," Aguilar said, holding up the drive. "Or her, for that matter."

"You couldn't control her, even in death." Cassie had to keep herself from sneering. There was a fine line between forcing the conversation and pissing off Aguilar enough that he pulled the trigger on it completely. "That must've driven you crazy, knowing the evidence was still out there, that Natasha might've known where it was."

"And it turned out she didn't." Aguilar chuckled. "Instead, you got it for me. Really, I should be thanking you."

Cassie ground her teeth together, but before she could come up with a retort, they heard glass shattering from the other room. Both the bearded men marched through the open door to investigate. Cassie had just enough time to see the darkened bar beyond before it disappeared behind the closing door.

But Aguilar wasn't looking in that direction. He was still looking at Cassie. "What did you do?"

"Do?" Cassie stammered. "I don't know what you mean."

"You told someone where we were meeting, didn't you? It wasn't the cops." Aguilar's eyes narrowed. "It was Bianchi, wasn't it?"

"Who?" Cassie forced herself to appear confused, but she wasn't the best liar. "I don't know who that is. We didn't tell anyone."

"It doesn't matter. I got what I came for." There was another crash from the other room, followed by a startled shout and then a roar of anger. Aguilar's grin was sharp, and it cut a line of fear through Cassie's body. "And I even got to put down that detective of yours. She got what she earned—a slow death. Alone and forgotten." He drew himself up to his full height. "It was nice meeting you, Ms. Quinn, but I'm afraid your evening ends here."

Several things happened in quick succession. First, Aguilar looked over at the guard still holding onto Jason and nodded his head. Cassie didn't need to read minds to know it was the signal to kill them both.

Before anyone could make a move, however, the door to the bar burst opened. Nicolas Bianchi rushed in, nose bleeding, eyes wild. Two of his men were on his heels. Aguilar's other guards were nowhere to be seen.

Aguilar cursed and sprang for the other door. Just as soon as he opened it, Bianchi raised his pistol and took aim. The crack of a gunshot made Cassie jump, even though she'd been expecting it. Aguilar cried out and gripped his arm, never letting go of the hard drive in his hand. He dashed down the hallway to the kitchens, Bianchi tailing him.

There was a dull thud, and Cassie turned to see Jason standing over the remaining guard, his boot pressed against the man's neck. Two more shots rang from outside, followed by a primal scream that told Cassie her worst fear had been realized. Aguilar had slipped out of Bianchi's grasp.

A few seconds later, Bianchi came storming back in, his eyes finding his men. "Brown was with him. They have a head start, but we can catch up. Let's go."

"Wait!" Cassie launched herself forward and latched onto Bianchi's arm before she could think better of it. "Don't let anything happen to the hard drive. Please."

Bianchi looked down at her, impatient but not uncaring. "I'm not making any promises I can't keep."

With that, he shook her loose, and left with his men the way they had come in. Cassie turned to face Jason, who still had Aguilar's guard pinned to the floor. Her head was filled with alarm signals and panicked thoughts. The proximity of Detective Green's spirit exhausted her, but she only had one thing on her mind.

She leaned over the man on the floor, who had no choice but to look directly into her face. She might not have been as threatening as Aguilar, but she was this guy's only hope—answer her one question, or go to jail for the rest of his life.

With that, she put as much venom into her words as she could muster.

"Where is Aguilar keeping Detective Adelaide Harris?"

39

CASSIE DIDN'T LIKE TRUSTING BIANCHI TO GO AFTER AGUILAR. NOT ONLY would Bianchi kill the man on sight, but she had no faith he'd recover the hard drive. Even if he did, why would Bianchi hand it over? He was likely in there somewhere, so they'd have a criminal case against him, too.

Harris' wellbeing was more important. The detective would never forgive Cassie if Aguilar slipped away, but they'd both have to live with that. Cassie could hardly think straight, worrying about what Aguilar had done to her and whether it was already too late.

Jason laid a reassuring hand on Cassie's leg. Normally, it would send an army of butterflies bursting throughout her entire being, but tonight, she experienced it as though she were in a deep fog. The sensation was there, but it felt like it belonged to someone else.

Aguilar's man was in the back, laying horizontally on the seat. They had found duct tape and bound his hands and wrists, then wrapped his arms and legs together. He could hardly move, let alone escape, and they'd taped his mouth shut for good measure.

But he wasn't struggling. Either he was leading them into a trap, or he'd given up hope of Aguilar coming back to rescue him. Maybe being abandoned by his boss had given him perspective, and the man realized that if he just gave Cassie and Jason what they wanted, he had a better chance of making it out of this unscathed.

It didn't hurt that they'd promised to let him go the minute they found Harris.

Cassie was still trying to decide if they were going to follow through on that promise as they drove toward the address the man had provided. On the one hand, all he'd done was guard the door while Aguilar talked to them. On the other, he was clearly a trusted member of the operation, and he had probably committed his fair share of crimes while in his boss' employ. At the very least, they could use him as a witness against Aguilar.

No, Cassie wasn't going to let him walk easily.

But it all depended on Harris, and what kind of condition she was in. Cassie couldn't even think the words *whether she was still alive*. There was no other option. She couldn't lose anyone else. As she looked over at Jason, she realized her circle was growing. The chances of losing someone else were getting higher, especially as she continued working with the Savannah PD. And especially if Jason started up his own PI business.

Cassie hadn't been paying attention to where they were until the car stopped. She looked around, noting a slew of typical looking suburban houses. It hadn't taken them long to get here, right outside the city to a middle-class neighborhood. Had Aguilar been conducting his business out here, right under everyone's noses? Or were his neighbors in on it? It seemed unlikely he owned the entire neighborhood, but she wouldn't put it past him to pay off a few people to mind their own business.

Jason pointed to a house halfway down the road. It was white with blue shutters, and a single vehicle sat in the driveway. "That's the one," he said, checking once more against the map on his phone. He twisted to look at the man in the back. "Anyone guarding the house? How many?"

The man thought for a second, then held out two fingers, which was about all he could move in his current condition. After another brief pause, he laid his hand flat and wobbled it side to side, like he wasn't sure that was the case. It wasn't the answer they wanted, but at least he was cooperating.

Jason reached over to the glove box and pulled it open. Inside sat a matte black handgun and its magazine. He grabbed both and loaded the gun, chambering a round, and then checked that the safety was still on. "Any chance I can convince you to stay in the car?" he asked.

Cassie rolled her eyes and popped open her door. "No."

"Didn't think so." Jason turned to the man in the back. "We'll be back soon. Don't try to escape. You won't get far." He held up the man's wallet. "And we know who you are. When we come back with Harris, we return this and let you go. That's the deal."

The man nodded his head, and even gave them a thumbs up for good measure. With one last look, Jason followed Cassie out of the car. It was still light out, but as the sun sunk farther below the horizon, visibility would drop. That could be good for them if they played their cards right.

Jason led Cassie around the block to approach the house from the back. Without knowing what they were getting into, it was better to sneak inside than storm the front. Especially if they only had one weapon between them.

As they got closer, Jason slowed and pointed ahead of him. Cassie peered past his frame and saw a man standing outside in the chilly winter air, smoking a cigarette and watching a video on his phone. Cassie couldn't hear what it was, but it kept his attention. He laughed, and the cigarette smoke blew out around his face.

"Wait here." Jason slid the safety off his gun and slipped forward into the shadows. A line of bushes separated one house from the other. Jason crept along them, and when he got even with the man, he rustled the branches until their target looked up. Cassie could just about make out the confused expression on the man's face as he walked over, probably thinking it was a rabbit or the neighbor's cat.

When he was close enough, Jason launched through the bushes and tackled the man, and they both landed on the ground with a dull thud. Jason struck him once in the temple, and the guard went limp, his phone tumbling from his hand. Jason stomped on the loose cigarette that had fallen from between his fingers, then motioned for Cassie.

Armed with their trusty duct tape, Cassie crept forward, and the pair of them got to work fashioning restraints around the man's arms and legs. Just as he regained consciousness, they slapped tape across his mouth so he couldn't cry out and warn anyone in the house.

Their eyes met, and Cassie stood and stepped back in shock. "I recognize him," she whispered. He wasn't in uniform, but there was no mistaking the crooked set of his nose. "Officer Billings. He worked with David."

Jason cracked a smile. "Let's hope we come out on top here, because I don't want to be arrested for assaulting a police officer."

Cassie didn't respond. It was hard to look at the man, to know he'd been friends with David and working with Aguilar the whole time. What if Billings had been one of the people to betray David? Aguilar was behind all of this, but there were plenty of people responsible for what had happened.

"Come on," Jason said, tugging lightly on Cassie's arm. "We have to keep moving."

Cassie tore her gaze away, and they entered through the back door. The house was empty. The kitchen didn't have any furniture or appliances or decorations. She could see into the living room, which had no couch or chair. No television or picture frames. This wasn't a place where Aguilar and his men met to conduct business. It was a façade to hide whatever dirty deeds he wanted to accomplish.

Murmuring voices sounded from overhead, and there was a creak in the floorboard, like someone shifting around upstairs. It sounded like more than two voices. Not for the first time, Cassie wondered if the man they had stashed in their car had been telling them the truth. But it was too late now. They came here to rescue Harris, and neither one of them would leave without her.

Jason moved first, sliding along the wall and stepping close to it to avoid creaking floorboards. Cassie did her best to follow in his footsteps, taking her time and listening for the sound of anyone coming in from around the corner or down the stairs.

When they got to the bottom of the staircase, they froze as footsteps pounded from overhead, like a heavyset person was pacing up and down in one of the rooms. Cassie wondered who it was and if she'd recognize them, too. At this point, she was becoming numb to the pain of betrayal. All she wanted was to find Harris.

They waited until the footsteps stopped and the person on the second floor presumably settled back into their seat. Jason ascended the stairs one at a time, careful to stick to the outside edges and avoid making noise. Cassie was sweating with the effort, but she hardly noticed.

At the top, they kept to the outside wall again. Now that she was closer, Cassie could tell the murmuring voices came from a television from inside the room across from the staircase. She couldn't make out the program, but she hoped that meant Aguilar's man hadn't been lying about there only being one of them.

She could see the rise and fall of Jason's shoulders as he took a breath to steady himself before making his next move. Just as he took his first step forward, the floor creaked and the man in the other room shifted, calling out to them.

"You bring me a beer?" he asked.

They both froze, neither one knowing whether to push forward or retreat. But the decision was made for them. At the sound of the other man standing up with a groan, Jason whipped around the corner, raising his gun so it pointed straight out in front of him.

"Who the fuck are you?" the man demanded.

"Hands on your head," Jason stated. Then to Cassie, still hiding around the corner, "It's okay, he's not armed."

Cassie stepped into the room and came face to face with the man. "Officer Crawford." She spat out his name. David hadn't liked him very much, and neither did she. "I'm not surprised."

"Quinn." The man sneered, and the set of his shoulders told her he wasn't worried about the fact that Jason had his gun trained on him. "It's too late to rescue the detective. You're not getting out of this one alive either."

"Get on your knees," Jason said, saving Cassie from whatever retort she was about to spit back into the man's face. "Hands behind your head."

"Who the fuck do you think you are, telling me what to do? You have five seconds to—"

Cassie didn't let him finish. Crawford might've been taller and well over a hundred pounds bigger than her, but he was old and didn't move like he used to. She stalked across the room, and before either of the men knew what she was doing, she landed a knee to his groin. As he leaned forward, Cassie used his momentum to send him to the ground. Jason was there in seconds, helping her push Crawford the rest of the way down and pulling his arms behind his back.

"You're going to regret this, Quinn. I'll have the whole department come down on you. I'll—"

Cassie slapped a piece of tape over his mouth, and then sighed dramatically at the sound of silence that ensued. Jason had his knee in the man's back, and each time Crawford struggled, he ratcheted his arms up higher.

Within a few minutes, they had Crawford duct taped to the chair. He was spitting and swearing behind the tape over his mouth, but Cassie wasn't afraid of him. She simply looked down on him in disgust. "How can you call yourself an officer of the law? How could you betray David like that?"

If Crawford had ever felt any guilt over what had happened to David, he didn't show it now. He just kept struggling and swearing and trying to kick his legs, to no avail. Jason tugged on a few spots, but the tape held. The man wasn't going anywhere.

"Let's clear the house."

Cassie's heart hammered in her chest. For a moment, she considered pleading with Crawford to tell them what they'd done to the detective. But there was no guarantee he'd tell her the truth, and he'd be more likely to use the detective's well-being against her. She felt sick to her stomach, wondering what they were about to walk in on.

Following Jason from the room, she spotted two more doors on the second floor. Both were open, and the first room held nothing more than a few empty boxes and some garbage. Jason checked behind the door and inside the closet, but no one was there, and there was no indication that anyone had been held against their will.

The second room was just as empty.

Cassie looked up at Jason, tears in her eyes and words stuck in her throat. He gave her hand a squeeze before leading her back downstairs, clearing the other rooms one at a time. When they came up empty handed, they both stopped in front of the door to the basement. It was the only place left to check, but the mustiness wafting up from its depths didn't bode well. If that's where Harris was being held, they hadn't worried about keeping her alive to trade.

Jason hauled Billings back into the house and tossed him in the living room. He hadn't tried to escape, but then again, where would he go? What would he say? If Cassie called Clementine, the officers who'd come to their rescue wouldn't be buddies of him and Crawford.

When the other man was settled against the wall, Jason pulled open the basement door and began his slow descent, with Cassie right behind him. Before she got to the bottom, she knew Harris was down there. Whether it was female intuition or supernatural instinct, she couldn't say. But the basement blurred as she took in the form of her friend lying on a dirty mattress on the floor.

Harris lay on her stomach, her face tilted to the side. From what Cassie could see of her, bruises formed along her cheek and down her arms. A splatter of blood leaked from her nose. Her hands were tied with rope behind her back and linked to another rope that twisted around her ankles.

Cassie launched herself at the detective, careful not to jostle her as she felt for a pulse. It was there, though it felt thready and uneven. A slight sheen of sweat coated Harris' face and neck, and she felt hot to the touch. Her eyes barely flickered when Cassie pressed a hand to her cheek, but she was alive. For now, at least.

Jason checked the rest of the basement, clearing the remaining part of the house, and then ran upstairs to get Harris some water. Cassie untied the ropes from around her ankles first, releasing the pressure on Harris' shoulders, then removed the ties from her wrists.

Harris groaned in relief, and it was enough for her to open her eyes and gaze up at Cassie.

"Hey," Harris said, her voice barely coming out as a whisper. "What are you doing here?"

"Came to rescue you." Cassie tried to keep her voice steady and confident. "Took down two cops to do it."

"Alone?" Harris asked, managing to push herself onto her back so she could breathe better. "Badass."

"Jason's here." As if on cue, he ran back down the stairs with a bottle of water from the fridge. "But I did all the work."

"Sounds about right." Harris allowed the two of them to sit her up and lean her against the wall. She chugged half the water, and when she talked again, her voice sounded stronger. "Crawford and Billings?"

"Secure," Jason said. "They're not going anywhere."

"Crawford has my phone," she said. "Call Clementine to pick them up. You can trust her."

Jason looked to Cassie and waited for her nod of reassurance before he bounded back upstairs.

When she turned her attention back to Harris, the detective had her eyes closed and her face scrunched in pain. "Are you okay?" Cassie asked. "Did they hurt you?"

"They tried." Harris laughed, then winced. "Think I have a broken rib, but I'll live." Her eyes snapped open, and they were already clearer than they'd been before. "Where's Aguilar?"

"He made us trade the hard drive for you," Cassie said, forcing herself to look Harris in the eye, no matter how difficult it was to tell her the truth. "We figured it was a trap, but we had no other choice."

Harris groaned. "You should've known better."

"We didn't have another option," Cassie snapped. "I know you would've risked your life for that evidence, but I wasn't willing to make that sacrifice."

"So, we lost it?" Harris asked. Her voice was tight with pain. "That's it? The evidence is gone?"

"Not quite." Cassie couldn't help but smirk. Aguilar hadn't given them a lot of time to get over to the cantina for the trade-off, but they'd been able to make one pit-stop along the way. "We've got an ace up our sleeve. Think you can walk? I'll fill you in on the way."

Harris took a deep breath to steady herself, then used Cassie to push up to her feet. "Yeah, I think I can manage." After a little bit of a wobble, she looked at the stairs like it was Mount Everest. "I'm getting too old for this shit."

Cassie laughed. "Now you're starting to sound like David."

40

"YOU PUT A TRACKING DEVICE IN THE HARD DRIVE?" HARRIS ASKED.

"Wasn't that hard," Jason said, glancing over his shoulder at Harris in the backseat.

Lying down on her back, one arm slung over her eyes, Cassie thought she still looked pale and sweaty. They hadn't talked about what Crawford and Billings had done to her, and Cassie didn't want to press.

"Had everything I needed at home. Only took a couple minutes."

"That was a risk." Harris was trying to be reproachful, but she didn't have the energy. "What if they'd found it?"

"We didn't have a ton of options," Cassie added. "You were my priority. But I knew you wouldn't be happy if we lost it." She looked down at her phone, where she'd been watching the dot move on the screen. "Turn here," she told Jason. "Stay on this road for a mile."

They were outside the city proper now. Jason had tossed Aguilar's man from the backseat into the house with Crawford and Billings. Cassie didn't feel guilty for going back on her word and not releasing him. Jason had laid the man's wallet on the kitchen counter for Clementine.

For a while, they had been traveling south, following Aguilar's path, and Cassie worried he would jump on a boat and head out into the open ocean. She'd envisioned them commandeering some poor family's yacht and accidentally crashing it, allowing Aguilar to get away for a second time. Harris would never let her live that down.

Luckily, the little dot on her phone had turned inland, heading west. As she watched, it came to a sudden stop. She waited for it to move, but when it stayed in place for another minute, she looked over at Jason. "I think they got to wherever they're going."

"What's out here?" Harris said from the back seat. "It's been nothing but trees for miles."

Cassie zoomed in on the map. "Not much. Some houses. A few churches. More trees." She sucked in a breath. "And a private airstrip."

Jason tightened his hands on the wheel. "Where?"

"Turn right," she said, almost missing the road. Jason slammed on the brakes and spun the wheel. Harris groaned from the backseat. "Follow this road until the end, then turn right again."

"And it's still here?" he asked. "Hasn't moved at all?"

Cassie had been keeping her eyes peeled for any planes taking off, though it was nearly impossible in the dark. When she looked back down at her phone, she couldn't find the dot they'd been following. She zoomed out, hoping she had accidentally moved the map too far in one direction, but it had vanished. "It's not there anymore."

"What do you mean it's not there?" Harris asked, her voice sounding weak but annoyed. "How could it disappear?"

"Maybe they found the chip," Jason said. "Or put it in a Faraday cage until they could look at it more closely."

Cassie stuck her phone in her pocket. It was no use to them now. "Here," she said, pointing out an old paved road leading to the airstrip. "We can't let them take off."

"On it." Jason floored the gas pedal.

As the engine revved and they launched forward, Cassie kept her eyes on the sky. They had a fighting chance if they could get to Aguilar before he took off, but once he was in the air, they'd lose him in a heartbeat. He could go anywhere, land at any other airstrip, and hop on a new plane before they had a chance to track him. From there, he could disappear to Canada or Mexico within a matter of hours. He might lose his throne in Savannah, but he'd already proven to have enough resources to settle into one of his other territories or build a new one from the ground up.

No, Cassie thought, it was now or never. This was their only shot.

The airstrip was nothing more than a large hangar in the middle of a field surrounded by trees. The paved road turned into a dirt path opening into a rudimentary parking lot. There were two cars there, and one matched what Aguilar had escaped in after they saw him at the cantina. If there was any doubt in Cassie's mind that they were hot on his heels, there wasn't anymore. The other one most likely belonged to Bianchi, and Cassie wondered how he'd fared going up against Aguilar.

Jason blocked Aguilar's vehicle by parking behind it, but it wouldn't stop them, just slow them down. Cassie turned in her seat to look at Harris, who was sitting up and had pushed the loose hair around her face back into her ponytail. She was breathing heavily from the exertion.

When Cassie opened her mouth to speak, Harris glared at her. "If you're about to tell me to stay in the car, you can shove it right back up your—"

"Adelaide," Cassie said calmly, having expected this reaction. "You're not doing well. Are you going to be able to stand? Run? Fight? What if someone attacks us?"

"Then you can protect me for once," she said, resolutely. "I'm coming."

Cassie wondered what Harris would do if she found a way to hand-cuff her to the seat but thought better of it. If the detective thought she could hold her own, Cassie wasn't going to argue. Even if she wasn't much good in a fight, they would need all the help they could get. Maybe if Aguilar saw he was outnumbered, he'd give up right then and there.

Yeah, right. Their luck so far made Cassie think that wasn't in the cards for them.

A loud rumbling shook her from her thoughts, and a small plane pulled out into the open. Before her brain caught up and talked her out of it, Cassie threw her door open and rushed forward. She hadn't made it more than a dozen steps before the plane halted. It was still running, but they were waiting for their passengers to board.

With Jason and Harris behind her now, the three of them flattened themselves against the wall of the hangar, and Cassie prayed she hadn't been seen. Turning to the others, she had to yell to be heard over the engine of the plane. "We need to find Aguilar."

"And the evidence," Harris said. Leaning against the wall to remain upright, it looked like the fresh air had wiped some of the sweat from her brow. "If they destroyed it—"

"They'll want to know what's on it," Jason said. "They might not believe we didn't make copies. Maybe even keep the original to alter, make it harder to prove which is the real one."

A voice from behind Cassie made her jump. "That's not a bad idea, really."

Spinning around, Cassie came face to face with Francisco Aguilar himself, holding a gun aimed at her chest. From this range, there was no way she'd be able to escape that bullet.

"It's good to see all three of you together." He leaned a little to the side to get a better look at Harris. "Detective, how are you feeling?"

"Never better," Harris said. Though her voice was still weak, it was tinged with anger. "This is the end of the line for you, Aguilar. It's over."

"I don't think so." He stepped to the side, swinging his gun at Harris now. He looked at Cassie and Jason with a wide smile. "I want nothing more than to kill the good detective here, but it's bad for business. If I let any of you go in my attempt to escape, I'll be constantly looking over my shoulder. I can't have that. If I kill you here, they'll find your bodies and trace it back to me." He pretended to think for a moment. "No, I think the best solution is for you to come with me."

Cassie froze. Getting on that plane was a death sentence. She had to keep him talking. "What? Why?"

Instead of answering right away, Aguilar looked past them and nodded. Cassie turned to see a tall, thin Black man step out of Aguilar's car. Holding a gun in one hand, he aimed it straight at Cassie. She could feel Jason tense beside her.

"Please meet my associate, Jasper Brown." After a moment's pause, he continued in a lazy voice. "Here's how I see it. You get on the plane with me, I let you live. I'll drop you off in the middle of the Colorado wilderness. Give you a fighting chance. You'll die within a day or so from exposure, but at least my conscience will be clear."

Harris attempted to laugh, but it came out more like a strangled cough. "You don't have a conscience."

Aguilar shrugged, unbothered. "Either way, it's the end you deserve. The alternative is to kill you now." He raised the gun to point directly at Harris' forehead. "You decide."

41

If Cassie had any doubt about how much money Aguilar had, then his private plane confirmed otherwise. The seats were cream with gold accents, and each headrest was monogrammed with his initials. There were only eight seats in the main compartment, but through a velvet curtain, she could see four more in the private room. No part of her desired to know what he did back there.

Aguilar led the way down the aisle, pointing Cassie and Jason to seats on the left and guiding Harris to one on the right. Jasper was behind them, watching their every move. When they were all settled and Aguilar gave his man the go-ahead, Jasper stepped into the cockpit to talk to the captain. Cassie wondered if the man flying the plane was one of Aguilar's, or if he was just doing his job.

Aguilar looked down at them. "Comfortable? Does anyone want any water? Complimentary snacks?"

Cassie fumed. It was a strange juxtaposition to be surrounded by opulence while Aguilar held them at gunpoint. These were the most comfortable seats she had ever sat on in a plane, and that was to say nothing about the extra leg room. Strange what your mind notices when all your senses are heightened.

But what really stole her attention was Harris' weakening form. She looked gray, and where she'd been sweating before, now her lips were cracked as though she'd expunged all the moisture from her body. Whatever had happened to her in that basement was more than just a cracked rib and a bruised face.

The last thing Cassie wanted to do was beg anything from Aguilar, but if she didn't get Harris to a hospital soon, the detective wouldn't even survive the flight. "Please," Cassie asked, "can I sit with her? She's not going to make it."

"Not my problem." Aguilar glanced down at Harris and curled his lip back in disgust. "I'm surprised she survived this long."

Something clicked. "What did you do to her?"

"Me? Nothing." He laughed. "Crawford, on the other hand, slipped a little something into her bloodstream. I don't ask questions. I just expect results."

Cassie stood and walked across the aisle. Every muscle in her body was poised to hit Aguilar, but she restrained herself. Even when he raised the gun in her direction, she didn't flinch. "You're not going to shoot us." Sitting down next to Harris, she pushed some of the woman's flyaway hair out of her face. "Even you're not that stupid."

"You have no idea what I'm capable of." Aguilar waved the gun. "A shot aimed in the right direction at the right angle? I could kill all three of you and still make it to Cabo by dinnertime."

"So that's your play?" Cassie asked, feeling Harris' pulse. It was weaker than before. "Mexico?"

"For now." Aguilar leaned back against the wall, relaxed. All three of them were still in his sights. "And then anywhere I want. I have a lot of friends in a lot of places."

"But you'll never be able to come back to Savannah."

He shrugged. "We'll see. People forget. They move on. They stop caring. Money solves a lot of problems."

The plane lurched as it started moving forward, and Cassie had to make sure Harris didn't slip out of her seat. She wanted to put on her seatbelt, but if there was any opening to get the upper hand against Aguilar, she needed to be able to take it.

The engine roared as the plane sped up, and Cassie felt the moment they left the ground and lifted into the air. Whatever hope she'd had vanished, swept away in the wind. If they did manage to take Aguilar down, Jasper and the pilot made sure the numbers were even. As far as she knew, no one else knew how to fly the plane. Even if they overwhelmed Aguilar and Jasper, they'd be at the mercy of the captain.

As soon as the plane leveled out, Jasper returned to the main cabin. There was no weapon in view, but the way he stood with his hands folded in front of him made Cassie think he was more dangerous than he looked. Cassie was scrappy, but she wasn't trained like Harris or Jason.

But she did have one talent no one else did.

Clearing her throat, she made sure Aguilar was looking her in the eye before she spoke. "Emily would be so disappointed in you."

The moment the words registered, Aguilar's eyes hardened. "Shut up."

"She's been inside my head," Cassie taunted. "And I've been inside hers. Did you know that at the end of her life, all she could think about was the ocean and her sister? Well," Cassie said, pretending to be thoughtful, "that and her excruciating death."

"I had nothing to do with that."

"You had everything to do with that." Cassie had trouble keeping the anger out of her voice now. "Just like David. Maybe you didn't pull the trigger, but you're the reason they're dead." She tried to even out her voice. "Look, I get it. David was a cop. He was a mole. You couldn't trust him. But Emily? Everything I've heard—everything I've seen—tells me that you loved her. Trusted her."

"That's why she needed to die!" Aguilar stepped forward, and Cassie couldn't help but flatten herself against her seat. "She betrayed me." Taking a moment to calm his voice, the emotion left his eyes. "I didn't have another option. That's what happens when people cross me."

"I know you regret that decision." Cassie forced her heart rate to calm down. "Even Zbirak did."

Aguilar laughed. "Zbirak was a machine. He regretted nothing."

"He regretted killing Emily." Cassie thought back to her vision of him carrying the woman's body. "That's why he prayed over her. He didn't want her to die. Didn't think she deserved it, even though she'd betrayed you."

Aguilar was silent for a moment, watching her. She got the impression he was trying to read her mind, trying to figure out what went on inside her head. "They say you're a psychic."

"I've always preferred the term medium," she said, "but if the shoe fits—"

"Prove it."

She couldn't help but laugh. "Zbirak asked me to do that, too."

Aguilar shifted the gun to Jason. "Did he have a gun to your friend's head?"

Cassie refused to let her panic show. "Actually, he had a knife in someone else's chest. In terms of intimidation, I think he's got you beat."

"Considering I'm the one left standing," Aguilar sneered, "I think I win this one." He reset his face to something more neutral. "Let's make this trip a little more interesting, shall we? I'll give you two minutes to prove to me you're psychic, or I'll throw one of your friends out the door. We're far enough away at this point that no one will be able to trace it back to me."

Jasper stalked forward and hauled Jason to his feet, leading him over to the door of the plane. Cassie shot to her feet, but Aguilar swung the gun around to point at Harris. The instructions were clear.

The same feeling of pressure she'd gotten with Zbirak hovering over her came back in full force. Only this time, two of the closest people in her life were in danger. She wracked her brain for anything she knew about Aguilar, anything she could latch onto. But Emily hadn't thought of him much at the end of her life. She'd been in too much pain to think clearly, and when she did, she chose to focus on the good parts. She hadn't stuck around to haunt Aguilar. Instead, she'd found Cassie to help take him down. Even in death, she was trying to help.

Unlike someone else she knew.

Cassie let out a small gasp. She hadn't seen him since their first meeting with Aguilar, but she knew Detective Green was never far away. He'd chosen to haunt her, either out of anger or regret, she wasn't sure. At every turn, he'd tried to drain her energy, to feed off it. It was like the man from Texas at the Hotel Cecil. Thinking of him reminded her of the young woman who'd helped her. Who'd shown her another way to use her powers.

Cassie looked up at Aguilar, still running through the possibilities, still searching for another way. It might be too risky, but she didn't have a ton of options. "What was the deal with Detective Green?"

The question must've taken Aguilar by surprise. "What?"

"Detective Green. You were both involved with Apex. What did he want?"

"What all people who deal with Apex want. More power."

"And that's why he was working with you?" Cassie asked.

Aguilar's eyes flicked to Jasper and Jason behind her. "He was a means to an end."

Cassie had learned early on that Aguilar didn't like loose ends. "And after the evidence was recovered, what was going to happen to him?" Cassie could feel Green's presence beside her. "A promotion?"

Aguilar snorted. "I doubt it. He was an upstart. Good looking, easy to parade in front of the cameras. But he'd never done anything notable in his life. At least nothing that wasn't handed to him on a silver platter." Aguilar's eyes narrowed. "If this is your way of proving you're anything but a hack, you're not doing a very good job of it."

Aguilar's words about Green had their intended effect. Cassie felt her anger rise, knowing that it was Green's effect on her. Instead of fighting it, she let it grow, nurturing the flame until it flushed her entire body.

"He's here with us now," Cassie told Aguilar. "I can feel him. He's not happy."

Aguilar laughed but didn't break eye contact. "You expect me to believe that?"

"Believe what you want." Her breath was shallower than it had been a few seconds ago. As the heat rose, her energy drained. Letting him feed off her, with every passing second, he grew stronger. "But I don't think he liked what you said about him."

"He can go to hell. Or wait." Aguilar grinned. "Is he already there?"

The anger flared, and Cassie could read the message in it. "You sent him there. It was your fault." As Cassie sagged in her chair, she saw

Harris stir. Their eyes met, and the detective's were brighter than she'd expected. Harris' hand fell to her side, and for a second, Cassie thought she was going to reach out to her. "He didn't want to die," Cassie continued. "But he had no choice. You did that."

"He did that to himself." Aguilar threw up his hands, taking his pistol off them for a split second. "He put the gun to his head and pulled the trigger. I just wasn't sorry when it happened."

Another flare of anger, and this time, Cassie pushed into it, feeding Green as much as she could handle. He was there now, next to her—his face a mask of fury, his hands balled up into fists. Unsure how much she could handle without losing herself to him, she was so close to accomplishing what she'd set out to do, she couldn't stop now.

"His death meant nothing to you." Cassie slumped further, losing feeling in her hands and feet. Green's shape was solid along the edges, brighter than she'd ever seen him. "He was just a pawn in your game."

"Yes." Aguilar's voice held no regret. "Haven't you been paying attention?"

A sound like a distant roar echoed around the cabin as the overhead lights flickered. Green charged forward, and Cassie saw the moment Aguilar saw the spirit. The King of Savannah's mouth dropped open in a silent scream, and he took a step back, the gun held limply at his sides and his focus no longer on the living.

Harris had been waiting for that exact moment. With the final bit of her energy, she pushed off her chair and dove at Aguilar. Cassie saw her raise a syringe before driving it into Aguilar's neck, pressing the plunger down until all the liquid was gone. Aguilar roared in anger and surprise, the gun knocked from his hand. The pair of them landed on the floor in a heap, and Aguilar pushed the detective off, yanking the syringe from his neck.

He stared down at it, first in confusion and then in terror. "What did you do?" he shouted, aiming a kick into Harris' stomach. "What the fuck did you do?"

"Same thing you did to me," Harris coughed out. "Only with a concentrated dose. Crawford wanted me to die slowly. I want to make sure you don't have a chance." Coughing again, her eyes were deadly sharp. "For David."

Aguilar growled, but Cassie could see the sheer panic in his eyes. He looked up at Jasper, and she took the time to find the gun on the floor. In a few seconds, he would get desperate, and she needed to be ready.

Closing her eyes, Cassie felt for Green, who silently howled in anguish. She reached out to him with her powers, gathering back every ounce of strength he had taken from her. Taking his pain, his anger, his desperation, she swallowed it down, letting it gather in her chest until the numbness fled from her hands and feet. Her legs felt steady under her, and her head cleared, just in time to see Green fade away.

Aguilar noticed the moment she came back to herself and looked for his gun. But Cassie was quick, and whatever Harris had injected him with was working fast. He stumbled sideways, and that was all the opening she needed. Rushing forward, Cassie brought a knee to his groin. When he doubled over, she held his head in place as she brought her leg up a second time, feeling the satisfying crunch of his nose. He fell forward, disoriented, and she moved out of the way, allowing him to crash to the floor.

There was the sound of struggling behind her, and Cassie picked up the gun, facing Jasper and Jason. But Jason didn't need any of her help. He had Jasper in a headlock, and after a few seconds, the man went limp. Jason laid him on the floor, then brought his arms up behind his back and placed his knee there to hold him. When he looked up at her, he gave her a curt nod.

Cassie leaned over Harris, checking her pulse again. "Are you okay? What was that?"

"Not sure." Harris tried to push herself up into a sitting position but fell back to the floor. "Good moves back there. You're getting better at this."

"We need to get you to the hospital," Cassie said, then looked at Aguilar. "And him too, if he makes it."

"Evidence?" Harris coughed out.

Cassie looked up and around, then spotted the velvet curtain Aguilar had been standing in front of. When she pushed it aside, she was surprised to see an unconscious Nicolas Bianchi strapped to one of the seats. Rushing forward, she felt his pulse and was relieved he was still alive. Looking around, she spotted a large safe that had been sealed shut. "Ten bucks it's in there," Cassie called out. "But we'll need someone to crack it open for us. I don't think Aguilar is going to give us the code willingly."

Harris made a noncommittal noise that sounded weaker than it had before. It was time to turn the plane around. She only hoped the captain didn't give her any trouble.

Stalking down the aisle, Cassie opened the door to the cockpit, leaning forward and letting the man sitting at the controls see the gun in her hand. His eyes widened, and when he looked up at her, she could tell he was in no mood to give her any trouble.

"There's been a change in schedule," she said. "Six tickets to Savannah, please. One way."

42

SAVANNAH HAD ALWAYS HELD PAINFUL MEMORIES FOR CASSIE, FROM HER attack to her recovery to the years of isolation afterward. Dozens of ghosts had moved through her house, some choosing to stay longer than others. She'd tried her best to make it her sanctuary, a place she could truly be any version of herself she wanted. But the horrors of the outside world had often followed her home.

Now, nearly a week after everything that had happened on that plane, home was exactly where she wanted to be. Going to New Orleans, then Chicago, and finally Los Angeles had drained her of all her energy. The run-in with Detective Green's spirit didn't help, though he appeared to be gone for good. Those first few days back, she'd slept till noon and gone to bed by nine every night. She'd never felt so well-rested.

Apollo and Bear followed her around the house like she might disappear at any second. Bear would lie at her feet, no matter which room she was in, while Apollo would watch her from a distance, feet tucked under him and purring softly just at the sight of her. Now, the cat was curled on her lap, while the dog rested with his nose pressed against her ankle.

Next to her was Jason, his arm slung around her shoulders and his head resting on top of hers. They hadn't seen much of each other over the past few days between hospital visits, work, and setting up the new PI business. Jason had been meeting with old friends and colleagues all week, while Cassie had been putting her life back together.

Jason had walked into work the day after they got home and quit on the spot. What had happened in California had changed him, and Cassie was happy to have witnessed it. She could tell he was still worried about stepping back into that world, but the draw of helping people outweighed any of the bad he would see. He was good at this, and the world was going to be a better place with him back on the streets, doing what the police couldn't—or wouldn't—do.

Her own work situation was an anvil hanging over her head. She had called Jane Livingston, the collections manager at the museum, and George Schafer, the curator, to talk to them about her future at the SCAD Museum of Art. After listening to her story—from David's death to her partnership with Detective Harris while they looked for answers, and even a slimmed down version of her travels across the country—they had given her a few extra days to get herself back on her feet. After that, they'd requested she come into work for a formal meeting. It was as bad as a partner saying they needed to have a talk about your future together. Cassie wondered what would happen if she just didn't show up.

"You're worrying again," Jason said, looking down at the scrunch of her face. "Work?"

Cassie grimaced. "Just going over disaster scenarios in my head."

"So, the usual." He grinned, and then curled her into his side. "What's the worst that could happen?"

That was easy. "They fire me."

"So, you get a new job. You have a degree, you have work experience, you're talented and a hard worker. Jane and George would give you a recommendation, even if you had to part ways. They don't hate you."

"I know." Cassie shifted in her seat, and Apollo opened his eyes to stare up at her. "I love my job. But I just don't know how viable it is for me to stay there and still help you and Adelaide."

Jason kissed the top of her head. "We'll figure it out."

Cassie's heart fluttered. It'd been a long time since she was in a relationship, and even longer since she'd been in a stable one. Used to doing everything by herself, it was a habit she wouldn't be able to break easily, but it felt good knowing that Jason supported whatever came next. She wished David was around to get to know him. Cassie could just imagine her and Jason going over to David and Lisa's house, laughing together over a homecooked meal. That image in her head felt right, even if it would never be real.

She'd gone to see Lisa a few times over the last week. Slowly, and with tears running down both their faces, Cassie had explained everything she'd learned about David—the good and the bad. Lisa hadn't seemed surprised, and at the end of the story, she'd thanked Cassie for figuring out what had happened to him. It didn't make the hurt go away, but the wound could start closing.

"Hey, it's on," Jason said, bringing Cassie out of her thoughts. Grabbing the remote for the television, he turned the volume up. "What do you think they'll say?"

"Hopefully something close to the truth."

Cassie turned to the screen in time to see them pan over to a reporter sitting behind a large desk. Her smile was polite, and her blonde curls cascaded perfectly around her shoulders. An argyle sweater made her look sharp and sophisticated. Cassie knew all too well how capable she was, after she had reported on Harris' past investigations, which had been anything but helpful.

"Annette Campbell, evening news." The woman nodded once, preparing herself for what came next. "Over the last few days, Savannah has been rocked by a series of events that has turned the city on its head. Francisco Aguilar, long suspected to be more than just a savvy businessman, has been tied to several high-profile crimes, including the deaths of multiple police officers. Although Aguilar himself will not face any criminal charges due to his death at the hands of Detective Adelaide Harris, who bravely defended the other victims aboard the private plane he had boarded to escape authorities, the last twenty-four hours have proven fruitful for the criminal justice system. With more than thirty of Aguilar's associates arrested and detained, including his right-hand man Jasper Brown, thanks to key evidence and several eyewitnesses, some say the city feels a little safer at night."

"Here we go," Cassie whispered as she clocked the woman's change in tone. Harris had told them to tune into the broadcast tonight, but she hadn't said why. The detective had been keeping them up to date on the investigation, both from her hospital room as she recovered from the poison Crawford had administered, and once she'd been sent home to rest. Most people knew what had happened following Aguilar's death, but for the first time, the Savannah Police Department would comment on the events.

"Others, however, feel as though Savannah has been left to flounder," the reporter continued. Her voice was sharp, but it was with disappointment more than animosity. "On the eve of Nicolas Bianchi and other persons of interest having escaped custody, Savannah's Chief of Police, Sandra Clementine, fired more than half her staff in response to additional evidence of widespread corruption within the police department. Additionally, a dozen officers have been arrested alongside Aguilar's associates, and an internal affairs investigation has been launched to clear the men and women who remain on staff. For her part in bringing down Francisco Aguilar's criminal empire and uncovering the corruption within her department, Adelaide Harris has been promoted to Assistant Chief of Police, effective immediately."

Cassie sat up a little straighter, jostling Apollo and causing him to meow in surprise. Bear lifted his head to watch them both closely. "What? She didn't mention a promotion."

"To be fair, she has been busy the last few days," Jason replied.

"We go live now to the Chief of Police," the reporter continued.

The camera switched to the front of the police station. A crowd of reporters gathered close to a podium, which held at least half a dozen microphones. Clementine stood at the podium, Detective Harris behind her. Adelaide still wore a few of the bruises Crawford and Billings had given her, and she used a cane to relieve some of the pressure of standing, but she looked stronger than she had in days. Cassie couldn't help but smile at the sight of her.

"I'll make this short," Clementine said, her voice commanding everyone's attention. "What happened here, under my watch, is an atrocity. I'm ashamed to say that I trusted in those who did not deserve it. But we will see justice, and moving forward, there will be no room for mistakes. This will be a new era for the Savannah PD. I promise to work tirelessly to ensure we protect and serve the people of this city and earn back the faith you have put in us."

"You're not resigning?" someone shouted from the crowd.

"No." Clementine seemed to look at every single person individually before she moved on. "I have spoken to the mayor, who has given me and my team clearly defined goals. I have one year to remake the police department and take measures to assure this never happens again. After one year, if I have failed to do my job, I will step down. Until then, I'll be putting in the work. We all will. Thank you."

Though there was a clamor from the reporters gathered around her, Clementine turned and walked side-by-side with Harris back into the police building, letting the door shut behind them.

Cassie let out a breath she didn't realize she was holding. "Well," she said. "Harris has her work cut out for her. She'll be doing more administrative work now, less investigating."

"Good thing there's a new investigator on the streets then," Jason said, winking. Cassie tipped her head back and laughed. His excitement for the future was contagious, and for a moment, she stopped worrying about what came next.

43

CASSIE TOOK A DEEP BREATH BEFORE KNOCKING ON GEORGE SCHAFER'S door. She had barely slept the night before, worrying about what she would do if they fired her. It would hurt—she'd never been fired from a job before—but the idea of starting over was freeing. She wasn't the same person she was when she'd started, and part of her wanted to know what else was out there.

The door muffled George's voice when he answered. "Come in."

Squaring her shoulders, Cassie pulled the door open and stepped inside, letting it swing closed behind her. She opened her mouth to greet everyone, noticing there was one more body in the room than expected. George sat behind his desk, and a chair had been pulled off to the side, occupied by Jane Livingston. An empty chair sat opposite them on the other side of the desk, but the seat to the left held a third person.

"Adelaide?" Cassie asked, blinking a few times to make sure she wasn't hallucinating. "What are you doing here?"

Harris turned in her chair, giving Cassie a bright smile. "Hope you don't mind, but I decided to crash your meeting."

Cassie's gaze flickered first to Jane's face, which was unreadable, and then to George's, which seemed to be somewhat amused. "Oh?" she said, taking the chair next to her. "Why's that?"

"Apparently, you have quite an advocate in the Assistant Chief of Police." George leaned back in his chair and folded his hands over his stomach. "I don't know whether to be impressed or intimidated."

"Hopefully the former," Harris said, turning her award-winning smile on him. "It was just a suggestion. It's up to Cassie, after all."

"Up to me?" Cassie asked, looking from one face to the next. "What do you mean?"

George and Jane exchanged a glance before Jane leaned forward, crossing her legs at the ankles. "First of all, we both wanted to say how very sorry we are to hear about Detective Klein's passing. Both Mr. Broussard and Detective Harris have given us some further context, including how close you were to him and his wife. The museum would love to donate money to a charity of your choice, in his name."

"Oh." Cassie felt tears prick her eyes. She had expected to be reprimanded. "Thank you. Of course. I can ask Lisa if there's one she would prefer."

"Good." Jane made a note in her phone before looking back up at her. "Please, have a seat."

Cassie took her spot in the empty chair, still feeling some trepidation at Harris' surprise visit.

"Now, having spent time with you over the last few years, I've come to know your work ethic." Though Jane's voice was unreadable, Cassie couldn't help but feel like the other shoe was about to drop. "You're a talented, dedicated worker who has always gone above and beyond. The last few weeks, however, you haven't seemed like yourself."

"I'm so sorry," Cassie said, leaning forward, hoping they both saw how much she regretted that. "I should've—"

Jane held up a hand, cutting her off. "Detective Harris here has told us that you've been working two jobs. During the day you're at the museum, and in your free time, you're at the police station as a consultant."

"Well, I'm not technically a consultant," Cassie said, clearing her throat. "But yes, that's correct."

"Would you like to be?" Harris asked.

Cassie turned to her, blinking in confusion. "Like to be what?"

"A consultant." Harris couldn't contain her excitement. "I've spoken with Chief Clementine. We're severely understaffed. We're hiring some temporary replacements until we can find officers willing to take permanent positions. Regardless, your *skills*"—emphasizing it in a way that made Cassie squirm in her chair—"are invaluable to us. We've appreciated your voluntary service in the past, but we'd like to bring you on board in a more official capacity."

"Official?" Cassie asked. She was having trouble keeping up.

"We'd like to pay you for your work," Harris clarified.

Cassie turned to George and Jane. "But the museum?"

"It's up to you," George said, "but we would be willing to cut back your hours to a part-time position with a flexible schedule so you have more time consulting with the police department."

"It'll take a few adjustments," Jane said, "and we'll need to hire someone else to pick up some of your work, but I've wanted to establish a wider outreach program with some of the SCAD students for a while now. We don't have any in our department, and this would be an excellent way for them to gain some experience. What do you say?"

Cassie turned to Harris. "You'd want me to consult? With you?"

"I'm stuck behind a desk for now," Harris said, raising her cane for everyone to see, "but yes. We'd love to have you."

"And Clementine is on board?" Cassie asked, hoping Harris could read between the lines.

"She took some convincing, but she trusts me." Harris' smile widened. "And I trust you."

George stood and held out his hand. "Well, Ms. Quinn. Do we have a deal?"

Cassie thought back on anxious days and sleepless nights, trying to balance both sides of her life. It wasn't easy keeping her secret from her friends and colleagues, but sometimes it was the best way to protect herself. Except now, she could embrace both sides of that life. Harris and Jason—and now Chief Clementine—accepted her for who she was, and she could follow her passions at the museum without giving up her calling to help the living and the dead with her two closest friends. If that wasn't a win-win, she didn't know what was.

Standing and placing her hand in George's, she couldn't hold back the excitement in her voice. "Yes," she said. "We have a deal."

44

That night, Cassie helped Jason set up his office in downtown Savannah. He'd found a good deal on a tiny space that needed some serious TLC, but between the two of them, they gave it a new coat of paint and patched some holes in the wall. The electric wiring was old and needed replacing, but Jason wasn't hopeful it'd be done to his standards any time soon.

Cassie had also helped him haul furniture up two flights of stairs and rearrange the room at least half a dozen times before he'd been satisfied. First impressions were important, and the room needed to be as professional as it was comfortable.

While the location of the building was ideal—just off the main stretch downtown—they would have to work hard on advertising if they wanted anyone to know they were there. The rest of the building was a hodge-podge of apartments and small businesses, and Cassie was more than a little curious to find out who their neighbors were.

But there would be plenty of time for that. For now, their biggest worry was whether there were enough outlets for all their equipment, and if they would blow any circuits after they plugged everything in.

As the sinking sun drenched the room in a golden glow, Jason stood back and surveyed their progress. Cassie watched him from the comfort of the loveseat they had somehow wrestled into the center of the room. Calm fell over her.

"A lot of this will need to be replaced eventually, but I'll worry about that when we start making some money," Jason said. Then he caught sight of her staring. "What?"

"You're going to be great. You're gonna help a lot of people." Cassie had never seen him so excited. "This looks good on you."

"You're not looking so bad yourself," he said, stalking over to the couch and pulling her legs onto his lap. "Any regrets?"

"About this?" she said. "None."

"About us?" Jason asked in a playful tone.

"None," she said.

They'd spent every day of the last week together, working on getting the business up and running and spending time at her house with Apollo and Bear. The three of them had bonded while Cassie was in Chicago, and whenever they were all in the same room, Cassie couldn't help feeling like a little family. She was so happy, her chest hurt, and even though that scared the shit out of her, she knew there was nothing she wouldn't do to keep chasing that feeling.

If Jason had any clue what she was thinking, he didn't show it. "What about work?" he asked. "Any regrets going part-time at the museum?"

"I think it'll be a good fit for me," she said. "I think if I didn't have a chance to work with art, I'd be unhappy. And this way, I can still help people. It'll be a better balance."

"But?" he prompted.

"Well, there's Magdalena."

"You told me yourself she was happy for you. For us both."

"She was absolutely *delighted* to rub all of this in my face." Cassie took on the older woman's mocking tone. "*I told you from the beginning you two were meant for each other, and now look at you!*" Cassie shook her head. "She says she has some pictures for us to hang on the wall here. Stuff she photographed when she was in college. Said it would fit our *vibe*."

"So, Magdalena doesn't hate you for leaving," Jason said, steering them back to the topic at hand. "What else?"

"Jane and George are really going out on a limb for me, trying to make this work." Cassie shrugged. "And Harris and Clementine are doing their best to accommodate me, too. It feels nice. But it's a lot to take in."

"Are you that surprised that people care about you?" Jason asked, poking her in the side. "That they'd go out of their way to help you after all the hard work you've put in for them?"

Cassie rolled her eyes. "What about you? How are you feeling about all of this?"

"Nervous," he answered right away. Then, after a pause, "but happy. Excited." He turned that goofy grin of his on her again. "Excited to be doing it with you."

"Me too."

His face fell, and for a second, she was worried he regretted what he'd said. "Is this place haunted? Do you see anything?"

Cassie couldn't help the laugh that escaped her mouth. "There are a few spirits hanging around," she said, "but I'd be more surprised if there weren't. Especially in a building this old."

"Anything evil?" he asked, and he sounded deadly serious now. "Poltergeist-y? Say the word now. I've got twenty-four hours to terminate my lease on this place."

"Nothing evil," she assured him. "And no poltergeists. For now."

Jason looked dubious, but before he could say anything else, there was a sharp knock at the door and Harris pushed her way inside, carrying a large paper bag in one hand and a pizza box in the other. She stopped dead in her tracks when she caught sight of them cuddling on the couch.

Then she plastered a fake smile on her face as she looked them over. "Aw, don't you look cute."

Cassie didn't take it personally. Laura had called her the night before, and the two sisters had a long-overdue heart-to-heart. Cassie shared her support for Laura dating whomever she wanted, as long as the relationship was healthy. Laura was grateful but didn't say much, claiming she was still trying to figure it out and didn't want to put a label on anything.

Cassie had asked about Laura and Harris' relationship—whether they would keep talking or try to do the long-distance thing—and Laura had broken down into tears. Harris had talked to her earlier in the day and had been honest about everything, including the feelings she had for

Laura and the amount of work she would be putting into her job now that she'd been offered a new role. They both wanted to remain friends, but Cassie could hear the heartbreak in Laura's voice. And she could see it on Harris' face too.

Cassie extricated herself from Jason's embrace with the excuse of finding a place for the pizza and drinks Harris had brought as part of their grand opening. The detective looked grateful for the help.

"Someone needs to fix the elevator," Harris said, holding up her cane. "The lack of accessibility is atrocious."

"I've already put in a work order." Jason held up his hands in surrender. "But I'm sure it'll go faster if the *Assistant Chief of Police* gives the building supervisor a call."

Cassie jumped at the change of subject. "How's it going?" she asked. "Still liking it?"

"*Like* is a strong word." Harris leaned up against a table and looked out the sunset lit window. "It's a lot of work, but I feel like I'm doing something, you know? Clementine wasn't joking when she said she wants to change the entire department. It'll take some getting used to, but at the end of the day, we'll be a better force because of it."

"That's good to hear," Cassie said. "And your injuries? Taking your meds every day? Getting plenty of rest?"

Harris rolled her eyes. "Yes, Mother. I've been taking care of myself."

Cassie harrumphed. She knew Harris better than that. "I'll believe it when I see it."

Jason opened the pizza box and grabbed a slice. "Any luck finding Bianchi?"

"Not yet," Harris said. "He'll pop up sooner or later. If you hear anything—"

"You'll be the first I tell."

The detective nodded her head in thanks. "Congratulations, by the way." She gestured to the room. "You got this place up and running pretty fast."

The lights flickered for a moment, and Jason shook his head. "Up, yes," he said. "Running, maybe not. I'll put in another work order."

Cassie watched as he retreated to the far corner of the room and pulled out his cell.

Harris' voice brought her attention back around. "Hey, I've been meaning to talk to you about something," the detective said. "If you've got a minute?"

Harris wasn't usually so cautious, and it made Cassie nervous. "Yeah, of course."

"These last few weeks have been a lot. For both of us." Harris swallowed, and it took her a second to find her voice again. "And I just wanted to apologize to you."

"You don't have to do that." Cassie's face went red, but from guilt or embarrassment, she wasn't sure. "We both did things. Said things—"

"I know. But I still want to." When Cassie didn't argue, Harris took a deep breath and continued. "I wasn't always myself these last couple of weeks, and I feel like you bore the brunt of that. I don't think I can handle there being hard feelings between us. I never had a ton of friends. It's not easy for me to trust people. David was the only one I ever really liked, you know? He was always there when I needed him." Harris broke off, and she had to wait a few seconds to regain her composure. "I'm grateful you're in my life, Cassie. And it kills me to think that I might've done something to hurt you."

With tears already forming in her eyes, the only thing Cassie wanted to do was hug Harris, and that's exactly what she did. "I didn't make things easy, either. I'm sorry, too." She stepped back and looked Harris in the eyes. "I miss him so much," she said, trying to hold back a sob, "but he would be proud of us. He wanted to take down Aguilar, and we did that for him."

"We're total messes," Harris said, and it came out half laugh, half sob.

"A little worse for wear," Cassie agreed, "but together. That would make him happy."

Harris looked like she was weighing her next words carefully, but Cassie could see the hope forming in her eyes. "You really never saw him? Never felt him?"

"No." She wished she had the answer Harris was looking for. "But he never wanted that. At the end of the day, he died doing what he thought was right."

"I don't think it's over yet," Harris said, wiping away her tears. "I've got some news."

"Oh?" Dozens of worst-case scenarios popped into Cassie's head. "What kind of news?"

"I'm not entirely sure." Harris was somber now. "I got a call from someone at Apex. She didn't give me her name, but it seems as though they've taken care of all my *indiscretions*."

Cassie blanched. "What does that mean?"

"First and foremost, there's no proof I killed Zbirak. I looked up his death records myself. Wiped clean. His murder case has been closed, despite them never apprehending a suspect."

"Apex doesn't do anything for free," Cassie said. "What else did they say?"

"They made sure all of my activities in Chicago and Los Angeles were above board." Harris shrugged, like she hadn't been that worried about it, but Cassie knew better. "Long story short, Internal Affairs won't find any wrongdoing on my end. As far as they're concerned, I was suspended and went on a nice little vacation, then came home just in time to become a hero."

"This person who called you from Apex," Cassie said, "what did they want from you?"

Harris leveled her with a look. "All they said was for you to give them a call sometime."

Cassie waited for more, but when it didn't come, she shook her head in confusion. "That's it? That's all they said?"

"That's it," Harris repeated.

Before Cassie could ask any more questions, someone banged on the door. Jason was the first to make a move, tucking his phone away and crossing the room. "That was fast," he said. "Management said they'd send someone up soon, but I didn't think it'd be tonight."

When Jason opened the door, however, it wasn't a maintenance worker on the other side. In fact, it was probably the last person on the entire planet Cassie had expected to show up at her threshold. It was so strange seeing her here in Savannah that it took Cassie several seconds to realize who it was.

The long dark hair. The black glasses. The sly grin on her face that told them the shock on their faces was totally worth the trip.

"Cassie Quinn," the woman said. "You're not an easy woman to find."

"Piper McLaren," Cassie said, dredging the name up from her hazy memory of the two crime scenes where she'd met the passionate podcaster. "What are you doing here?"

Piper stepped past Jason without waiting for an invitation. "I have a proposal."

Harris folded her arms over her chest. "Which is what, exactly?"

"You make a guest appearance on my podcast," Piper said to Cassie, her eyes sharp and excited. "And I tell you everything I know about Apex Publicity."

Cassie Quinn returns in *Born from Ashes*! Pre-order your copy now: https://www.amazon.com/dp/B0BDQHBSQY

Join the LT Ryan reader family & receive a free copy of the Cassie Quinn story, *Through the Veil*. Click the link below to get started: https://ltryan.com/cassie-quinn-newsletter-signup-1

LOVE CASSIE? **Hatch? Noble? Maddie?** Get your very own L.T. Ryan merchandise today! Click the link below to find coffee mugs, t-shirts, and even signed copies of your favorite thrillers! https://ltryan.ink/EvG_

THE CASSIE QUINN SERIES

Path of Bones

Whisper of Bones

Symphony of Bones

Etched in Shadow

Concealed in Shadow

Betrayed in Shadow

Born from Ashes

Love Cassie? Hatch? Noble? Maddie? Get your very own Cassie Quinn merchandise today! Click the link below to find coffee mugs, t-shirts, and even signed copies of your favorite L.T. Ryan thrillers! https://ltryan.ink/EvG_

ALSO BY L.T. RYAN

Find All of L.T. Ryan's Books on Amazon Today!

The Jack Noble Series

The Recruit (free)

The First Deception (Prequel 1)

Noble Beginnings

A Deadly Distance

Ripple Effect (Bear Logan)

Thin Line

Noble Intentions

When Dead in Greece

Noble Retribution

Noble Betrayal

Never Go Home

Beyond Betrayal (Clarissa Abbot)

Noble Judgment

Never Cry Mercy

Deadline

End Game

Noble Ultimatum

Noble Legend

Noble Revenge

Never Look Back (Coming Soon)

Bear Logan Series

Ripple Effect

Blowback

Take Down

Deep State

Bear & Mandy Logan Series

Close to Home

Under the Surface

The Last Stop

Over the Edge

Between the Lies (Coming Soon)

Rachel Hatch Series

Drift

Downburst

Fever Burn

Smoke Signal

Firewalk

Whitewater

Aftershock

Whirlwind

Tsunami

Fastrope

Sidewinder (Coming Soon)

Mitch Tanner Series

The Depth of Darkness

Into The Darkness

Deliver Us From Darkness

Cassie Quinn Series

Path of Bones

Whisper of Bones

Symphony of Bones

Etched in Shadow

Concealed in Shadow

Betrayed in Shadow

Born from Ashes

Blake Brier Series

Unmasked

Unleashed

Uncharted

Drawpoint

Contrail

Detachment

Clear

Quarry (Coming Soon)

Dalton Savage Series

Savage Grounds

Scorched Earth

Cold Sky

The Frost Killer (Coming Soon)

Maddie Castle Series

The Handler

Tracking Justice

Hunting Grounds

Vanished Trails (Coming Soon)

Affliction Z Series

Affliction Z: Patient Zero

Affliction Z: Abandoned Hope

Affliction Z: Descended in Blood

Affliction Z : Fractured Part 1

Affliction Z: Fractured Part 2 (Fall 2021)

Love Cassie? Hatch? Noble? Maddie? Get your very own L.T. Ryan merchandise today! Click the link below to find coffee mugs, t-shirts, and even signed copies of your favorite thrillers! https://ltryan.ink/EvG_

Receive a free copy of The Recruit. Visit:

https://ltryan.com/jack-noble-newsletter-signup-1

ABOUT THE AUTHOR

L.T. Ryan is a *USA Today* and international bestselling author. The new age of publishing offered L.T. the opportunity to blend his passions for creating, marketing, and technology to reach audiences with his popular Jack Noble series.

Living in central Virginia with his wife, the youngest of his three daughters, and their three dogs, L.T. enjoys staring out his window at the trees and mountains while he should be writing, as well as reading, hiking, running, and playing with gadgets. See what he's up to at http://ltryan.com.

Social Medial Links:

- Facebook (L.T. Ryan): https://www.facebook.com/LTRyanAuthor

- Facebook (Jack Noble Page): https://www.facebook.com/JackNobleBooks/

- Twitter: https://twitter.com/LTRyanWrites

- Goodreads: http://www.goodreads.com/author/show/6151659.L_T_Ryan